# THE RECKONING
# OF JACK THE RIPPER

## ENTITY UNKNOWN

MARK BARRESI

authorHOUSE®

*AuthorHouse*™
*1663 Liberty Drive*
*Bloomington, IN 47403*
*www.authorhouse.com*
*Phone: 1-800-839-8640*

*Published by AuthorHouse  6/1/2012*

*ISBN: 978-1-4772-1287-5 (sc)*
*ISBN: 978-1-4772-1286-8 (hc)*
*ISBN: 978-1-4772-1285-1 (e)*

*Library of Congress Control Number: 2012909591*

When a series of multiple murders of mutilated females throws the city of Sand Diego, into a Panic stricken frenzy a city wide task force is put in place to uncover the unknown killer, who the police have called; "The Entity", for concealing his identity from police, forensics and witnesses up to his latest victim. Until detective Ed Brooks, confronted the "Entity", in a bloody last ditch effort to stop the mass killer. An encounter that almost cost Brooks his own life, now four years later, the "Entity", murders have started again. As Brooks and his team are once again charged to stop the killer, and unearth his reasoning for committing the most brutal serial slayings since the original; "Jack the Ripper", style murders. Over a century before in Whitechaple England, with the help of FBI profiler Stephanie Morgan. They will uncover a connection between the recent murders now, to the original Ripper suspect so many years ago. A link that will connect modern forensics and the history of the world's most infamous first serial killer will all culminate together with the action and fury, for a shocking ending in, "The Reckoning of Jack the Ripper."

Combining both fiction and historical facts of the; "Jack the Ripper", murders of 1888, England. Author Mark Barresi, has set out on his own personal quest to name the most likely suspect of the world's most elusive and first serial killer ever known.

# History of Researchers of, "Jack The Ripper"

I want to first say, I never intended to write a book about "Jack the Ripper". My first thoughts were to write a novel, about a serial killer in San Diego that was possessed by a demon. But I stopped and thought about this idea, and it didn't sound very appealing to me, and then I knew at that point. That kind of story would not be very interesting to all my readers. So I began to investigate the history of, "Jack the Ripper". As we all know his identity was never discovered by all the lead detectives on Scotland Yard, most notable of all, Inspector Frederick Abberline, and a whole list of other prominent police detectives and officials who all worked the case. Even beyond the year the murders began and ended in 1888, Whitechaple, England. I read many books about the Ripper, and watched many documentaries about him. With a whole list of the known suspects and many potential suspects that keep being mentioned every year to present day. Some suspects and theories sound believable, and most are very ridiculous that lead investigators and researchers to just laugh and not even bother to follow these leads. The best known researches who I give my most admiration and respect to believe and follow their works are; Martin Fido, Paul Begg, Stewart Evans, Richard Jones and Donald Rumbelow. I have read their works, watched them being interviewed and give their personal thoughts on who the Ripper could have been. From 1888, to how our advanced criminology system has taken us to DNA evidence now. We can list up to six plausible suspects; we may believe to have committed the slayings. Some of these suspects were even named in secret archived notes locked away In Scotland Yard, to more recent years. But as the years passed, we have no DNA evidence to link any suspect or any confession that was ever made by the suspects that were arrested at the time, or any valuable witnesses to the crimes being done in the act of the murders. Until the day comes, we can find something truly linking one outstanding suspect to the crimes, and we can all just give our own opinions and suggestions as to whom really was; "Jack the Ripper". As I will write in my book, this is only my opinion who I feel committed the most brutal serial slayings of all time, but after two years of research and investigations. I agree with some of the best researchers and authors, we might have found our suspect. In all I dedicate this book to all "Jack the Ripper"; Authors and Researchers around.

Mark Barresi

# Acknowledgements

I want to thank my family and close friends, who helped me and supported me, in writing this book. As I was facing some personal hardships along the way, as I was writing this book. I will always be indebted to you all, and mostly to my Mother, for her love and support.

# Discovery of the Journal

It was a very dark night, as the strong winds carried the down poor of heavy rain. All throughout the massive city of San Diego, It was just passed eleven PM, as he sat at his desk, reading the latest news on his lap top computer. The headlines read, "Prominent physician, for the pharmaceutical company, Quasar Pharmaceuticals , Was terminated yesterday for his ongoing illegal attempts to bring in GHB and other drugs that are not legal for most American, and other companies. Who sell and distribute a wide variety of brands, of drugs and pharmaceuticals around the world. The doctor, whose name is being withheld at this time by the board of directors of, Quasar."

He laughed to himself, as he took a long drag of his, Dunhill fine cigarette. As he placed it down in the glass ashtray to his left hand side on the desk. He then picked up a shot glass of, Wild Turkey vodka. He took a fast gulp of it, as he squeezed his eyes tight from the effects of the strong alcohol. He stopped reading the online news article about him, as he already knew what was printed about him to follow. He would wait to be brought up on federal charges, to distribute illegal uses of prescribed drugs. Both steroids and other GHB preforming enhancing drugs, to sports athletes and other well-known physicians to give to their patients.

As the illegal distribution, made him a wealth of money and made him many powerful influential friends. As he now was about to lose all his money, and his luxurious home and cars not to mention all his, personal things he gathered other the years. He thought of being alone now, in a federal prison. Unable to access any of the enjoyable, comforts even the everyday person has. As he knows he will be found guilty, and sentenced to many years in prison. Losing his freedom, and his will to live, he clenched his fists and banged them down, hard on the wooden desk. As he thought to himself and smiled; "If I'm about to lose everything I have built all around me, to those who feel they are the champions of good and just of the people. I will not give in to them, without extracting my bold taste of vengeance against these fools."

"I have long held my hatred for men and women, who achieved the happiness in life I was never able to cherish and enjoy. As money and power did not bring me, true love I never found. Just a short brief failed marriage to that bitch!" "Who never loved me, but gave all her love and devotion to our only child. I have longed for her to suffer in hell, from the day she passed away from Alzheimer's disease." He was overjoyed the way he watched her suffer, as she lost all memory of her loved ones and happy life.

To him, her suffering was well deserved as he blamed her for their divorce and his many years of unhappiness together. As she took him for so much money due to their divorce which she received in her settlement, along with custody of their only child, the one thing he only truly loved in his bitter and twisted life. His disdain for women started with her, as he now knows the true blood line of hatred and vengeance. All began within his own family tree so many years ago. Due to his recent discovery of an old box, he discovered as he removed the many personal items from his family, as he went through an old trunk from the early 1900's. That belonged to his father, which was stowed away for many years unopened till just the other day. As he spun around in his, leather chair to reach the old 19th century wooden box, made of dark Calamander wood. He opened the box, and took out the very old journal and two imitation brass rings, that belonged to a female at one time.

The journal was from the 1800's, as it was leather bound and brass latched in the center. As he opened the latch to read the very worn and frail pages of the journal, the journal belonged to a distant relative, as he read the name of its owner and author on the inside cover. The name signed with a fine fountain pen, period to the time of the book. As the ink was still legible to read, the water-based liquid ink, written in fine script in the color blue; "Francis J. Tumblety", was the author of the journal. It held a total of two hundred pages, but only one hundred thirty seven pages. Were completed with detailed written passages by Tumblety, who happened to be in fact, a physician himself, dealing in ancient Indian herbs and other forms of medicines found in that era.

But it was the last twenty pages or so, that really caught his attention. As Francis Tumblety recounted his visits to Europe in the mid to late 1800's, as he described traveling to a poverty stricken area, known as Whitechaple, England. There he spent time in late 1888, as one of the most infamous crimes to the world and history was taking place.  He admitted that Whitechaple, was home to the immigration of a large population of Polish Jews. Who found refuge in abundance in very cheap lodging houses, known as doss-houses. That would result in very tight quarters for the occupants. Who would result in sharing, a toilet to a floor, or out-houses.  He went on to write that these, people where below him and found them repulsive to his stomach. As he hated them, as they would all drink heavily and become violent towards one another, in an area that was already very tight to live and streets that were over crowded and very small alleys. He noted the drink of choice for them was gin, as the women would have very puffed out cheeks from heavy drinking. That the ones, who took to prostitution, in order to make a living, walked the streets of Whitechaple, to find a few pennies to cover the cost for the means of lodging for the nights, he wrote in his hatred for these women, "I have become sick to my insides, of these grotesque and foul women. Who need to sell themselves to earn refuge for a night's stay.  For my first wife, was a woman of the street, whom she never admitted to me, until after we were already husband and wife. I shall fix these women while I am here in Whitechaple."

Tumblety went on to say; how he committed the most unspeakable act one can do to another person. The act of bloody murder and how he got away with it after he savagely taken five women's lives, Till he escaped England and then onto France, making his way by boat, across the Atlantic Ocean. To come back to New York and be in America again, he smiled as he read who his distant uncle really was.

"I escaped the fools in England, right after I slaughtered the last whore. I managed to slip by the great detectives of Scotland Yard. As they gave me my true name, "Jack the Ripper".

He looked up from the journal, and spoke to himself. "My dear great uncle, how true do I hold what you did so many years ago to my heart. I will carry on your legacy of vengeance, to rid the world of these foul women, and all others who will get in my way. For the Ripper, shall be born again!" He put down the journal, and picked up a very sharp, stainless steel Post-Mortem knife, as he smiled and said; "A century ago you were immortalized then, and now I will join you in the present time!"

# Chapter 1

Veronica Wood was walking the unsafe streets of National City. Just south of Downtown, San Diego, this area was both a mixture of commercial and residential areas. As Veronica would earn her living by meeting men, along the truck stops and rest areas, and take her charges back to either one of the many, cheap motels or better class hotels. To accommodate her men as to their tastes, Veronica was a very attractive twenty six year old brunette. She was about five foot four, with long black hair and dark brown eyes. She wore very short daisy duke denim shorts, with a black button down blouse, under a short leather jacket, with black pump heeled shoes. She wanted to bare as much of her body as she could, for any man walking by her, or driving by. To catch their attention to her very slim and athletic body.

She was walking around the corner of the diner, a spot most frequented of truck drivers as they would stop and park to go in and get a bite to eat or coffee. As they would get ready to embark of their long journeys on the interstates to head north out of San Diego, it was just past one AM, as Veronica looked up and noticed the four door sedan drive slowly passed her from her back. She did smile at the driver if indeed he was a male, to get his attention. As she smiled to herself, hoping she didn't have to walk the streets for long to find a man this particular cool night of, May the seventeenth. She would charge him the usual amount for a three hour meeting;

she would ask him for four hundred dollars cash. Not an expensive amount these days she thought, for an escort to ask. She stopped in place, as the car came to a stop and made a u-turn over the double yellow lines, to come back in her direction.

His heart started to beat faster, as this was to be his first meeting with a prostitute and his first cleansing of the low class women he has come to hate. For he did not think of it as murder that he was about to commit, but a cleansing of scum and pure trash, that he wanted to think of them as, just like his great uncle did. So many years before, he was taken by Veronica's, exquisite body, and nice shapely long legs. As he slowed to a stop and lowered the passenger side window to greet her; "Hello sugar," she said with a wide smile, showing off all nice white teeth. She asked him, if he was interested in a good time tonight.

"Hello my dear, how are you this fine evening?" The doctor asked her, "I'm sorry, but I am nervous being that this is my first time meeting a young lady in this manner". Veronica, amused by his innocent demeanor, she thought he was to well mannered and too soft spoken to be an undercover cop, out to bust her tonight.

"Well, why don't you open the door and let me in, and we can talk about it sugar." She replied with a laugh, as he unlocked the passenger side door and she gently opened it and slid so gently into the leather seat. She thought to herself, this was a nice car and he was very pleasant and mature. This was a good catch for her tonight.

"I'm Veronica, thank you for stopping by and meeting me". She told him, as he smiled and said it was a pleasure to meet a very beautiful woman on this pleasant early morning.

"So what's you're name?" She asked him. He told her his name was Nathan.

"Is that you're first name, or last name, Nathan?"

"Does that really matter? I don't mean to sound rude, but I don't like to be very open to you right now. Being this is my first time I have ever met with one, like you." He replied, with a nervous look in his eyes.

"It's all right Nathan, no need to be nervous with me. I just want you to relax and give you the experience, of the first time you will never forget". With that reaction from her, Nathan becomes more confident, as he got to know her more each moment. He asked her, if she would meet her men, at her place or at motels only? She remarked, she only met her contacts at motels and hotels only, especially being this was their first meeting together, she felt safer being in a public place. He smiled, and asked if they could meet at the, Twin Palms motel. That was less than a mile away; she smiled at him and said that motel was fine with her. As Nathan, told her; "great". He drove off to the motel.

"What made you pick that motel"? She asked him.

"It is small and kind of cozy I thought, being this is my first time. I just wanted to be in a very comfortable setting for myself". He replied to her.

Veronica, asked him to tell her about himself. What he did for work and how old he was. He told her, he was fifty six years old, and divorced with no children. As for work, he told her he was in medicine. But did not go into any details, as to what he actually did. As they entered the small motel that held twenty four rooms on two floors. Nathan parked his car, in the middle row. He instructed, he would go into the office and secure a room for them that seemed to be very empty except for two other vehicles parked in the motel's lot. As he exited the car, Veronica thought to herself that Nathan kept himself in very good shape for his age. He gave her the appearance he exercised and ate well, to be fit.

He had a full head of dark gray hair, which was brushed straight back. As his height was just under six feet tall. She watched as he entered into the office as she opened her small purse and took out her compact powder and lipstick. As he lowered her passenger side visor, to open the mirror as she added more makeup to her beautiful face. As she noticed him returning to the car with a key in his right hand, she quickly placed the items back in her small purse. As he went to the back of the car and opened the trunk, he took out a carry vinyl bag, about eighteen inches long. As Veronica exited the car to meet him, he told her, their room was number twelve just straight ahead from where he parked. As she told him first, the amount of her donation, she would not only meet with him for that amount and for only three hours. As he agreed, that was all right with him. She looked at the bag in his left hand puzzled.

"I hope you're not into anything kinky? Because I'm not into that sought of thing." She said with a look, of seriousness in her eyes.

"Neither Am I", he replied as they both smiled and he motioned for them to enter the room, that he opened with his key. Veronica went over to the king sized bed, as she removed her jacket and placed her purse on the side table next to the lamp. That she turned on, as Nathan left only the light to the foyer of the room on. As he watched her remove her blouse and shorts. As she kicked off her pumps, she was now stand in her black laced matching bra and panties. As Nathan opened his wallet, and took out four, crisp hundred dollar bills. As he handed them to her, and Veronica pleasantly took it from him, as she placed the money in her purse and returned it back top the side table.

"Come on handsome, don't you want to have the time of your life now?" She said, as she slid back the top comforter and sheets to the bed, and relaxed her sexy body, to entice him to join her on the bed. As he began to take off his button down denim shirt and he kicked off his black leather shoes and removed his jeans. Veronica, was stunned as she expected to see him in his underwear, he was now wearing what seemed to be dark black hospital scrubs. She asked in surprise what he was wearing. He replied, they were cotton pajamas that made him feel very comfortable to wear, before they got started. As he joined her on the bed, he glided his hand up her very smooth left thigh to her left hand, as she pulled him towards her face and kissed one another deeply. As she pushed him down onto the bed, where he removed her bra, and while they were still kissing. He gently removed her panties.

As Veronica, had wanted to remove his top, he stopped her hands and just held them down as he kept kissing her. As she then tried to remove his bottoms, but again he stopped her hands, as he spread them against her sides. Uneasy about how this was going she asked, "hey now, what's with you? Are we going to get on with it or what sugar"? He looked into her eyes, and smiled.

"Can we first play a nice game?" He asked her, as she made a face and asked if he wanted to role-play? That she wasn't into that sought of thing.

"No not role-play, just a very romantic game of blindfolded sex". She asked what he had in mind, as Nathan instructed he would blindfold her, with a dark black scarf while they had sex. Amused by this she smiled at him.

"You really are, nervous about this being you're first time? Aren't you handsome?" She said, as fond of the idea she agreed to have him blindfold her. As he reached into his bag, and took out the scarf. As he placed it around her eyes and double knotted it in the back of her head. To make sure it was secured. As he pushed her back down to the bed gently, he began to kiss her deeply again. As he reached down to his carry bag, which he left on the floor near the bed. As he took out a stainless steel sharp knife in his right hand, as he very quickly covered her mouth very tightly with his left hand. As he muttered to her ear softly; "Whore!" As he cut her throat deep, with the very sharp blade from left to right and again very deep from right to left. As he squeezed his hand very tight over Veronica's mouth. She was flailing her hands about, as all he could hear was her gasping for air, and choking on her blood.

Till she stopped, gasping and her hands fell down to her sides. He watched in peace now, as she looked at him in shock and closed her eyelids shut. He watched as the blood gushed out all over her neck in the two open straight cuts on her throat. As he removed his hand, from her mouth, he quickly got up from the bed, and pulled open the bag, he produced a few white gauze pads, and a bottle of sterile water. As he put on long latex gloves, to cover his hands, and he produced two sterile, shoe covers. As he quickly covered his feet, he was now secure, not to leave any of his DNA behind. As he wet the pads with the water, he quickly washed her body with the water, her legs, her face and hands. Her lips, as he then wiped down the inside of the room, the room key and the inside doorknob and light switch. He knew he would finally clean his hands up when he was done. But now, it was time for the real cleansing to commence.

With anger in his eyes, he took out a sterile black cap and full plastic visor mask. As he picked up the knife again, he took her right hand as he inserted the blade under her index finer nail, and violently pulled it off her skin, he dropped the finger nail into a clear plastic bag, as hid did the same to the next finger. As he repeated the process for the other hand, he laughed to himself. "No DNA evidence people." As he placed the plastic bag, in the side pouch of his carry bag. He looked at the time on the digital face of the clock on the table, as it read. Two twenty five AM. Still enough time for him to finish what he set out to do, so long ago now.

He took hold of her left breast, as he remembered what his great uncle did to his last victim in England, "Mary Jane Kelly". He brutally, decade her body of all her flesh and organs to leave her faceless and a death that no one deserved. But this was the start of no remorse for him; this was his way of continuing Francis's, hatred towards women. He thrust the blade into the edge of her breast, and sliced all around tissue and ligaments, as her blood darkened her whole chest red with her blood. He removed her breast and placed it at the head of the bed, and did the same to the other breast. He stopped and thought to himself again.

"The ripper took trophies of his victims. Their uterus and a kidney, they deserved to have their bodies cleansed, from the whores they became in life!" He shouted the idea to himself, as he spread her leg wide open and inserted the blade deep into her vagina, he wants her womb out. As he uses both hands to open her vagina cavity apart, being well schooled as a medical doctor, he knows the insides of the human bodies. He takes hold of her fallopian tubes. As he cuts and tears them off from the womb. He rips her insides out of her, as he extracts her uterus from her. He holds it in his hand and smiles, as he looks at her lifeless body.

"This is what makes a woman a whore!" As he wants to take the bloody organ with him, as Francis wrote in his journal, he had a large collection of female wombs in glass jars. But Nathan couldn't take it with him, for it was to bloody and messy. As he placed it at the foot of the bed, next to the extracted breasts, till he turned her over on her side, he tore into her lower backside as he wanted both her kidneys out of her. He thrust and tore through skin and muscle till he knew he felt her left kidney, for he just cut all away the organs that held it. As he took it out of her body, till he stopped and paused again and thought.

"From Hell": the letter that was mailed along with a bloody kidney to George Lusk. Who was the head of the, Whitechaple vigilance committee at the time. He placed the kidney next to the other organs as he knew now, he needed to stop. For this was modern day, San Diego. People will be up early for work and he needed to hurry and clean up now. He hurried and tore into the body again, and extracted her right kidney, wet with blood. He placed in a neat row, next to both breasts and the other kidney. As he turned her over on the backside once again, Nathan quickly took out a large black plastic, garbage bag. As he took off all his sterile garments off and placed them along with the bloody surgical knife in the bag. As he took out a small bottle of clear hand sanitizer, and rubbed his hands clean very well. As he took out one last sterile gauze pad, and stopped and looked at his amazing, and bloody work. But for him, it was an art of true wonder. How this act, proved himself to be a true man, and personal hero to his own cause like; "Jack the Ripper". He laughed as he left her eyes blindfolded, and walked to the door and used the gauze pad to turn the brass doorknob and close it behind him. As he dropped it into the black garbage bag, and opened his car door and sat inside, and started the vehicle up.

As he put the car into reverse and then into drive, he drives out of the parking lot so slowly, as there was not a soul around at two fifty, in the AM. Nathan smiled to himself, "I have done it, my first murder of a whore! But it will not be my last. I will go home and burn my scrubs and knife. As I will always follow the same pattern to strike a new whore each time, the fools will not catch me!" As he made is way onto the on ramp of the interstate, to take him home and hide.

It was just after eight AM in the morning, as homicide detective Edward Brooks, got the call from central division headquarters, that a body was discovered at the Twin Palms Motel, just south of downtown San Diego, but still under the jurisdiction of the central division. As Ed's partner, Robert Cullen picked him up in their unmarked sedan, and pulled into the motel's parking lot. To see it swarming of central command squad cruisers and the county coroners' forensic van, ad Brooks and Cullen exited their vehicle to be briefed as to what happened inside room twelve.

Ed Brooks, was six foot one and very muscular. He had a vigorous exercise routine to life weights every night at his house and run up to five miles on the weekends. Ed was a Navy veteran, serving just less than six years. That earned himself the rank of Petty Officer Second Class, E—5 pay grade. Ed has been with central command P.D. for eighteen years, as he was a patrol officer and sergeant for ten years, and has been now lead homicide detective for the division for the last eight years. As he was now forty one years old, for his partner Rob, was just 36, joining the force straight out of college at the age of twenty four. The two have been partners for four years now, as Rob replaced Ed's last partner who had retired. As the first squad officer on the scene walked up to them, to brief them on what was known so far.

"Hey guys, we got ourselves a bad scene here. According to the victim's driver's license found inside her purse, she is twenty six year old female, Veronica Wood. A known prostitute from the area as we picked her up a few times for solicitation on the streets; Rob, asked him who was in the room so far, and who discovered the body.

"The body was first discovered by a housekeeper, Betty Flores. As she screamed and ran into the office and notified the night manager who was still on duty, who intern called us. First call came into dispatch at 07:23 AM. Forensic team just entered the room, to gather evidence only, as per you're boss. Lieutenant Stanford."

"Was the night manager on duty, if any guests came to rent this room during the night?" Ed asked him.

"He was on duty, as he assigned room twelve to a gentleman by the name of, Mason Albert. Probably a fake name, but we are checking on that. The manager stated he came into the office alone, paid cash for the room, a total of $65.00. And he was alone. He signed for the room at 01:50 AM." The officer read from his notes, as Ed and Rob said they would interview him once they were done looking at the body.

With that, both Ed and Rob entered the room and closed the door behind them. As the three man forensic team was busy dusty for prints in the bathroom and around the foyer to the room, both detective put on latex gloves and sterile foot coverings. Before they moved any where near the body that was on the bed, still with the black scarf, tied around her head and eyes. Ed and Rob just looked at one another when they saw the amount of blood that had seeped all over the bed and onto the carpeting of the room. Rob just clenched his teeth in surprise when se saw, the organs spread out at the foot of the bed. As Ed whispered to him, "the killer posed them in his own symbolic way, to show us. He has no fear of law enforcement I can tell right away". As Rob just nodded to him in agreement, Ed approached the lead forensic specialist and asked him, how long ago was the murder committed by, the bodies temperature.

"I estimate the murder was done between one and 2:30 AM. So just about five hours ago, not a long time at all", He told Ed.

"Any signs of a struggle and skin tissue under her fingernails?" Rob asked him.

"We will never be able to tell, the killer removed all ten of her fingernails. The cause of death was two sharp straight deep cuts to the throat of the larynx. From ear to ear, left to right first, and then right to left. That makes our killer; right handed". Stated the forensic specialist, Ed gathering all the information known so far as he is looking around the room for any clues as he walks over to the body and lifts up the blindfold on Veronica's head.

"So no, signs of a struggle, no fingerprints so far, and are all these organs removed with the same weapon, if you had to guess?" Ed asks him.

"Well I didn't turn her body over to look at the wounds from her back, as it appeared the killer turned her on her backside again, once he removed her kidneys. But what I can see from the throat lacerations and the deep sharp penetrating cuts to her vagina, to remove her womb. I can tell you, this guy knows what he is doing, he's smart and he had it planned out very well".

Ed takes a breath and lets it out slowly, "I agree with you on that. Look bag the blindfold; send it with all the DNA swabs of the body and blood. If we are lucky, they had sexual intercourse, and maybe his seamen was left on her vaginal wall, and get lots of pictures of the body and room. Let's hope this is the first and last victim, but my guess it's the start of a serial pattern to come". Ed tells them, as the lead forensic specialist acknowledges his requests. As Rob tells Ed, to look at her eyes. They are closed peacefully, no fear on her face. Ed just looks and thinks to himself, what a very pretty girl, what a waste of a young life.

"She has no fear in her eyes, because of the blindfold and she was very comfortable with him. This means our man, is well groomed and mannered and well spoken to persuade any young lady to be with him. Another thing for us to worry for, if he is indeed a serial killer," Ed explains to Rob, who agrees with him. As Ed's cell phone is ringing, he takes it out of his inside pocket and answers it. It's their boss, lieutenant in charge of the homicide division, Rick Stanford. He instructs Ed, he is on site and is coming in the room now.

As Rick enters, putting on the latex gloves and sterile shoe covers. He approaches his two detectives, ad Ed and Rob brief him up to this point. Rick himself a very skilled detective, has been on the force for over twenty years. He enjoys his job and the nice weather of San Diego, and likes every one of his men in his division. Rick has no means of retirement. As Rick looks around the room and body, he agrees with Ed and the forensic team. That maybe the killer made a mistake by not taking the blindfold with him, and hopes he touched it before he used any sterile gloves on his hands. As the three men, exited the room to go and talk to the night manager.

Rob was going over with the night manager, for him to describe to him and their forensic sketch artist. To make a detailed composite drawing of the suspect, as Rob went naming all the aspects of height, weight, hair style, mustache, side burns. If he was Caucasian or black, or any Hispanic descent, as he replied to his list of questions.

"Look as I already stated before to the other policemen, the guy walked in here at ten minutes to two AM. He paid cash for the room and signed the ledger, Mason Albert. The guy was white; He was about five foot nine to five eleven. Full head of straight back gray hair that was kind of high. He had a dark gray mustache and long sideburns I believe. As far as what he was wearing, I think a dark shirt and a jacket I believe. Look I only dealt with him for about three minutes, he paid me I gave him the room key. I didn't see him with her or if he was with another guy. As we have no surveillance camera system here. That I know is a violation to the state by the owner of the motel". He admitted to Rob and Ed. As Rob said, "yes it is a very big violation."

As the forensic artist was finishing up his sketch of the suspect, Rob thanked the manger as rick wanted to talk to them outside, as the artist was done. He handed the sketch to Ed, as he thanked him for it and showed it to both Rick and Rob as they walked outside the office, and were now standing in the parking lot right outside of the room, as they watched the body being removed in a body bag and placed into the county coroners' white van.

"So what do you guys think so far?" Rick asks them.

"Well he scouted this location out before hand, knowing they didn't have any surveillance camera system. He parked his vehicle right in the lane by room twelve, for an easy in and out getaway. And just by looking at the sketch, my guess is he was wearing a fake mustache and wig, along with sideburns". Ed explains his thoughts of the killer to them.

"And by the looks of the patterns of the wounds, and the knowledge it would have taken to find and extract the victim's organs. I say we are dealing with a doctor or some person with anatomical knowledge of the human body". Rob suggest to them, as both rick and Ed agree with him.

"Okay, we will wait and see if Dr. Cate Adams finds anything with the gathered swabs and the blindfold. Till then, run this guys face against our database of known convicts. Plus check around and fellow counties and states to see if there have been any similar killings like this one guys." Rick instructs them, as Ed tells Rob to go back to the precinct and to begin work there, as they will also contact Veronica Wood's, next of kin to break the sad news to them.

That night he was watching the evening news, as he was sitting at home in his living room, smoking another fine, Dunhill cigarette. As he exhaled a long puff of smoke so slowly from his mouth and into the air, He listened to the female newscaster tell of the horrific find of a young female body, at the Twin Palms Motel, as police are holding back the victims name at this time, and the grizzly details of the murder. He was just about finished with the cigarette, and smashed it out into the glass ashtray on his marble coffee table. He then picked up the old journal from his distant uncle, and read more of it's chilling passages.

"I was able to get by the fools, by using other men's names to hide my own. I even went as far as to grow my mustache very long, and wear clothing the fools would not have known I was to wear. I am a true hider of my own identity and a traveler who escapes all those who seek me out. For I am the one, who did not end with five, as the fools do believe me to have murdered, I continued until the number ten."

He read the passage in the journal that made him feel as if he was now equal to Francis Tumblety, in more ways than one. He has achieved his goal of concealing his identity so far, and able to disguise himself and means of murder. As he looked up from the journal and laughed out loud.

"Dear uncle, I wish to surpass you at number ten! Till I can kill a great number of whores that will shock not only this large city but shake the world by the core of its foundations," he laughed again, as he thought and planned to wait for his next murder. He would allow the space of timing of days, as did the Ripper did with his victims.

# Chapter 2

It has been two days since the murder, as Ed Brooks and his partner Rob Cullen, were going over the DNA results found at the crime scene, by county medical forensic scientist, Dr. Cate Adams. As Rob was reading off her findings to Ed, "no fingerprints were on the blindfold because Dr. Adams, found that the blindfold had been dampened with sterile water. Maybe before or after the killer, place it over her eyes". Ed just looked up at Rob from his desk, that faces Rob's and said, this guy is very clever.

"So if he is to follow this same pattern again, avoid surveillance cameras, and disguise himself good. We are going to need an eye witness to his next killing to identify him. That will be the only way we will have any thing to go on about him, but I am sorry to say this. There will be another murder to happen soon." Ed tells Rob, as just then, Lieutenant Stanford came by. As he already knew of all the DNA findings, being he was in a relationship with Dr. Adams for quite some time. As Ed, threw out an idea for him to think about, on how to catch the killer in the act.

"Hey boss, how about the idea of using female under covers as prostitutes to flush him out? We have done it before on while on raids of male solicitors in the downtown area, why not for this case?" Ed questions him.

"I already talked to the captain about that idea, and for now he said no. He doesn't want to place any one's life on the line in undercover work on this just yet. But being as we have little to nothing to go on in leads, I agree with you, that there will be another murder bound to happen. So for now, we are heating up the patrols by our uniformed cops, through late evening till early mornings. To see if we just spot any suspicious men, driving around the downtown areas;" Stanford informs them, as he tells them to stay sharp, that they will get a break eventually.

He had picked up the very lovely Sharon Kessler, just after six PM, on Monday June twenty second. More than a month ago since he had first picked up Veronica Wood, this time he planned his routine different. He met Sharon, as she was walking through a strip mall and the thought crossed his mind she was a street walker, being she was wearing skin tight leather pants and high black suede boots. Just to about her knees, as she had on a dark blue sweater, which had a large neck line to show off her bare shoulders. Sharon was a beautiful, African American woman, who has nice wavy long hair to her shoulders. With a body that was almost identical to that of, Veronica Wood. He was not nervous this time as before, as when he slowed his sedan up to her in the parking lot. He used his same mellow voice and charm, to ask her if she wanted to show him a good time tonight. As Sharon entered his car, he agreed on her donation of six hundred dollars for five hours. But he just made one different request than the first time; he asked if they could meet at her residence instead of a motel.

Sharon gave some consideration to the thought. As she felt that Nathan, was a man who seemed harmless for his older age, as she agreed to his request, and she told him were she lived. As they drove off to her residence in the northern district of San Diego. They come upon the nice apartment house, she shared with her roommate. Just off Carlton Hills Blvd. as they entered her nice spacious two bedroom apartment, Sharon informed Nathan. That her roommate would not be home until later this evening, and if he was still here when she would arrive. For he shouldn't worry, that her roommate was also an escort and would keep the men's names who they met.

Very confidential from each other, as Nathan told her, that made him very comfortable indeed. As Sharon closed and locked the door behind them, she asked Nathan, what was with the nylon carry bag he had strapped over his shoulder.

"Oh, this is just a change of cloths and clean underwear I have for myself, so my wife would not be suspicious of me when I return home". He answered her, as they entered her bedroom and she closed the door behind them.

"You're wife? But I thought you said you were divorced now? She answered him as her back was to him as she dimmed the room's lights. As all of a sudden, a gloved hand came over her mouth very fast and held it shut very strong in his powerful grip.

"Yes I made a mistake whore! He spoke very softly into her left ear, as his right hand held another steel, post mortem knife, as the sharp blade came across her neck, dug deep into her flesh. As it cut very easy, as her blood covered his left arm red, as it flowed down the open wound. Sharon didn't even have time to react or make a sound. As she couldn't gasp for air, and lost all life in her muscles and collapsed in Nathan's arms. He quickly picked her up in his arms and carried her still body to her bed, and laid her down. He then undressed himself, till he was again in dark black, sterile scrubs and fixed the head cap and clear face mask, along with the shoe coverings. To be certain again, none of his DNA would be exposed to the body, and left in the room.

"Just like the first bitch I cleansed, I have plenty of time to destroy this whore's body, and cleanse all the shameful acts she has reaped and sew in her wretched life!" He snarled and whispered softly, as he took hold of the sharp knife, and stabbed hard into her chest. As the blood flew up into his face mask and all over the nice cotton sheets, as he stabbed again. The blood flew upwards even higher now, being the open wound to her chest dripped out her dark blood. He wanted to extract the most valuable organ to the human body. He wanted her heart first, as he found the still heart. He then began to cut away its arteries and muscles that held it in the thoracic cavity, when he was done. He pulled it out of her chest cavity, in the enormous open wound he had cut and tore into her chest, to extract the bloody heart he now held in his left hand.

"My prize gift to myself that I have taken from this foul bitch, for I remember what he done to those women one at a time, I will do the same now. As he again whispered to himself in a dark and evil voice, He charged at her ears, and slit the sharp blade behind her back earlobe. As the blade sheared away her muscle as blood oozed down his blade and gloved hand, as it was now severed off from her head. He held it in his hand, bloody still with its gold looped earring, dangling down the left ear. He smiled to himself again, as he placed it right under the heart. As he repeated the extraction of her right ear, and also displayed it at the foot of the bet along with her other organs, as he smiled as he looked at her body over, still not satisfied with his work.

"What else does she still have, that I would need to take from her, to prove to these street walkers. This life they lead is true filth! He spoke softly to himself, as he looked at her eyes and then knew what he wanted to take next. As he also knew he had to work fast, and extract her fingernails just like the first whore.

It was nine thirty seven, when Linda Rivera opened the door with her key. As she entered her apartment she only saw a few lights on in the living room, and no lights coming from her roommate's room as she passed by the closed door. She didn't know what time Sharon would be home, so she decided to give her a call on her cell phone. As she pressed the saved number into her phone, only three seconds passed till the sound of a musical ring, came from within Sharon's bedroom. As Linda stunned by the sound of the phone, went back over to Sharon's room and knocked light on the door. As she called her name;"Sharon?" But there was no answer from her.

Concerned now, Linda turned the doorknob slowly to the right as the door was unlocked. She slowly pushed the door inwards halfway, till she reached her hand out and found the light-switch on the wall and turned the lights on. As her eyes were fixed on the purse on the floor, where it contained the cell phone that was still playing its musical ring, Linda then looked at the bed, as her eyes shot open wide in horror as she let out a loud piercing scream into the room, at the top of her lungs. As she could not keep herself to look at the bloody corpse on the bed, she ran out of the apartment into the hallway, the other neighbor from the apartment above. Came to her door, and looked down the stairs to see what the course of the loud scream was. As Linda looked up and saw her, she calmed herself down enough to yell up to her; "call the police!" she screamed to her.

At eleven o'clock, Ed Brooks was just relaxing on his leather sofa, listening to one of his favorite Jimi Hendrix songs, "Hey Joe". From the sound system of his deluxe, Bose stereo system, as he was drinking a cup of coffee, as his wife Kayla came into the living room, wearing her short silver silk robe, over some nice lingerie she had just put on. As Ed's eyes were fixed on his beautiful wife. Her long red hair, and sparkling hazel colored eyes. Kayla was just less than five feet, nine inches tall. She was a middle school teacher. As she came over and sat in Ed's lap, as he placed the hot mug of coffee on the end table next to him.

"So is there something you would rather do tonight, than listen to Jimi Hendrix CD's all night? Or would you rather join me for some fun?" Kayla asks him with a gleaming smile on her face, as Ed grasps her tight around her waist and pulls her face close to his, as they kiss deeply. As Ed, asks her what kind of lingerie she has on, under her robe. Kayla smiles at him, and answers.

"Well I will give you a hint; you got it for me as a gift this past Valentines Day." She says, as Ed raised his eyebrows and knows what it is.

"Wow, so I think we better make sure it was a special gift I got you". As Ed uses his remote control to turn off the CD player, as he picks Kayla up in his strong arms as they kiss deeply again. As Ed was carrying her to their bedroom, he heard his home phone start to ring. As Kayla, broke their kiss, and told him softly not to answer it. But Ed told her, he didn't want to answer it but he has to. As he sat Kayla back down on the couch, and picked up the phone just after the fourth ring. As Ed, answered; "hello".

"Ed, its Rick, look come meet me along with Rob at 475, Carlton Hills Blvd. We have another similar style case on our hands". Rick informs him. As Ed, looks at Kayla who just makes a sad look on her face, as he tells Rick he will be there as soon as he can.

He hangs up the phone, and bends down to her holding her hands with his. "Hey, I got to go out for a while, but I will be back as soon as I can. I'm sorry sweetheart." He told her, as Kayla had a tear run down her right cheek.

"Go Ed, I will be up waiting for you. Just be careful please." She told him, as Ed kissed his wife again gently and went and got his 9 MM, sidearm and his jacket, as he headed out the door.

Ed arrived at the crime scene just short of a half hour, after he got the call from Rick. He saw the whole block was blocked off from both ends by Northern Division, squad cars. As he glimpsed another county coroners van parked out from the apartment house, as Rick and Rob walked over to him as he got out of his, GMC Envoy. Ed knew this wasn't their jurisdiction, being this latest murder happened in the Northern part of, San Diego. So he knew then, the crime had to be very similar to the Veronica Wood murder.

"The forensic crew is already inside doing the whole ten yards on the scene and the victim". Rick tells Ed and that the two detectives from this division are already interview the victim's roommate and neighbors about any suspects seen with her this evening. As Rob asks Rick, for the victim's name.

"The latest casualty is, twenty nine year old, Sharon Kessler. She lived here with her roommate, thirty two year old, Linda Rivera. Both women are escorts, who really advertised privately on the internet for their services, so it looks like either our suspect sought her out through an online search, or maybe he happened to approach her on the street. As Linda told one of the other investigating detectives, that Sharon had told her, she had no clients set for this evening". Rick told him all he knew so far from what information he was told up to this point.

"So how is this case similar to ours?" Ed asks them. As Rick tells them to glove up, and cover their shoes. That this scene is far worse than the other one, as the three detectives were ready they entered through the door of the apartment and walked through the living room, were they saw Linda Rivera, crying as she was talking to the detectives. As the door to the bedroom was closed, Rick knocked on it, as one crime scene technician opened the door, they saw three other technicians as one was taking photographs of the body and the room, the others were dusting for prints and gathering swab traces for DNA evidence. As Ed and Rob just stood still in place, in absolute shock and horror as they were speechless as they looked at this poor girls remains.

"Oh my God", Rob just muttered softly, as they then walked closer to the bed. The head technician, who worked the first crime scene, removed his mask to talk to Rick and his men. As he explained, just like the first victim, her fingernails were removed and taken by the killer. As he left the other organs he removed from the body, placed at the foot of the bed like the last girl. As Ed, just looked at the organs placed about, her eyes and heart, along with both ears, they were placed in such a way, the eyes and the two ears made what looked like a happy face. As Ed was thinking to himself, he thought of a famous crime committed, years before. As Rick called his name and Ed didn't respond. Rick called his name more loud a second time; "Ed!" As Ed turned to his boss, he was standing next two the two lead detectives assigned to this case. As the men all huddled around to talk and share notes and knowledge of both cases.

"Guys, these are detectives Jack Kerns and Ken Rogers. I filled them in depth of what we know so far, on Veronica Wood. So we are already in agreement that this is the same suspect". All five men agreed, on that so far.

"So he prays on escorts so far, he travels all around the city, not worried about sticking to one sector or pattern of where to commit the murder. He takes the victim's fingernails with him as both a trophy of the crime, and mostly not to leave is DNA, scraped under the fingernails." Ed tells them, as he looks at Ken Roger's shirt that seemed to be stained with water. His partner just looked at Ed and said.

"Ken and I were so shocked by the nature of the crime, he threw up on himself." As Ken admitted he is still in shock by the brutality of this killer's work.

"So do you think the Chief, would want to set up a task force now? Or do we need more murders on our hands as I'm sure he's smart enough to know, we have a serial killer on the loose now in the state of, San Diego." Rob tells them.

"Okay guys just relax for a minute; I need to talk with these guys Lieutenant, about this, since the first crime happened in our division. We would take point lead on this investigation, as far as a task force goes. That is up to Chief John Chase, so I will be briefing him and his staff tonight. Let Kerns and Rogers here; take care of the crime scene and witnesses contact information. As I will make a brief statement to the media about what we know so far", Rick instructs them, as Ed smiles and says to himself, "what is he going to tell them? We don't know any thing ourselves about this guy just yet".

As detective Kerns, tells Rick. The crime scene crew will forward everything to Dr. Adams for a complete DNA analysis like the first murder, and she will brief them all when she gets her results back. As the men are in agreement to stay in touch, they exchange their cell and office numbers and say goodbye for the time being.

It was just two AM, when Ed got home. He parked his Envoy in his garage right next to Kayla's car. As the garage door closed, Ed glanced, a smile at his prized, Fat-boy motorcycle, which was custom painted black with chrome trim. As Ed exited through the garage and up the stairs, he knew Kayla was sleeping so he was quiet as he took off his jacket and his gun, out from his right side holster, and went into his office and turned on his computer. He closed the door not to awake his wife, as he sat back down at his desk and then did a search of; "Jack the Ripper". Ed started to read the history of the Ripper's victims, as he read their names and the passage states. There were five known victims of the Ripper, but maybe as many as eight all together. But the police officials who investigated the crimes in the Whitechaple section of England, in the autumn of 1888. Ed kept on reading about the lead investigators assigned to the case from, Scotland Yard, when the door slowly pushed open inwards as

Kayla entered his office. Ed quickly closed the screen to his lap top computer, not wanting to show her what he was looking at. As she pulled a chair from the corner, to sit next to him, as she knew he was disturbed by something by the look on his face.

"Ed are you all right? I know you can't discuss any thing with me about the cases, but I watched the eleven o'clock news, and they talked about another young woman was found brutally murdered. I'm scared now living here; I'm scared for you being involved in this case". Kayla whispered to him.

"Look, nothing is going to happen to me or you. You know I will never let anyone harm you Kayla. But this is part of my job and so far after all my time on the force here in this city. We are faced with the worst serial killer in decades. But don't worry, because we have so many cops and forensic specialists working the case, we will get a top lead and then we will get him. I promise you." Ed trying to sound positive to Kayla, as they both get up and embrace one another, as Ed tells her, "let us finish, what we didn't start before I left". As he kissed Kayla gently, and picked her up in his broad arms and carried her to the master bedroom.

He read from the old journal again, as he was reading again how his great uncle; Francis Tumblety. He was born in Ireland and grew up in a small town in upstate, Rochester New York, and how he traveled across the states selling his Indian herd remedies, as he called himself a doctor of herbal medicines. He wrote how he treated patients for minor ailments, but the fools were so taken by his persuasion act as a physician, they bought his remedies in hopes they would be cured. From Detroit, to Washington D.C., parts of Maryland and across Europe he would travel, gaining knowledge of how to perfect his con-scheme and meeting very important figures in history he stated; Charles Dickens, and he even was awarded for treating; Louis Napoleon. The second President of the republic of France, at the time, and he was also mentioned as a suspect in the assassination of president; Abraham Lincoln. In St. Louis, in May of 1865, as he was thought by the federal police and Union Soldiers, his false name he was going under at the time, was some how involved with the assignation plot, orchestrated, by John Wilkes Booth and others. But he wrote he was released, when it was known he was using a false name and there was no evidence to charge him with any conspiracy crimes. As Nathan, read more of a passage that really intrigued him greatly.

"The fools thought they had me, days after I decayed the body of Mary, the fools had me. But when they could not hold me, I escaped and to France. Where I boarded the ship back to America, and used the hidden name, Frank Townset. I then fled to Brooklyn, when the fools came looking for me, and I evaded them once again. The great police of Scotland Yard, was too late and powerless to capture me a second time." Francis wrote this passage with an arrogance and novice, as he praised himself for his choice of disguising his names and appearances, to elude capture from Scotland Yard. Who had sent detectives to New York, to apprehend Francis Tumblety, in December 1888, but were too late as he had already moved out of his apartment in Brooklyn, and fled to another state. Very impressed by the way Francis, was so clever and cunning to have never been caught, and was a master of disguise. Nathan; smiled as he looked up from the journal, and stared out the window and wondered.

"So now that I have taken two whores, to sicken them even more and shock the great police of this city. I will plan to move on the next one soon. "For I can't wait to start to cleanse again;" Nathan laughed out loud, as he closed the journal and locked its latch into place.

At eleven thirty AM, two days after the shocking murder of Sharon Kessler. Ed Brooks and his partner Rob Cullen had just been briefed along with the other two investigating officers, Rogers and Kerns. Who came over to central division headquarters to listen to the latest crime scene findings by Dr. Cate Adams. As she found, like the first victim. The body had been cleaned with sterile water, and the killer had to be in complete scrubs or sterile suit, as he was very smart but it was stomach turning to take all ten of her fingernails, just like Veronica Wood. Both Rogers and Kerns said they were returning to the strip mall where, Sharon Kessler was last scene and may have encountered the killer. They were going to see if there were any surveillance cameras in the parking lot, from the malls businesses and interview witnesses if any that night.

As it was now an hour later, noon time, Rob looked up from his computer and asked Ed, what he felt like for lunch, as Rob saw Ed deep into his reading of a book, he had opened on his desk. As Rob, then saw another book face up on Ed's desk. As Rob was surprised as he read the book's title; "History of Jack the Ripper". As Rob looked back at Ed who was still deep into his read.

"Ed, come on now; don't tell me you think this guy now is a copycat of the original Ripper from way back when?" Rob asks his partner, as Ed just looks up at him with a serious look in his eyes.

"Well look, he mutilated his victims just like our suspect now, and if you read about Jack the Ripper's last victim, Mary Kelly. He just hacked this poor women's body and including her face. So there is no doubt in my mind, our man now has been reading up on the original Ripper crimes." Ed responds to him, as Rob asks him if he could look at the book Ed is reading. As Rob looks at the photograph of the crime scene of Mary Kelly, as she lied on her bed in her one room flat, as her body and face were completely destroyed, as her flesh was taken off her face and her intestines and flesh. Was placed on the night table, beside the bed. As Rob read the caption under the picture, and it stated the crime scene even shocked the most veteran detectives of Scotland Yard. Rob, now agrees with Ed, that their suspect now has knowledge of the Ripper, and his style of body mutilation. As they saw Lieutenant Stanford, walk over to their desks, as they quickly put the books away. As Rick was about to inform them of another victim.

"Guys, we just got a call from western division unit. It looks like another body was discovered in Shoreline Park. It's a female, with more similarities to our cases now." Both Ed and Rob just logged off their computers, and put the books and files away. The trio was now on their way, to see the latest victim's body.

Again as they entered the park's main road, there were many squad cars and county medical examiners team. As they were allowed in, by four patrol officers keep out only the police investigators into the crime scene. Ed noticed the two northern division offices being briefed by two other plain closed detectives, as he knew those two had to be with the western division unit. As Rick told his men, let's see what they are talking about, as they approached the four men.

They all greeted one another, as detective Jack Kerns, introduced the two detectives now assigned to this latest murder; "Ed and Rob, this is Skip Jones and Julie O'Keefe from homicide, they will be working on this case now". As they all shook hands and introduced themselves, Rick was called away by a uniformed officer, to go meet with higher ups in the departments. As Ed asked the two new cops, what are the known details about this victim, as Julie O'Keefe read off the details to them.

"The body was discovered around eight AM, by an elderly female walking her dog. The victim is thirty two year old, Lauren Morton. Her neck has multiple deep stab wounds, and her head was decapitated from the body." She read to them very softly, with remorse and shock in her voice. As the macho men, just looked at one another and now knew, their suspect has no fear of the police or anyone else. To leave the body, in a very public place as a park.

Skip Jones led them under the police caution tape, which was lined out many yards away from the crime scene. As they walked into the grassy and wooded park, which it's grass was still wet from the due of the early day. As the victim was laid on her back, spread eagle in position, as the crime scene unit was taking pictures of the body, but already there to take DNA samples and examine the body; was county medical examiner. Dr. Cate Adams. As she greeted all the detectives, as Rick Stanford walked into the crime scene, to join them as he smiled at his girlfriend; Dr. Adams. Cate was telling them the similarities of this body and the other two.

"This young woman's fingernails were also removed. It looks like the same kind of knife to make the deep inflicting wounds. But the decapitation weapon has to be a small axe. I can tell that by the clean sharp edged wound to her neck. But what makes this murder different from the others; it seems she tried to fight him off, due to bruising on her arms and hands, with a deep bruise to her right cheek. That tells me, he killed her somewhere else and placed her body here". Dr. Adams told the group. As Rick had something important to tell them;

"Okay everyone this is coming straight from Chief Chase and his office. He is going to have a press conference within the hour at Central Division headquarters, and after the press conference that we all will be present at. He will be briefing us, as he has charged us as the task force to investigate and apprehend our suspect, as he will be giving us more details in our confidential briefing." Ed just shakes his head in agreement with his Lieutenant, as he looks at the body of Lauren Morton and becomes enraged that another young woman's life has been cut short for no reason, by a mad psychopath on the loose in his city.

Just a half hour after the major press conference that the Police Chief of San Diego, and the mayor conducted at Central Division headquarters. The briefing of the organized task force of detectives, was about to take place in the large conference room. Present were the two team lead detectives of each division where the three murders happened, and as far his overwhelming experience on the force and a longtime resident of San Diego, LT. Rick Stanford, was made lead Lieutenant of the squad. As they were all seated around the large oval wooden table, as they viewed the large LCD projected map of San Diego, where all the points were marked of where the three bodies were found. As each detective had a folder with the crime scene photos, and names of the victims placed in front of them. As there was also a sketch of the only known suspect, and some other details about the forensic findings. As Dr. Cate Adams, was also present for the briefing as chief, John Chase walked into the room with Rick and closed and locked the door behind them. As he took his seat at the front of the table, and Rick sat beside him. All the partners were seated next to one another, as Chase went over with them what he told the media a short time ago. That he told the public, the names and ages of all three women, that they were escorts. That they are dealing with a male serial killer, with a release of his composite sketch of his face. That he is a white male, about five feet nine to six feet tall. As he may use fake mustaches and beards to disguise and conceal his true identity, and that he stated that the police are doing all in their power now. To make sure every citizen of San Diego to safe and not to venture out alone late at night, as all divisions will have more patrol units on the streets round the clock. As he now looked up at all the seated detectives and introduced them to one another, Ed Brooks and Robert Cullen from central division, Ken Rogers and Jack Kerns from the northern division. And from the western division, Julie O'Keeffe and Skip Jones, as he now laid out who was the point team for the task force.

"Okay people, since the first murder happened right here in central division's jurisdiction, Ed and Rob are the lead detectives for the task force. As we have now dubbed our suspect; "The Entity". For his use of disguises and concealing his identity and every move from us up to this point," Chief Chase tells them.

"Rick Stanford is you're leading Lieutenant as he will forward everything over to me and my staff, as I want only a small number of people in on this task force. The smaller I keep people out of it, the better it is and less confusing it will be for you six to work together. As Dr. Adams, will now go over what she has found out so far in the forensic findings of each woman". John chase concludes talking, as Dr. Adams takes out her folders with many pages of DNA analysis findings and she begins to speak to the group.

"Well so far he has the same pattern for removing the fingernails for each victim, which gives me a less of a chance to find any of his skin cells under the women's nails. He has washed the first two bodies clean with a sterile pad or gauze and sterile water. So he knows how not to leave any of his DNA around, as I also believe he wears latex or vinyl gloves and wears some sort of sterile suit for when he gets ready to disembowel the bodies. From the patterns of the knife wounds, he is right handed, very strong from the bruising we have found on the third females skin. I believe she got into the car with him and tried to fight him off once she knew she was in trouble or didn't want to go to the location he suggested. So he killed her in his own car, placed her body in Shoreline Park. Where he then decapitated her with a sharp edged axe I believe. But he stabbed her in the chest with eleven deep knife wounds, as I believe he held her down in his vehicle very strongly as he stabbed her. To leave the multiple bruising marks on her arms and face", Dr. Adams finishes reading off her results of the case.

As the group were all looking at the crime scene photos, Julie O'Keefe asked Dr. Adams what kind of knife did she think was used, as Dr. Adams stated she thought he was using a very sharp; post mortem knife. Made of stainless steel and they must be disposable ones, as he would be smart to use a new one for each victim. As Ed, whispered to Rob under his breath; "just like Jack the Ripper". As Rick asked Ed, if he had a comment and Ed said no, that he just agreed with Dr. Adams.

"So by looking at the map of where he supposedly, meets and then kills his victims, he knows the city well and he doesn't seem to follow any symbolic ritual or any patterns on where to leave the bodies, nor does he care if we find them. It seems he wants us to see how he mutilates the bodies, and then the way he can cover his tracks as if he is daring us to try and stop him." Ed comes out and adds his opinion, as Detective Rogers asks the Chief, if he has any plans to bring in the FBI on this?

"As long as the murders don't go beyond our city limits we can keep this all right here in our city jurisdiction. But if he happens to kill someone beyond our limits, then I'm certain the FBI will get involved. But this is why I decided to bring us all together and stop this now, and keep this whole thing from getting into national headlines, making the San Diego police, inadequate of finding this serial killer. Another reason why I don't want the FBI involved in this one," Chief Chase adds, sounding upset if the FBI and over media exposure takes hold of his city. As he doesn't want any more negative press here;

"So if he is very cunning and knows we are out looking for him now, I say we don't just sit around and hope our uniforms are able to seek him out and stop him in the dead of night. We need a way to draw him out into the open, and conceal ourselves if we are to get the drop on him". Rob Cullen, openly tells them, the task force can't be in a wait and see game with the; "Entity". They need to do something now, to stop him. As Chief Chase and Rick look at one another, and then they stare at the very attractive detective; Julie O'Keefe, as she smiles back at them, and then all the men look at her and smile. As they know what the chief and Rick have in mind, to draw out their suspect in the open.

# Chapter 3

He was frustrated that he wasn't able to have his way with the last female; he wanted to get her alone in a place where he could have had time to perfect his wish. Of having his fun, to open her up and gut her insides out like the first two women. But no, this young woman was smart. She knew something was wrong when Nathan, suggested they go to a secluded location rather than the hotel she suggested as she first got in the car with him. If it wasn't that he locked the doors to his car, she would have gotten away and told the police about him. She fought back hard against him, scratching his face as he tried to hold her hands down, but she was strong and in good shape. He had no choice but to stab her hard many times with his knife, as her blood shot out all over himself and into the dashboard and upholstery. He just took her to the park, after he had killed her and quickly beheaded her, and took her fingernails and washed her body clean. This was the most disappointing victim of the three he thought to himself, as he sat at his desk reading more of the journal. He read how Francis, wasn't able to enjoy one of his victims either. The Ripper's third victim, Elizabeth Stride, whom Francis approached at the early morning hours on September 30th, 1888, he read the passage describing how he was disturbed and unable to enjoy this whore. "I first met this tall and slender street walker, at Berner Street. I talked with her a few minutes as I was wearing my long wool coat and deerstalker hat. I had proposed we go to a cheap lodging house, but she refused when she saw I had my satchel bag, of knives and instruments for my work. She grew loud as I was forced to push her into Dutfield's Yard, and I slit her throat deep with one sharp stroke of my blade. As he body fell to the cold pavement, I took out my other knives and bullseye lantern to give me light to see, in the pitch of darkness and fog of this night. As I was about to gut her up, I heard the steps of the beast and carriage coming close. I quickly saved my tools in my bag, and hid behind the wood fence in the dark. As I saw the rider and pony come into view, as the rider's beast. Reared and bellowed loud in fright, as he was unable to move forward as the body of the whore startled him. As his rider, got off the carriage and lit a match to see what startled his pony, there he saw what I have done, slit the woman's throat as he called for a constable to come and help him. I quietly slid out from the alley way, and walked quickly till I was far away from them, and I found a new whore to deal with, and this time I had my way with her."

Nathan, just read what lead to the night of what is known as the double event. How Francis Tumblety was interrupted with his first victim, by the passing of Louis Diemschutz on his cart and pony. As he wasn't able to mutilate the body of his third victim Elizabeth Stride, but he walked a mile away to he found his fourth victim, Catherine Eddowes, and this time he was able to not only slit her throat deep, but have time to mutilate her in Mitre Square. Where her remains were found just a short time after the body of Stride was discovered. He was satisfied with this cleansing he wrote, as he also took two brass rings he found among Catherine Eddowes, possessions. Francis wrote, "This night was not a total loss, I was able to find another streetwalker and cleanse her good. As I even took a small memento of my two kills. Two cheap brass rings, one for each whore"; he wrote, as Nathan takes hold of the old brass rings in his hand. He smiles to himself, as he now knows he has to make plans to either move on from San Diego, feeling the police may close in on him at any moment. Or maybe they already know, who he really is now, and his moments are counting down as he may be caught soon enough. But he will not be taken alive, no he will go down to death before, he is to be dragged through a police cell and mocked in the media.

"Oh Francis, how I tried to be like you, in disguise and good with your skills of cleaning their foul bodies, but I am against more modern times and better skilled policeman than you dealt with. Oh I will make certain they will not capture me alive, but I will have at least one more thrill to enjoy, unlike the last. I will truly enjoy, opening this next whores insides out, as I will take my time, and behold a last kill. Even more shocking then my uncle's last victim; Mary Kelly", Nathan closes his hand tight on the two rings, as he closes the journal for what may be the last time. And places it with the rings back into the calamander wood box, and locked it closed. He knew he had to prepare to either move on, or get ready to meet his uncle in Hell.

"I will plan one more kill, but I hope it will not be my last. This Friday night, will be the perfect time for it to happen, as I will plan a direct avenue of escape for these fools, who think they can stop me. I will have my name remembered in infamy!" He swears to himself, as Nathan get up from his desk and gets ready to make, what he feels will be his last murder and his coming death.

Kayla had just made dinner for herself and Ed, who were seated together in the dining room. As Kayla looked up at Ed, and who just seemed distant and was barely touching his food, he just kept drinking his ice water, as Kayla was getting upset with him now that he has been acting this way since the last murder. As she also wanted to confront him about something that was bothering her; "Ed, can you please talk to me, for almost four days now we have just talked about certain things around the house and what's for dinner. Please talk to me; I want to support you through all of this." Kayla pleaded to him, as Ed just put down his fork in his plate and pushed his chair up and got up from the table.

"What do you want me to say, I have a murdering psychopath on the loose, I am the lead detective of this new unit we hope will bring him in, plus we are about to do a sting operation I'm not in favor of.

Of course I'm mad and upset, but not with you Kayla. You know I still love you." Ed tells her, as he is now standing in the living room as Kayla gets up and walks over to him, as Ed sees her frustration in her face.

"Ed, besides all this I am tired of you avoiding the issue of when are we going to have a baby. I'm not getting any younger and we have been married a while now, as all my friends and sisters are mothers now, and very happy. I want us to have at least one child together." She tells him, as Ed just rolls his eyes and sits down on his leather couch, as Kayla comes and sits with him.

"Look, this isn't the time to be talking about this now, I know how you feel and you want a baby, but we lost the first one when you miscarried remember, so let me get through this and we will talk about it then okay?" Ed tells her, as Kayla starts to cry, as she remembers when she lost their baby two years before when she was in the early stages of pregnancy.

"So then let's talk about something else, the thing you have been devoting all you're time to ever since these murders happened. I know you been reading and researching the, Jack the Ripper murders from years ago. What the hell is this all about, as I'm not comfortable with these books and you reading up on this stuff in my own house!" She yells at him, as Ed just rubs his hand on his forehead.

"I don't know yet, but these crimes now are very similar to the ripper murders years ago. I haven't told anyone else in the unit except for Rob and now you. I feel there is a pattern here with both cases, then and now". Ed tells her, as Kayla just shakes her head in disbelief.

"Ed, I'm sorry, but I can't be here with you while all this is going on. I am going to stay with my parents for now until this is over, as I don't feel safe being here alone while you're out looking for this person." Kayla tells him, as she gets up and walks quickly to their bedroom, as Ed calls out after her but she just walks away from him. As he curses to himself; "Fuck, Dammit!"

As his cell phone starts to ring, Ed goes over to it on the coffee table where it was sitting right next to his Smith and Wesson 9 mm black gun. As he answers the phone, it was Rick. Telling him to come down to central division that the chief has given the go ahead to their sting operation for this evening, as Ed tells him he understands. He just gets his gun and a few other things together, as he hears Kayla taking out her suitcases from the closet, to pack them with clothes for herself. She is getting ready to move out of the house, as Ed picks up his Envoy keys and just shakes his head as he slams the door behind him. Kayla stopped packing and heard the door close, as she just said a prayer softly; "God please look over Ed for me," As she started to cry again.

It was Friday evening, June the twenty ninth. As Ed and Rob walked into the conference room, as they passed the other cops in the hallway, they all saw the serious look they had on their faces, knowing something was going down tonight. As they entered the room, they saw Rick Stanford and Chief John Chase, along with one of his deputy chiefs. As all the detectives in the task force were seated except for Julie O'Keefe, as Ed and Rob took their seats. Chief Chase began to talk about the operation, which was going to take place tonight, as the lights dimmed and the LCD screen, lit up a huge image of of city of San Diego.

"Thanks for coming so quickly, I'm sorry we couldn't call you guys sooner, but the mayor just gave us to go ahead on this a short time ago. As Rick and my staff have been busy pulling the top patrol teams from each division we feel, will be best suited to work on this operation with you people. So as we know, he doesn't seem to have a particular pattern to stay in when he meets a woman, and then kills her. But we feel, since the last murder took place in the western area of La Playa, where we felt he met Lauren Morton, and then left her body in Shore Line Park. We feel this is the area we want to concentrate our focus on tonight, and see if he will take the bait we will set for him." The Chief informs them, as he tells Rick now to go over the plan of action they both devised.

"We will have our female operative work this area of Liberty station, we feel it's a great industrial sector of the city, where truck drivers and cabbies meet people and stop on their way to, nearby San Diego International Airport. We feel if we have our patrol men, cordon off this seven mile radius of Liberty Station, and have cruisers set on all ramp points and exit ways off of Lanning Drive, and North Harbor Road. We can contain him in this square pattern of seven miles. As myself the chief and you men only, will be the only units close by to our operative, in plain colored cars. As we will be on a one channel radio to ourselves, as I and the chief will be the only ones to communicate with the cruisers if we have to box him in, to avoid too much radio confusion. We have the best in body armor for all you guys to wear, as we want you to carry one side arm only with extra clips, and the small ear piece radio only. Just in case we have to give a foot chase, we can move swiftly with less to carry. Do we all agree with this assignment, or any questions?" Rick asks them, as all the detectives look at one another and seem very comfortable with this plan. As Ken Rogers raises his hand and asks, Rick, who is their decoy?

Rick and the chief smile, as Rick asks for Skip Jones to bring her in. Skip leaves the conference room and comes back with Julie O'Keefe, who is wearing a long black raincoat. As Skip closes the door behind them, Julie smiles at them as she takes off the coat, revealing to them her undercover uniform. She is wearing a short black skirt, just above her knees, with black stockings and short black leather boots. With a black sweater, and short dark blue denim jacket, as he medium length brown hair is made up very nice, and her face done nice with makeup and her brown eyes, are glowing in the rooms light. As Rob and Jack Kerns, whistle loud. To let them all know they think Julie looks very attractive as she places her hands on her hips and smiles at them.

"So you men didn't think, I was good enough to be the undercover target for this creep? Did you guys?" She asks them being very coy and laughs, as all the men agree she is the right choice for the decoy. As Rick, instructs Julie and the team how they are going to set this up now.

"Julie, this is where you're going to walk on the main stretch of Central Ave. As it has two lanes of opposite traffic, and we want you to walk on the northbound side, so it will be easy for us to pick up any vehicle that comes in contact with you. We will be in three unmarked vehicles, myself and Skip, Ed and Rob, followed by Ken and Jack. All three units will be no less than two blocks apart, as we will have you under surveillance from all vehicles with night vision scopes, and we will have our helicopter airborne once your picked up by any vehicle, so they can detect you by FLARE night vision from above. You will have the small ear piece radio and microphone disguised as the gold butterfly broach on your jacket, but you will only have mace, to carry in your small hand purse. So you will be vulnerable if we lose track of you, and he has you cornered alone somewhere. So are you certain, you want to carry on with this plan? Rick asks her, concerned for her safety.

"Look Rick, I know all you guys will be there looking after me. But I also know this might be the only way to stop this person. I am afraid to put myself in this position, but I'm also mad he took three young lives for no reason. I want to do this, I will be fine, I promise you all." Julie tells them, sounding confident she will be able to pull this sting operation off.

As chief Chase, looks at the time on the wall and his watch he knows they have to move into positions now, as he gives some last directions on what to do. "All right, Rick I will be in mobile command unit one, situated right off of North Harbor Drive. My team and I will be listening to all your radio transmissions, and viewing you all with our monitors. I will not break into radio transmission until Julie, is picked up by a vehicle and we can start to have our units blocking off the main intersections to box the suspect's vehicle in. Any questions people?" No one answers the chief, as he says good and let's move then. As all the men rise from their seats and gather their things and walk out to the parking lot. As Rick instructs Julie, she will ride with himself and Skip and drop her off on Central Ave. As she is putting on her raincoat, Ed comes over to her, and whispers to her softly.

"Hey don't worry, we have you're back covered and I will not let you get hurt tonight, you got that." Ed tells her, as Julie smiles at him and places a hand on Ed's chest.

"I know Ed, just you be careful yourself and no big hero stuff for either of us if it does happen that way, promise me?" She asks him, as

Ed smiles at her and says; "I promise, come on let's go." He tells her as they walk out the back entrance to the parking lot, and get into their vehicles and drive towards the target location.

Rick is able to watch Julie, with is single night vision scope, as she walks up and down the street smiling at passing cars. As Rick, stays in communication with the other two vehicles, all they have scene for over an hour's time now, has been four vehicles approach Julie, but the male drivers just complimented on her sexy figure, and they did not offer to pick her up. As Ed and Rob were talking to one another, that maybe he will not show up tonight. As Rob told him to just be patient, that it was only eleven forty five PM that the chief instructed the operation will be cold off by one AM, if they made no contact with any suspects by then.

"I see she is using her cell phone, was she instructed to have it visible?" Rob asks Ed, as he nods yes to him.

"The chief and Rick thought by her being on her cell phone, talking and texting. It would really make it look like, she is an escort in contact with a client to set up a date for tonight. Besides, they told her if she was in a vehicle with a suspicious person, to text Rick a quick description if she could to him. Being she can't say it out loud to get his attention that she is a cop." Ed informs Rob, as he tells Ed, the chief and Rick thought of a good plan for this, but he hopes their suspect will show up.

Slowly Nathan drove on Lanning Road, as he had scanned for his next target. He passed a few females on the way, but none that really took his eyes to any interest. If this was to be his last offering, he wanted her to be very special, and he had the ultimate cleansing planned for her. As he drove in one of his other vehicles, a Jaguar X type, that was metallic gray. He didn't have time to clean and wash all the blood out of his, other car that had the smell of death in it still from the last meeting. He was looking for the perfect female tonight, as he was wearing a dark blue suit over his black scrubs. As he turned and looked at his bag in the backseat, he knew he would not make the same mistake like last time. He will earn her trust, and then get away from the populated roads, and once alone. He will slit her throat right away; don't even give her a chance to breathe so he could then take her to the place he had all picked out, so he could pick away at her body without worry and interruptions.

As he made a right turn onto Central Ave. He saw one female than another, but not satisfied until his right eye caught a glimpse of the female walking up ahead with her back to him. Even from behind he knew, this one was different from the rest. He started to slow his speed, as he got into the right lane. He was parallel to her left shoulder, as Julie noticed the gray jaguar to her left. As she put her cell phone in her bag and then looked directly into the vehicles passenger side window and gave the driver a smile, as she was smiling, she whispered into her microphone; "Rick, gray Jaguar, to my left". As rick responded to her, he sees the vehicle; "Approach him Julie; guys get ready to move". He instructs the team, as Julie walks over to the gray vehicle, as the driver lowers the window to greet her.

"Hello nice man, with the fine looking car". Julie says to him, as she looks at him good, ready to send back a detailed description to her fellow detectives. As she notices his short gray curly hair and long sideburns, but he was clean shaven and wearing a dark blue suit.

"Good evening my dear, would you care to have a nice getaway for the two of us, in this great cosmopolitan city of ours tonight?" He asks her, as Julie knows right away this man is educated and suave with his words, one thing the team thought he possessed to earn the victim's trust.

"My goodness, you're and educated man and very handsome. I will be honored to spend the evening with you." Julie answers him, as he opens the passenger door for her, as Julie slowly gets into the Jaguar and very slowly brings her legs together and rests her purse on her lap, as she closes the door. He smiles at her, and then looks for oncoming traffic as he slowly drives northbound on Central Ave. As Nathan and Julie introduce themselves, Rick and the others see them drive off, as he tells his men softly to follow them. As all three vehicles move onto Central Ave. Rick tells Skip, to stay two vehicle lengths behind the jaguar and for Rob and Ken, to stay three vehicle lengths behind them, not to raise the man's suspicions.

Chief John Chase, hearing all that is taking place, he orders the helicopter to take off, and follow the gray Jaguar and for his patrol vehicles to start to close off the intersections of Barnett Ave, and Rosecrans St. As he wants to get Julie out of that vehicle as quickly as possible, as Rick focuses on the vehicles license plate number, that reads, CBQ-7298, Rick tells mobile command the plate number, as the officer who is in contact with him. Confirms the number again, as they start to search the computer to find out who it's registered to, as the vehicles speed is only forty miles per hour, as they confirm he is being cautious.

"So where do you want to go tonight, any hotel you have in mind?" Julie asks him, as he looks over and smiles at her. Julie knows just by looking he is wearing a wig, with fake gray sideburns. As the color of gray in his hair, does not match the color of his sideburns very well. As she takes out her iPhone and sends Skip a quick text; "He's in a disguise, dark blue suit". As Skip holds up his cellphone, and reads the text to Rick. Rick then, tells everyone on the radio what the suspect is wearing.

Nathan taken by her stunning beauty knows this was the perfect catch tonight, as he already has this planned out now. "Julie my dear, on this perfect night how would you like to see the nice rays of the full moon, shines off the crystal blue waters of the Pacific Ocean at Ocean Beach." He asks her, as Julie quickly thinks, that area has many remote deserted locations this time of night. Knowing he has plans for her, she goes along with him.

"That sounds romantic for us; may I ask what you do for a living? Being a fine tailored educated man." She asks him, as he just turns and smiles at her, feeling uncomfortable she asked him this question as to way it would matter, and so far she didn't ask what her donation would be yet. As Nathan is already suspicious of her as Julie again texts in her lap, Nathan was about to answer her, he notices her sending a massage on her phone again. "I'm a real estate agent my dear, and who can you be texting again this late at night?" He asks her, as Julie sent the last text to skip quickly, as he read it to Rick.

"Ocean Beach, that's where he's taking her," Skip yelled to Rick, as he radioed it over to the other two cars and the mobile command. As Chief Chase, ordered patrol vehicles to Ocean Beach at once. Ed hearing all this, as he notices the Jaguar begin to pick up speed. He orders Rob to drive faster, as their car begins to pass Rick's vehicle on the left hand lane, as Rick becomes angry, as he tries to motion to Ed and Rob to stay back.

"Come on Ed, we can't get too close to his car. He might get tipped off we are tailing him." Rob explains, as Ed is convinced this has to be the suspect, as he yells back at Rob; "Rob it's him I know it! Just stay close to him now, and before he makes the left turn onto Barnett Ave. Cut him off!" Ed orders, as Rob tells him, they can't the man hasn't done anything wrong yet. As Ed screams again at him to just do it. As Rob shakes his head, his car now passes Rick's vehicle as they are now next to the Jaguar in the center lane, as Ed starts to stare at Nathan who is looking straight ahead at the road, waiting to make the left turn up ahead. As Julie, looks passed Nathan, and looks at Ed in confusion. Knowing this isn't going the way Rick and the Chief had planned it.

Rick furious with Ed and Rob, yells on the radio; "units close off Barnett Ave! Don't let him turn onto it! Ed, what the Fuck are you doing"! Rick yells on the radio, as mobile command acknowledges Rick's orders two squad cars quickly close in from the shoulders as Nathan turns to his left, and see's the vehicle keeping pace with his, his eyes then lock dead, with Ed's eyes; as Ed gives him a stare of deep hatred, he knows it's the Entity. "You Son of A Bitch"! Ed screams in anger, as Nathan then gives him an evil smile, he responds to Ed; "She's mine!"

As Nathan locks the doors to the car, he quickly slams on his breaks. As Rob passes his vehicle, and Skip stops short along with Ken's vehicle in the right hand lane. As Nathan turns into the opposite lane and now is heading southbound. As Ed screams to Rob to turn around and follow them, Rob screeches the tires hard as they turn around. The two patrol cars barely miss their vehicle, as Skip was also turning around, with Ken's car. All four vehicles collide head on in a violent collision. As Rob floors the gas, to keep up with the Jaguar, as Ed yells to him to hurry, stay with them, Julie's life is in peril.

Nathan looks behind at the black sedan gaining on them, as he turns to Julie, who is trying to open her side door, even though it's locked. Nathan, just looks over and screams to her; "You Bitch cop!" As he grabs her arm, and pulls her away from the door, and slaps her across the face as the force of the slap, cuts her bottom lip open, as blood starts to flow down the right side of her lip. As Nathan comes to the intersection, he thinks fast of what to do. He makes a hard right turn onto, North Harbor Drive. As he thinks of an escape route for himself, but he wants to kill Julie first. If this was to be his last day on Earth, he will take her life with him, he swore to himself. As Rob came to the intersection, and floored it hard to make the right turn. Barely missing another vehicle, as the chase continued now eastbound, towards San Diego International Airport, and where mobile command was based. As Ed yelled on the radio their position, the helicopter circled above and shown its blue searchlight down on the Jaguar, as Nathan cursed to himself, as he looked up at it. He was without a firearm to match the police, as he didn't think he would need to carry one, being he thought he would always get away with his crimes. As Julie, tried desperately to grab hold of the steering wheel and force him to crash. Nathan, punched her hard in the face, as Julie flew back into her seat, as he reached into his inside pocket, and produced a steel scalpel, as he was going to slit her throat. Julie, quickly, took out her small mace bottle, and sprayed him right into his left eye. As Nathan screams in pain, as it burns his eye. Julie again tries the door, as she was able to unlock it and pushed herself out onto the road, as she hit the hard pavement but kept her hands over her face, as she spun on the hard surface, as it burned her skin and scraped and cut her knees and arms. Nathan, was able to glimpse the airport up ahead, as he made a hard left into the entrance, smashing through the checkpoints gate arms. As Rob, came to a stop as they saw Julie, on the right shoulder on the side of the road. As he and Ed exited the vehicle and ran over to her.

"Julie, are you all right! Ed shouted to her, as he held her in his arms, as she started to come to, she started to cry as she held him tight. As Rob took out a clean handkerchief, and covered her right knee that was bleeding heavily. As Ed, thanked God she was alive, he then became enraged for this. "Rob, stay with her!" Ed screamed as he ran to the ford, he slammed both doors shut and took off after Nathan. As two squad cars came and stopped to aid Rob and Julie, as Rick and Skip were inside one of them. Rob told him, Ed was now in pursuit of the Jaguar, as the helicopter's co-pilot confirmed the suspects' vehicle has entered the airport. But they couldn't follow overhead; being air regulations forbids even police aircraft to fly over any free airspace for safety reason. As Ed, follows the path made by the Jaguar, he then slows down some, as he is in a very populated area, as he has to be careful not to endanger any innocent civilians. As Ed slowly drives down a service area of the airport, knowing this is where the suspect would have likely driven, being it's less populated.

As Rick and Rob arrived at mobile command with Julie, an ambulance was waiting there as they rushed her to the nearest medical center for treatment, she was in shock and had multiple cuts to her hands and face, along with that deep gash to her right knee, but as they loaded her into the ambulance, she was crying and thanked the team and most of all Ed, for saving her life. As Rick was on the radio with Ed, and twelve squad cars that entered the airport, they began to canvas and search the areas, as the security at all the checkpoints. Were given a description of the suspect, in case he tried to board a flight out of San Diego, as Ken and Jack were inside working with the security, Ed remained outside with the patrol cars, as Rick turned to Chief Chase, and told him that this guy is very smart. He knew by going into the airport they would lose him. As just then, they received all call that the suspect's vehicle had been found, as the west end of the airport. Ed raced over there, as he was met by two squad cars.

Ed quickly got out and gazed over the inside of the vehicle, as he saw marks of fresh blood, which had to be Julie's. As the bag that Nathan had in the backseat was gone, as Ed cursed to himself as he looks around that this is the area for returned rental vehicles, as Ed notices two uniformed officers talking with a rental agent. Asking him if he saw anything, Ed joins the conversation as the man says he didn't see anything as he was behind the counter with his back turned to the window. But he then heard the start of the engine to a car and drive away towards the west end gate. As Ed shouted at him; "what kind of vehicle was here?" The man replied, a new blue, Nissan Altima. As Ed, races to his Ford and drives out the west entrance, as he was now cutting through the, Midway district and heading onto the San Diego Freeway, that was going to take Ed, back westbound. As he radioed back, for any luck finding a blue Altima from above, by the helicopter, as they radioed back, he must have been keeping the speed limit not to draw attention to himself. As Ed curses to himself, and yells back to Rick. If there was any luck checking the vehicle's license plate number, as Rick was handed a print out by an officer; "we got something Ed! The vehicle is registered to a Dr. Nathan Malcolm; 8540, Hill Street, the Sunset Cliff Estates!" Rick yells to Ed over the radio, as Rick along with Rob head to a vehicle, Ken and Jack race out of the airport with the patrol vehicles as Chief Chase, renounces the suspects name and address over the radio, every unit is to converse on this location "the order is given to shoot the suspect, if he is deemed hostile!" Orders the Chief, as he races out of mobile command, and gets into a squad car that will meet with all the other units at the location of the suspect's home.

Ed who already has a head start beyond any other vehicle, just placed his flashes on as he gunned his car up to eighty miles per-hour. He knew this area of San Diego; he knows only well off people lived here. As he thought to himself, Dr. Nathan Malcolm, the man who us embroiled in that pharmaceutical drug case, that his trial was set to start at the end of the month. He was released on his own recognizance since he posted bail, and he wasn't charged with a crime to hurt another individual. As Ed came upon the exit for Chatsworth Blvd, it will take him right to Sun Cliff Estates.

Nathan had parked the car down the street, in order to buy him some time. As he entered his large home, he began to gather the two small carry bags he had made for himself. As he knew he couldn't carry anything larger to get away now, since he had to hurry. He quickly went over his desktop computer, and smashed it with a baseball bat. Want to destroy all evidence of searches on the hard drive, but he knew that wasn't good enough. He had to get his plan ready if he was to deceive them, he had to destroy his home. As he went behind the bar in his living room, he poured the contents of alcohol all over the walls and curtains of his home, as he ran to the kitchen and turned off the flames to the gas pilots of the stove heads, to let the gas seep into the air. As he lit a match and threw it down to the carpeting of the living room, igniting a flame that shot fast up to the curtains and walls. As fire now, engulfed the inside of his house, as Nathan tried to focus from his left eye, which was enflamed from the burning mace. He then, threw a bottle of vodka to the wood stairs, and lit another match that flamed the stairs with fire. As he then dowsed one last, object on the floor with more alcohol. He was about to pick up the bags as Ed, came crashing through the front door, as his gun flew out of his right hand, as he dropped it from the sheer force of breaking the wood framed door. Nathan, stood there in shock as both men locked eyes again, as Ed got to his feet, "You Bastard"! Ed yelled, as he charged at Nathan and both men collided together as they fell to the floor, with scorching flames all around them, as they rolled on the floor. Ed raised his hand back, and with a hard clenched fist drove it hard into Nathan's face, and again. As he hit him a third time. As he then raised his head off the floor and smashed it back down onto the hard wood floor, Ed without mercy for this man for the brutalities of murder he has done. Ed curses and swears as blood shot out of Nathan's nose and mouth, and from the back of his head. As he was able to reach the doubled edged sharp knife, he kept strapped to his left ankle. He took hold of the sharp blade, and thrust it deep into Ed's left side, and pushed it in deeper; "Die you foul cop! You're too late to stop me!" Nathan screams at Ed, as Ed falls off of him screaming in pain. As wet blood begins to rush out of the deep open wound in his side, as Ed looks for his gun, but can't see clearly as the smoke from the raging fire begins to blaze out of control as Nathan comes closer to Ed with the knife in his right hand.

He reaches down and grabs Ed's shirt with his left hand, as he was going to strike him in the neck with the steel knife. Ed blocked the swing with a roundhouse right hook, as the knife flew from Nathan's hand. Ed then hit him in the face hard, and again. As Ed grabbed him by his jacket, and flung Nathan into the raging fire. As he screamed in mortal pain, as Ed saw him burn from the waste up, As Ed was able to get to his feet and leap through the large window panes and crash through the glass and onto the front lawn of the home. As Rob and Rick had just pulled into the driveway with other units, they got Ed to his feet and they all ran behind the safety of the cars, as the home exploded outward with glass and debris. As they took cover just in time, as Rick looked up and saw the fire was out of control now. He reached into the car for his radio, and called for the fire department and an ambulance.

As Rob looked down at Ed, and saw he was shaking in pain. As Rob asked him what was wrong, as other vehicles arrived with Ken and Jack. As Ed didn't answer Rob, but kept shaking in pain, as Rob then felt wet blood all over his hands and knew Ed had a major stab wound to his left abdomen. "Shit!" Rob yelled as he took off his jacket and covered the wound, as Rick and the other detectives raced over to Ed. "The ambulance is coming!" Rick yelled, but Rob knew by the amount of blood Ed was losing they couldn't wait. "We have to take him ourselves to the hospital!" As the three men helped Ed into the backseat and Rick got into the driver's seat of the Ford, and floored the gas to the floor, as they took Ed to the Emergency Room, of the trauma center. As Rick made Ken call them on his cell phone, to be prepared for an incoming male patient, with a major stab wound to his left side. As they would be ready to take him into surgery on arrival.

As Ed lay on his back, in the backseat as Rob kept pressure on the wound. Ed started to close his eyes, as he was losing conscientious as he was going into body shock. "Ed stay with me! Don't you dare die! Rob yelled to him. As Rick, was weaving in and out of vehicles on the freeway, as he told Rob they were less than a mile away from the hospital. As Rob told Ed, he got the bastard. That the fire department arrived and was fighting the fire he set at his own home. As Rick told Rob, no to worry about that right now, as he pulled into the entrance of the E.R. there were four nurses and a trauma surgeon already there with a gurney, to take Ed to the O.R. As Rick screeched to a stop, the men pulled Ed from the car and onto the gurney. As they rolled him into the E.R. and towards the elevators, as Rick was answering the Doctors questions of what side, of his abdomen was punctured. As they headed up to the fourth floor, and hurried the stretcher inside the open double doors. As Rick and Rob, were told they couldn't go any further, as they watched the doors closed. Rob just looked at all the blood on his hands, as he then looked up at Rick, who answered him. "He's going to make it Rob, don't worry".

As the trauma team had prepared Ed, for surgery. The two head surgeons were looking at the wound while their team, prepared Ed with intravenous lines and he was given anesthesia. As the head nurse monitored his vital signs, she told the doctors he was stable now. As they prepared t look at the deep wound to his upper abdomen. As one surgeon announced his spleen had been punctured an artery was severed, as he asked for clamps to stop the blood, from gushing out of the deep wounds. As the nurses were changing bloody dressings around the wound, the other doctor asked what his blood type was, that they needed to start a flow of blood into the IV line for Ed, as he was losing too much blood. As the team raced around one another, the surgeon began trying to suture the artery closed first, but the spleen kept bleeding simultaneously. As the two doctors looked at one another, the head surgeon shook his head no to him, as the nurse told him his vitals are dropping.

"Look, we are going to have to close both wounds at the same time. If we don't we are going to lose him." Shouted the head surgeon, as the other agreed with him and asked what he should do.

"Here clamp the spleen in four places, and begin to close the wound from the smaller penetration gap up to the major gap. As I will work on the severed artery, it's the only way to save him!" As the staff, agreed with the lead surgeon, he then asked the head nurse to help keep the suction going on the blood as he began to work on the artery. As Rick, was in the waiting room of the O.R., along with all the detectives and Skip Jones had just joined them. As he was with Julie, who was admitted for observation after receiving stitches to her right knee and had other various cuts bandaged and clean. As she was now resting, unaware what had happened to Ed, as Skip and the others didn't want her to worry for now, as she was sedated and resting. As Rob's wife Antonella , met Kayla in the lobby as they walked into the waiting room together. As they were just called by Rob to get to the hospital as soon as possible as Rob and his wide embraced each other. Kayla, confused asked Rick where Ed was. As he just took her hands and sat with her on the couch, and told her what happened to him. But he hasn't received any word yet of what his status was from the doctors. As Kayla became hysterical and started to scream, as Rob and his wife tried to comfort her, Rick and his men just became full of remorse, as they just looked at the wall clock and noted that Ed has been in surgery going on over an hour now. As Rick felt, it didn't look good for his friend. But just said to himself, "come on Ed, you can make it buddy".

Over two hours later, the two surgeons entered the waiting room as they came over to Kayla, who was seated next to Antonella. As the lead surgeon, Dr. Stewart Foster held her hands, and spoke softly to her. "Mrs. Brooks, we were able to close the wounds to Ed's spleen and also one of its major arteries that was heavily torn open. He lost a tremendous amount of blood, and we had to administer blood into him, to keep his heart and other major organs functional while we operated on him. I'm happy to say, he will make it. But there will be a long amount of time for recuperating for him to come." As Kayla, smiled and began to cry, she hugged and thanked Dr. Foster for saving Ed's life, as all his friends gave each other handshakes and thanked God that he will be all right. As Chief Chase, was now at the hospital being briefed on the status of both detectives. He was now set to give his press conference of what had transpired tonight.

Chief John Chase took the podium as Rick and other top officials all lined behind him as he spoke, as this late breaking news conference going on at four o'clock in the morning. As he was instructed he could begin to talk now; "at exactly eleven PM last night, we set into motion a sting operation to try and flush out the suspect in the brutal slayings of three prostitutes in our city. As myself and others in my staff, formed an elite task force of veteran detectives to work this complex case. We were forced to take unorthodox measures to flush out our suspect; we had named the Entity for concealing his identity from us, through the use of many disguises and his medical knowledge of the crimes. We had to use a female operative to go undercover as an escort to lure the suspect into the open, as she was wired and under constant surveillance and contact with our team as she was picked up by our suspect in the Liberty station section of the city, that we had cordoned off for the operation to take place. Our female operative made contact with the suspect at around twelve ten AM, as she was picked up in his vehicle as he had plans to take her to a secluded location and carry out another mutilation as like the three previous victims. But our teams moved in to first save our detective, and then apprehend the suspect. In which time, our female detective, was assaulted in the vehicle and then was able to throw herself out of the moving car, as a car chased ensued within the area of San Diego International Airport. We were able to safely secure our operative, and get her medical attention right away, where she is currently admitted here at Mercy Hospital for several but non-life threatening injuries. As during the car chase, we were able to trace the suspects vehicles license plate number back it it's registered owner, as Dr. Nathan Malcolm. Who was currently set to stand trial in the Quasar Pharmaceutical scandal case, as our lead detective, followed Dr. Malcolm back to his residence in the Sunset Cliff Estates area. Where Dr. Malcolm attempted to escape but first to try and conceal his evidence of the crimes, he attempted to set fire to his home and destroy vital evidence of his involvement. Where our lead detective was able to confront the suspect in his home, and a violent struggle took place, where our operative was severely injured and the suspect ended up perishing in the fire, which caused a gas explosion that destroyed the house. As the fire department discovered the remains of the very charred body at two AM this morning and by medical and dental records of the suspect, we made a positive identification that the badly burned body was that of, Dr. Nathan Malcolm. As lead detective Edward Brooks, received a deep stab wound to his left abdomen that took surgeons hours of time to close and heal the wound. As he and our female operative whom we are withholding her name at this time for her safety, are both resting and expected to make full recoveries." As the Chief was done giving all the facts in the case, he then announced not only Brooks, but the whole task force will receive Stella awards for their work in this case, from the Mayor and city of San Diego.

# Chapter 4

## Four Years Later

Ed pushed up on the barbell, and let out a deep breath of air from his mouth. As he brought it back down to his chest, and raised it up high once again as he then placed the barbell that held two hundred and fifty pounds of weights. Back onto the rests of his free weight bench press unit, that was in his spare bedroom. He then sat up and started to drink some bottled water, to cool himself down. As he listened to heavy metal songs, playing loud from his stereo system for motivation as he worked out this early Tuesday morning. As Ed got up and went over and shut off the CD player, he used the towel to wipe all the sweat off his forehead and arms. As he went into his master bathroom, to shower and shave to get ready for work, he took off his white tank-top. As he stared at himself in the full mirror, Ed turned to his left to look at the remains of the scares he had from the only encounter with the serial slayer, Dr. Nathan Malcolm. As Ed, gently glided his hand over the long scare that didn't hurt him anymore, it was just a reminder to him how this case has affected his life now. As he then, took off his gray sweat bottoms and entered his glass enclosed shower, as the warm water relaxed him as he thought of what this day would bring him now at work.

At nine AM, Ed met Rob in the employee lounge as they sat down and talked over breakfast and coffee. As they made small talk, knowing they have been slow with no recent cases on their agenda's lately. As both men, didn't mind not being busy at all. As Rob, was telling Ed he and his wife are just busy these days with their four year old daughter, Megan. That his wife, wants her enrolled in modeling for toddler clothes adds and commercials as Antonella, feels she has the look and the early talent to be a future model and actress. As Ed, wishes them good luck, with Megan. As Rob thanks him, he notices Ed is still wearing his wedding band on his left ring finger. He knew this was the time to bring it up to him now; "hey Ed, you know I don't like to pry into your personal life. But it's been three years now that you and Kayla got divorced. It's time for you to ditch that ring and move on now, Antonella and I were talking about you last night. We want you to move on and be happy again, so get rid of that cheap gold ring and come out with us this Friday night for dinner." Rob told him, as Ed just looked at his partner and knew he was concerned about him.

"I know you guys really care for me, and I know I should take off my ring. But Kayla and I still talk, as she asked me to come over this weekend and paint the bedroom for her. Her fiancée is out of town on a business trip. So I agreed to do it for her, I don't mind. It gives me something to do besides of always lifting weights and playing my guitar." Ed tells him laughing.

"Well just think about coming over the house for dinner with us, Antonella is going to make another one of her top Italian pasta and veal dishes, so I know you don't want to miss a free meal like this one". Rob tells him, as Ed thanks him and says he will be at Rob's house six PM sharp, for dinner Friday night. As they get up from the lounge table and head to their desks in the homicide division.

As both men sat down at their desks, they were going over the recent cases they were assigned this week. No homicides just, two gang related assaults and one domestic violence case. That they could go interview the witnesses and the gang members who were involved, and maybe have this all done by three PM and call it an early day, as Rick came by to talk to them.

"Hey guys how's it going?" He asked them.

"Not much boss, anything new with you or around here today?" Rob asked him.

"Here it's been slow, so that's good. Getting married to Cate has been a blessing in my life. Because now I have her to make the bed in the morning and cook me dinner for when I get home." He says as they all laugh, as Rick suggests they all go out for some drinks after work. At the usual cop hangout bar, just three blocks down the street. As Ed and Rob agreed, to meet Rick there around eight PM in the evening.

Just after eight o'clock, the three cops were seated in the back of Four-Clover's Pub. Sharing drinks, and talking how they have to all get together with their wives to go out to eat at a restaurant sometime soon. As Rob knew he shouldn't have mentioned the word wives, being Ed wasn't married any more. But he looked at Ed's ring finger, and noticed he had taken off his wedding band. As rob was pleased, that Ed had listened to him. As he was going to let Rick be the one to ask Ed this question, and the real reason they wanted to get him alone tonight at the pub. As Rob glanced at Rick, and he knew it was time to talk to Ed.

"Hey Ed, Rob and I have been talking lately. We know you been through a lot not only being alone again. But we know what happened four years ago is still haunting you now, maybe it's time you considered retiring and moving on with your life. Find a new woman and settle down again, while you're still young and able to have kids like us." Rick asks him, as Ed just looks up and smiles at them.

"I know I can retire any time now and get my full pension, but I need to still be active with the job. It keeps me busy and I just want to be able to help our city being out there, from preventing any more murders and bad crimes." Ed reacts to their suggestion that he retire now. As Rob, was getting frustrated over this, he had to come out and tell his partner how he really felt what was going on in his life the last four years.

"Ed, it's over with! You got him four years ago, now let it go! It almost cost you your life, it round up costing you you're marriage. You need to let this go, there is no connection here with Malcolm and Jack the Ripper, over a hundred years ago! Now move on for your own sake of mind." Rob tells him, in a bold voice. As when he mentioned, Jack the Ripper; a few people in the bar looked over at them. As Ed now shot Rob a cold stare, a look that told Rob to back off of him. As Rick, told Rob to relax.

"Look, I have looked into the ripper case for over four years now. And I'm convinced that Nathan Malcolm was related to one of the top suspects of the ripper murders then, and he must have found out recently before he started his own crazed rampage that gave him his motivation to kill those women". Ed responds to them. As Rick just shakes his head in disbelief.

"Ed, even if you're right about this. It doesn't matter anymore, Malcolm is dead. Jack the Ripper, even though we may never know who he really was, is long dead now. Unless Malcolm came back to life as him in reincarnation, so let it go! There is nothing left for you to prove, you should be very happy that you saved Julie's life that night. And God knows how many more innocent young women, at the time". Rick tells him, as Rob shakes his head yes in agreement with him. As Ed, just looks down at his cold glass of beer, and feels they may be right. That after four years of investigating the ripper murders on his own, it has consumed him and stressed himself out. As Ed was about to answer them, Rick's cell phone was going off. As Rick, got up and excused himself to answer his phone. Ed and rob, felt it maybe Cate asking him where he was at this time of night. As Ed, thanked Rob for his and Rick's concern about his wellbeing. As Rob, told him not to mention it. That he and Rick and their wives want nothing for the best for Ed.

As they looked over at Rick in the corner on his cell phone, they knew he wasn't talking to his wife by the serious look on his face as he was finishing his phone call. As he walked back over to their table, as Rob asked Ed, what is this all about now?

"Hey guys, we have a body that was just discovered a short time ago; a young female that looks like a homicide." Rick tells them as Ed studies the upset look in his eyes.

"Why do you look so upset over this? Is there something more to it? Ed asks him, as Rick hesitates to answer him.

"The body was discovered in Shoreline Park, and the victim has been badly mutilated". Rick tells them, as Ed and Rob's jaws just dropped open. Shoreline Park was the last place of the Dr. Nathan Malcolm murders was discovered four years ago. As the three detectives got up and shot out the door, to the parking lot and get to the crime scene right away.

At nine fifteen PM, the three detectives from Central Division. We're being briefed by the uniformed police from the Western Division, as two familiar detectives joined them to talk about the victim. Detectives Skip Jones and Julie O'Keefe, said there hellos to the detectives they used to work with on the task force in the original serial killings. As Julie, smiled at Ed Brooks who just smiled back and winked at her, as Julie is still very grateful Ed saved her life four years ago. As Skip Jones, began to give them the details on the latest victim.

"We were able to identify the victim by her driver's license, in her purse that was found near the body. A twenty four year old, Caucasian female, Ashley Cook, who is not a known prostitute but a waitress at; "Perlisis", Steakhouse in Old Town, we think she was picked up by the killer, who she might have known. Being there was no signs of a struggle to her hands, to indicate defensive wounds." Jones tells them. As Rob asks, what was the cause of death, and how was the body mutilated.

"Cause of death, was a sharp deep cut to the throat of the victim, with her fingernails removed, all ten of them were taken." Jones said, as all the men and Julie just made surprised looks on their faces that this recent murder is following a pattern of inflicted wounds they have seen before.

"Any other wounds or body parts taken by the killer?" Rick asked, as Julie told him, her breasts were also removed and she had a deep straight knife wound down the center of her chest. But besides this wound, and her neck being slashed. The only body parts removed was her fingernails and breasts, as the breasts were placed at the feet of the victim, and the fingernails are presumed taken by the killer. As Ed looks at Rob and then looks in the direction of the area of the body, which has been taped off by yellow caution tape. As Rick and the others go to look at the body that was very clear to see, as the forensic team had set up, mobile large flood lights. That illuminated the area of the park, even in the dark evening of night. As Ed, knew already this had to be a copycat killer. But just how were they going to approach this new case now, as he saw Rick talking to the side with one of the police Chief's staff members. As Rick seemed, to be agreeing with his orders, as he then returned to brief the detectives as he called for everyone to gather around him.

"Look people, I was just instructed by the Deputy Chief that there will be a press conference in the morning to announce the discovery of this victim. But the Chief, is not going to state any type of mutilation wounds to the victim, not to stir up panic in the city. He wants a complete autopsy done on the body, and then he will go from there on how he wants us to react on this new series, or possible series of murders." Rick informs them, as they watch the forensic team place the body of Ashley Cook in a body bag. As detective Jones, informs them he will contact the family of the victim. As Ed just think to himself, another young life taken away by a vicious unknown killer.

Just after two PM, at Central Division headquarters. Ed and Rob were contacted to come meet Rick and other in the conference room for a briefing. As they were walking in the hallway together, they noticed two other familiar faces to them. Northern Division homicide detectives, Jack Kerns and Ken Rogers, as the men greeted each other and entered the conference room, they saw Julie O'Keefe and Skip Jones already seated. Along with county medical examiner, Dr. Cate Adams, the original task force from four years ago. Was now back together, for what seemed to be an obvious copycat style mutilation copied from the Dr. Malcolm slayings. As everyone took their seats, Rick told everyone to listen to Dr. Adams brief them all first, before that had any questions. As Rick took his seat, Dr. Adams thanked her husband, and turned on the slide projected on the large screen, for the team to view the massive wounds, to the body of Ashley Cook.

"I want to first say, that whoever committed this murder now. Had some deep insight into the murders four years ago, just by looking at the wounds and type of sharp edged knife used. I also want to point out, that we didn't get any DNA evidence back yet. I don't expect we are going to find any DNA from the killer, as I don't believe there was any oral or vaginal sex preformed with the victim before she was killed. I do think that this killer now followed the same M.O. As the previous killer; Dr. Nathan Malcolm, as it's obvious enough to leave the body in the same park, that the last victim was left four years ago," as all the detectives in the room, just look at one another stunned. That whoever this killer is now, must have known Nathan Malcolm, and his ways of mutilating his victims. As Ed, raised his hand to ask Dr. Adams a question.

"Doc, the type of knife wounds here on this victim; how similar are these wounds to the other wounds four years ago?" Ed questions her.

"Just by looking at the wounds, I see the knife that was used to very similar. But the angles and the penetrating wounds are not as deep as the previous murders. So we definitely have a similar killer now, but we all know that Nathan Malcolm perished in the fire at his home, as his body was given a full autopsy by me and DNA analyst, Dr. Diana Farrell. We confirmed that Malcolm perished in the blaze, as his remains were cremated by order of the state." Dr. Adams said. As Rick was going to advise them, why the task force was called together again by Chief Chase.

"Okay, as order by Chief Chase, we are again forming the task force under top secret circumstances until we find out more about this new killer. We can all expect another murder to happen again soon, but when and where is the big question. As for precaution reasons to anticipate this new killer's style, to that of Nathan Malcolm, we contacted the FBI, and they are sending us their best profiler here on the west coast. To help us on this case, as the profiler will be working mostly with Ed and Rob, who will again be taking point charge of the task force." Rick instructs them, as Ed frowns to himself thinking, what an FBI profiler is going to find out, what he already knows about these murders now.  Rick asks for Ed and Rob to stay, as the others leave the conference room to look into any leads of the new killer now. As Rick and his wife, Dr. Adams wants to warn Ed about this new suspect.

"Look Ed, Cate and I were talking about this just between us. If this new killer has any ties to Nathan Malcolm, then he probably is going to target you for being the one who killed Malcolm." Rick advices him, as Cate also states that criminal physique is not her specialty. But the mind of a psychopath will always follow the pattern for murder and revenge. She tells him.

"Thanks for the warning, but I'm in this one again to the end like four years ago. I don't have any worries about whoever this new killer is, or if he is indeed related to, Dr. Malcolm. I just want to catch this person without any more bloodshed." Ed tells his lieutenant, as he asks Rick, when will this profiler be coming to work with Rob and himself.

"I was told by the Chief; he is leaving L.A. tonight on a flight, and will be here early tomorrow morning to start work with you and Rob". Rick told them, as they understood they have to work with the profiler. They walked out into the hallway, to catch up to the other detectives, to begin sharing notes on this new case. As Rob turns to Ed, and asks his opinion on the profiler.

"What do you think this profiler dude, is going to look like? I bet he will be in his fifties and all gray and overweight. These guys are always out of shape, being they are office bookworms." Rob tells Ed laughing, as Ed agrees with him, and just hopes this new case ends soon not want to make it a threes a crowd atmosphere with the profiler.

That night, Ed was home working on his computer as he was comparing the latest crime file to the past victims. As he was also checking the original Ripper victims, for any new patterns to compare to this victims now. Ed thinks to himself; "five victims that are known Ripper victims, but maybe seven or eight. Being there was two murders prior to the first known Ripper victim, Mary Ann Nichols. But some say the, Martha Tabram murder, was not related. Even though she was stabbed thirty nine times, she was not slashed or mutilated like the five noted Ripper victims." Ed reads to himself, as he looks at the time in the lower right hand corner of his computer, saying its, two ten in the morning. Ed just logs off his computer and knows he will not mutter a word, about his belief these crimes are in some way related to; Jack the Ripper. As he gets up and stretches his muscles, and heads to his bedroom for some sleep.

Wednesday, just after nine AM, Rick had left Ed a voicemail saying he was going to pick up the profiler at his hotel and bring him to the office, by early morning as Ed and Rob were just patiently waiting the profiler's arrival.

"So what do you think we should do for this guy when he gets here? Take him out to Starbucks or Dunkin Doughnuts? So he can stuff his face while we fill him in on the case." As Rob laughs, he looks up and notices Rick standing behind Ed with a very attractive female, as Rick makes a face of embarrassment and the very pretty brunette smiles and responds to Ed's remark.

"Well detective Brooks, I would like it if you please take me out to a nice diner along with your partner to fill me in on the case. But I have no intentions of stuffing my face, when I'm into a very healthy diet and exercise routine as you are". As Ed turns around and stares into the dark black eyes, of the FBI's lead profiler in their L.A. division. As Rick, introduces them to her.

"Ed and Rob, this is FBI profiler, Stephanie Morgan. And I apologize for Detective Brook's remarks." Rick tells her, as Ed and Rob get up from their seats to greet her. Stephanie tells Rick, that it is all right as she shakes Rob's hand and then shakes Ed's hand. As he is very upset with himself, as she smiles gingerly at him.

"I'm very sorry, I didn't mean that. I didn't know you were a?" Ed, wanted to finish his sentence but couldn't. As Stephanie finished it for him; "You didn't expect me to be a female? Is that it Ed? As Ed now feeling very embarrassed in front of Rick and Rob. He just smiled at Stephanie, as she broke a smile on her face.

"I know a good diner; we can all go and have some good coffee for the three of us to talk". Ed states, as Rob gets his jacket and car keys and says he will drive, as Ed shows Stephanie to the back door to the parking lot. As Rick grabs Ed's arm, and tells him to keep cool and behave himself with her. As Ed smiles back, and says he will treat her like a true lady.


An hour into sharing coffees and going over all the victims and forensic findings from all the four murders with Stephanie, she asked Ed and Rob if they did any checking on Dr. Malcolm if he had any know relatives or a wife. As she knew of his illegal doings in the Quasar Pharmaceutical, scandal he was involved in at the same time of the murders. As Rob, filled her in on what they knew about his private life, up until his death.

"Nathan Malcolm was the top international sales buyer and distributor for Quasar. He made a big fortune for himself and others as they were able to distribute many illegals drugs into the country and Mexico primarily. Drugs like illegal steroids and GHB, tablets and the drug Soma that is a heavy painkiller he would get to many pro-athletes without a prescription. As they would rely on it heavily to fight injuries, and keep it quiet from their teams physician's." Rob explains to her, as Stephanie asks Ed, if he was married or any known next of kin?

"We looked into this very heavily, but we found out he was divorced and his wife received a lot of money from him in their settlement as she passed away a few years later from Alzheimer's disease. They did have one child together, but it seems they must have changed their last name because we have not found any records on their child, or if their son or daughter is deceased now." Ed tells her, as Stephanie nods to him, and then looks back down to read the case file. As Ed, studies her face and appearance.

He thinks to himself; "she has to be around thirty eight or thirty nine years old. What a beautiful face and long black hair, and she has to work out often, to maintain that athletic physique". Ed thinks to himself, as Rob notices Ed staring at Stephanie, as he kicks him under the table. Not wanting to embarrass him again with her.

"So what are your personal thoughts about this killer now, and if you have a theory if he has a connection to Dr. Malcolm? Stephanie asks him, as Ed looks up and thinks to himself and stutters before he answers her.

"I guess being Malcolm had medical knowledge, when it came to remove the victim's organs and the way he was very cautious not to leave any DNA evidence behind, I feel this killer now has to possess medical skill. Along with insight to the killings for years ago, as to where to leave his victim in Shore Line Park, but I believe we are dealing with a copycat killer now." Ed gives her his opinion, as Rob says he agrees with his partner. As Ed looks at Stephanie's ring fingers on both hands, trying to see if she has an engagement ring or a wedding band. As he doesn't spot one, but that still doesn't mean she is single. As Stephanie, notices him looking at her from the corner of her eye. She just calmly ignores it, thinking that she is now working with two macho detectives. As she says the best thing for her, to get a feel for this killer, is to see the crime scene at Shore Line Park, along with the other crime scenes four years ago. As they all get up and gather their things, and head out to start working together.

The trio made their route, from the first murder at the Palms Motel, to the apartment of the second victim, Sharon Kessler. As they round up back at Shore Line Park, as the area of the body was still cordoned off by police tape. Stephanie was looking around the area trying to get a feel for the victims and killer. What could have drawn him to this park, besides being secluded and deserted late at night to kill his victims? As to why, the second killer would want to come back to the same area as the first killer. As Ed and Rob just look around for themselves, and Rob asks Ed what he thinks of Stephanie's work so far.

"Well, being a profiler she is very educated and sharp. But unless she has some psychic abilities that we don't know about, she can't figure this killer's methods or if he is some hoe tied to Malcolm, until we just catch him ourselves." Ed responds to Rob, as they see Stephanie coming towards them with her dark sunglasses covering her dark black eyes, in the bright sunny day on this afternoon. Ed smiled at her, as she joined them, "so we been going at this now for five hours, as it's now two thirty PM. We just had coffee for lunch, what do you want to do now Mrs. Morgan?" Ed, questions her, as Rob can't believe he threw out that remark, to see if she is indeed married or single, at Stephanie.

"For starters it's Miss Morgan, Mr. Brooks. And yes I know we have been all over the crimes scenes now, but I want you to take me to the county morgue, so I can view the body of Ashley Cook. As I have some questions for, Dr. Adams. Who conducted the autopsies of the **bodies**?" Ed agrees to take her to view the body at the county coroner's facility. As they are driving on the interstate, Stephanie asks Rob, if it's true that Rick is married to Dr. Adams; as Rob responds to her question.

"It's true; they got married right after the Entity murders had ended, a little less than four years now. Funny it's Rick's first marriage at his ripe young age of forty five". Rob tells her, as she absorbs the thought, and decides to make a comeback response for Ed's straight forward question earlier at her.

"Oh and Ed, hasn't it been three years now that you're divorced from Kayla? If I, may ask you?" As Ed slowly turns around in the passenger seat to face her, as Rob makes a face under his sunglasses as he looks straight ahead of the road. As Ed, glares at Stephanie and then smiles at her.

"You seem to know a lot about us, and including my private life Miss Morgan. As I will be honest with you, yes I have been divorced from my ex-wife going on three years now, if you really need to know that." As Stephanie smiles back at him.

"Well I really like to know whom I'm working with, when I'm in an unfamiliar city, and working a very important case with new men who I just met today." She tells him, as Ed just faces forward again as they pull into the parking lot of the facility.

Dr. Adams, lead them into the cold crypt room, where she opened the door in the wall to pull out; the remains of Ashley Cook. Stephanie was looking at the wounds to the body, and then at previous photographs of the other victims, to see if she can predict a pattern is the killer's styles of inflicting the wounds. As she asks Cate Adams, what are the differences from the knife wounds and gouges from this victim now, to the others before?

"From what I could tell, both killers are right handed. As Nathan Malcolm, was more powerful than this killer now, I can surmise. Being the wounds he inflicted on his three victims, were deeper lacerations and I feel, he took his time wanting to remove the organs and not hide his hatred for these women." Dr. Adams gives Stephanie her opinion.

"I can add that this killer now wants us to think he is like Nathan Malcolm. Not only in the sense of his similar style murder. But the way Malcolm thought and his use of disguises. I have no doubt that this killer now, wants to taunt the police, and make us play a game of cat and mouse with him. By not choosing a prostitute for his first victim, we can expect more series of murders to happen being he will be taking young women at random now, as his victims." Stephanie tells them, as Ed and Rob just shake their heads, hoping she is wrong on her hunch.

Ed thanked Dr. Adams for her time, as they left the county coroner's building and were now heading back to Central Division, to brief Rick on what they went over. As Ed asked Stephanie what hotel she was staying at, she told him for now she is staying at the Capri Hotel, on Mission Blvd. And that Chief Chase and Rick will find her a condo for herself, while she is here helping them on the case. As Rob, pulled into the parking lot of Central Division, as they all went into Rick's office and brief him on how Stephanie is helping them, and what Rick has planned for the task force set for tomorrow.

"So you guys saw the body of Ashley Cook, and spoke to my wife, Dr. Adams. I know Stephanie; you might have more insight as to what this new killer has in his thinking and methods as compared to Malcolm. I know it's late in the afternoon now, and you must be tired from you're flight late last night. So I'm going to let you go back to your hotel now, and we will have the task force here early in the morning so you can meet them and begin working with them all". Rick tells her, as he also tells Stephanie, he and the Chief have found her a condo for her to stay in, the area of Bird Rock. As Rick, asks Ed if he wouldn't mind taking her back to Capri Hotel, being it's on his way home. As Ed, agrees and Stephanie thanks Rick and tells him to thank Chief Chase for their kindness. As she leaves with Ed, as they get into his GMC Envoy, and head off to the interstate.

While driving, Stephanie is just looking out her window gazing around the beautiful sites of San Diego. As Ed asks her, if this is her first time here to the city? As Stephanie tells him yes, that she grew up in Encino California, which is a suburb outside of Los Angeles. As Ed, proposes to her if she would like for him to help her move her things into her condo now, being he lived only a few miles away in Lower Hermosa. As Stephanie told him, that would be great. That she didn't unpack yet and she doesn't care for hotels much anyway. As Ed, pulled into the Capri Hotel an went up to help her bring her bags down to his SUV, but Ed was shocked to find, Stephanie has five large bags, along with her briefcase and small carry bag for her lap top computer. As Ed, saw the smile on her face, as she knew she got back at him again for his behavior when they first met. As Ed secured the trunk, they took off for Bird Rock.

"Look Stephanie, I'm sorry for the way I acted when I thought we would be working with a male profiler. I'm not like that at all, I just wanted to let you know that" Ed tells her, hoping she will accept his apology as Stephanie just faces him and removes her sunglasses.

"Let me see, Detective Ed Brooks has a stellar naval record when you were enlisted in the Navy. You have received many awards and commendations on the force now, as you worked four very difficult homicide cases and you were able to solve them all. As to why, not only is the reason given you are the lead detective for the task force being the first murder happened in your division's precinct. But you're dedication and hard-nosed attitude to catch your suspect. How's that for a summed up profile, of yourself by me." Stephanie tells him, as Ed just stares at her shocked that she knows so much about him.

"So how is it you know so much about me, and I know nothing about you as of now?" Ed asks her, as Stephanie tells him; her boss filled her in on all the people she would be working with in the task force, and how Ed was almost killed by Nathan Malcolm, in the bloody sting operation that happened the night Ed killed him. As Stephanie tells him she was sorry for what he went through, and it cost him his marriage. As Ed just smiled, and thanked her as he said, can they be friends now. Stephanie smiles and says, we can be friendly and work together but as for friends, she will wait and see. As Ed pulled into the her nice condo complex, as he made a face, that he would have to unload all the bags and carry them to her apartment, as Stephanie read the key number and told him good news, her place is number 1-D, on the first floor, ad Ed whispers to himself; "Thank You Lord". As he helps her inside her spacious apartment, and places her bags down in her bedroom for her, as she thanks him and is walking him to the door, Ed looks at his watch and it's just after six PM now, he was going to suggest something to her.

"May I ask do you have plans for dinner? Unless you packed yourself many microwavable dinners in one of your bags?" Ed asks her, as she just smiles at him.

"No Ed, I don't have plans for dinner, and I don't have any food with me. I was going to look online for the best place to order food from". She told him, as Ed asked her if she would like to go out to dinner with him. That he knew a very nice Spanish restaurant in La Jolla Mesa, close to their location now. Stephanie just studies the handsome look on Ed's face, as she knows she is safe with him and feels this is a good way to earn his trust. She smiles, and says she would love some Spanish food for dinner, but she wants to shower and change first, as Ed tells her great, that he will be back to pick her up around eight o'clock sharp, as they exchange cell phone numbers. Ed walks to his truck and smiles to himself; "Thanks again God". He says to the good Lord, as he heads home to shower and change.

Just a little before eight PM, Ed arrived at Stephanie's door and was dressed in a casual black shirt and dark gray slacks and shoes. As he popped a Tic Tac into his mouth for fresh breath, as he was about to knock, Stephanie opened the door slowly, as Ed was stunned to see her dressed in a pure white dress, that was low-cut and sleeveless up to her knees, with nice black sandal type shoes. As her long hair flowed down, so softly to the back of her neck, Ed was just flawed by her beauty and Stephanie was also taken by his, tall clean shaven, handsome appearance. As Ed, couldn't talk and Stephanie laughed as she had her purse in her hands and said, how about we go to dinner, and Ed said yes of course, as he opened the door for her and she got into his truck. As Ed pulled out of the parking lot and said the name of the restaurant is, El Sabio. As Stephanie repeated the name, Ed thought she said it perfectly in Spanish, as he asked her if she spoke Spanish, and she said just a little.

Stephanie was taken by El Sabio's, old Spanish decor as she and Ed were seated in a small booth in the middle of the restaurant, as Ed thanked the male host for seating them. She knew Ed must have come here often before, as they read their menus, Ed asked her what she felt like, and she said she didn't know yet, and asked him what he felt like having as Ed showed her his menu and said this dish. That he couldn't pronounce the word, as Stephanie told him don't worry she will tell the waiter the name of the dish for him. As their waiter comes over to them, Stephanie tells him in Spanish that she will have the, Arroz negro, paella negra, seafood dish. And Ed will have the, Andalusia meat dish. As she tells the waiter, they will both have just water to drink. As she thanks him again in Spanish, Ed just felt like the words that came out of her mouth were, so sweet and polite, they should be put to music for her to sing.

"Wow, did you take Spanish in school?" He asked her, as Stephanie smiled and said yes and that she traveled to Mexico and Spain before for vacations. So she is very fluent in the language.

"So Ed, tell me you obviously have been here before with other women, I can tell." She asked, as he said it was one of his ex-wife's favorite places to come to for a nice dinner together on the weekends. As Stephanie made a sad face, when he mentioned his ex-wife, as Ed then asked her, why is she still Miss and not Mrs. Morgan as of now? She just made a frown and knew he would ask her this question.

"Because Ed, I just haven't found the right man as of yet. I was in a long relationship for a while, he was a nice guy it just didn't work out for us, as we are still dedicated to our careers and we decided to just move on. That was about a few months ago we ended our relationship, and I know you're going to ask me if he was an FBI person too. And the answer is no, he is a dentist if you wanted to know, and his name is none of your business." She says laughing as the waiter brings them their food. As they begin to eat, Ed raises his glass of water and says to new friends and good luck on this case, as she clings her glass with his. As they tell one another how good their food is, Stephanie asks him what are his thoughts on the case now, as Ed just talks about another similar style killer, but they will catch him with her help. As he didn't want to talk about the case, he just wanted to enjoy her company now. Stephanie felt he was holding something back from her or even hiding something. But she didn't want to press him on it. She was enjoying her dinner, and his company as they were now relaxing having coffee together. As Ed, asked her about her family.

"My parents live in Santa Monica, my father is retired LAPD, and my mother is still working as a behavioral therapist, in her own practice. So you can see how I had inspirations to become a profiler for the FBI. I have one brother, who is a captain in the Marine Corps, stationed overseas right now." As Ed smiles and says; "Semper Fi!" Meaning, always faithful a motto of the Marine Corps. As Stephanie asked Ed, about his family.

"My parents are retired, and living quietly in northern California. Where I was raised in Redding, I have one brother who is married with a family in San Francisco. He and his wife are both lawyers, and have two daughters. I moved here to San Diego when I left the Navy a long time ago, and been with the PD ever since." Ed tells her, as he briefly mentioned his short marriage to Kayla, as they still talk once in a while and she is now engaged to be married again. As Stephanie didn't want to ask him any more questions about Kayla, not wanting to upset Ed, as Ed received the check and paid the waiter and left him a generous tip. He knew it was getting late as he suggested he take her back to her place, as Stephanie had her arms over her shoulders, Ed knew she was cold as he didn't even ask her, he covered her shoulders with his leather jacket as she thanked him and they got into his truck.

"So here you are", Ed said as he pulled into her complex, and he got out to open her door and they walked to her door. As Stephanie opened the door, and they walked into the foyer together, she thanked him for dinner and said she had a nice time with him tonight, as she did have something on her mind.

"Ed, I know we just met and I also know besides working together we have to trust one another no matter what happens right?" She asks him, as Ed is confused and tells her; "right".

"So then tell me what's on your mind about this case now, because I know you're not afraid of anything, but you are holding something back from me, I sense it Ed." As Ed just takes a breath and lets it out slowly. He tells her in time, he will open up to her about something. As Stephanie just smiles and nods to him, "Okay, you better get going Detective Brooks." She tells him, as Ed smiles at her as they shake hands, Ed then pulls Stephanie around her waist, to his chest as he kisses her gently on the lips. Stephanie returns the kiss to Ed softly, as she pushes him off slowly with a hand to his chest.

"Ed, let's take this slow please? We just met, but I am attracted to you now." As Ed smiles into her dark eyes, and says; "I will pick you up at eight thirty in the morning, and I really like you, miss profiler." He tells her as they kiss gently again, as Stephanie pushes him out the door gently and closed it behind him. As Ed slowly walks back to his truck and whispers; "Thanks again God". Knowing he has granted Ed's prayer to meet another elegant woman in his life now.

# Chapter 5

Early morning of Thursday the tenth of August, the task force
was again assembled at Central Division's conference room.
As Chief John Chase and some of his staff was there to
brief his elite detectives and introduce them to Stephanie Morgan.
As she entered the conference room with Ed Brooks, Rick and
Rob just smiled at one another, feeling Ed has broken into more
than a friendship with Stephanie. As Ed took his seat next to Rob,
Stephanie went to the head of the podium to talk to the Detectives.
As the pictures of the three previous victims were brought up on
the large projected screen, along with the recent victim two days
ago, the dates of the victims were listed next to their names, of the
exact date they were discovered by the police. As Rick, then turns
over the podium to Stephanie.

"Good morning all, I had the privilege to meet a few of you
yesterday and speak with Chief Chase quite a bit on the phone about
these cases before I was brought in to assist you all. My name is;
Stephanie Morgan, I have been with the FBI for over twelve years
now as a profiler working in the L.A. office. I helped our agents
there and the Detectives of LAPD apprehend Louis Stolla, the serial
strangler who killed six young women. Along with the serial rapist;
Stan Wilson; who raped over eight women but did not kill them, as
I looked over the three murders committed four years ago, to the
recent victim now; I have no doubt that this killer wants to follow the

same methods and style of killings of Nathan Malcolm." Stephanie tells the task force, as she then explains this killer has done a lot of searching into the patterns of Malcolm, and now wants to taunt the police to think he and Nathan Malcolm are one in the same. As the detectives now begin to question Stephanie, on whom this new killer is, as Skip Jones is the first to ask his question to her.

"Stephanie, you said this new killer wants to match patterns of the killings as Malcolm, is there a chance he may be related to Nathan Malcolm somehow? Or could have Malcolm, revealed his ways of killing to a close friend? Jones asks her, as Ed said he would answer part of that question for her.

"Once we knew Nathan Malcolm was the serial killer, we did a complete thorough check on him. He was divorced and his wife passed away, and they had one child together. We tried to trace records to see who was their child, but we believe Mrs. Malcolm had the child's named officially changed being we can't find no records or DMV records of a surviving heir to Nathan Malcolm." Ed explains, as no next of kin even came forth to take possession of hid badly charred remains from the house fire, where he perished that night. As he was cremated by order of the county judge, after his autopsy was finished. As Stephanie, answers the second part of Jones question.

"You're asking me do I feel this killer has knowledge of Malcolm's patterns of murders. Yes I believe he does, and he is going to continue killing young women like this, until two things happen. We track him down and stop him first. Or, he is going to end up killing the same amount of victims as Malcolm did, stopping at three, but Malcolm did try to take one last victim who was; Detective Julie O'Keefe. So if this new killer is going to try for three more victims, and if he is not preying on prostitutes as Ashley Cook, was not a known escort. Trying to anticipate this killer's next move is going to be more difficult to counter". Stephanie tells them, as Julie asks her; so if they can't set up another sting operation as an operative as an escort. How are they going to have a chance to be a step ahead of the killer?

"Well we know the areas Malcolm met and took his victims, I suggest for now we have double patrols of all the areas the murders took place, and mostly secluded parks and recreation areas that would be an inviting way for a killer to stalk a young woman. We can have an operative, set up as a jogger, or walking a small dog all alone in one of these places. It's really the best shot we have right now if I had to make a judgment call on this." Stephanie tells them, as all the Detectives look at one another and Chief Chase and Rick, whisper to one another. As Chief Chase, gets up and tells Stephanie thank you, as he will brief the task force again.

"Thank you Stephanie, for giving us you detailed insight into this case. As I want to let you know, Rick and I will be considering having an undercover officer pose as a possible target for our suspect. But as what happened to Julie, four years ago and Ed Brooks, we almost lost two cops in one night. So this would be a last resort to draw this person out. I'm going to follow Stephanie's advice in patrolling those specific areas. We are going to look into Malcolm's personal past more in depth, and see if he had close friends whom he worked with, or a neighbor who he was close too. And all recently released convicts who are known killers. We have to find something soon people, because I don't want to get a call and be told we have another victim on our hands. So let's get a move on this quick!" The Chief tells them, as he leaves with his staff members. Ed and Rob go over to Stephanie who is gathering up her folders as Rick comes over to them, and asks what they are going to do now.

"Boss I think, we are going to pay a visit to Quasar Pharmaceuticals, and speak to their CEO or person who knew Malcolm, the best while he worked there. Stephanie thinks, he could have said something to a fellow co-worker who may know something or may even be our killer now." Ed tells him, as Rick tells them go for it. As the two detectives and Stephanie, head to Spring Valley, San Diego.

Ed led the way into the big commercial facility of Quasar, as they were checked in at the central security desk. The security guard made a call to the CEO's office, as he spoke to the secretary of Mr. Aaron Byrne, the CEO of the company. As his secretary advised, she will come down and escort them up to his office to meet with Mr. Byrne. As they waited a few moments, a middle aged woman wearing a business style dress skirt, welcomed the Detectives to Quasar as she told them to follow her to the elevators and up to the top floor, to Mr. Byrne's office. As they walked through the large floor of the facility, they saw many people working at work stations, with lab tables and cold storage units and freezers for their work with pharmaceuticals. As the secretary, told them that the work floors go as high as the fourth floor. And from the fourth floor up to the ninth floor, were all regular offices. As the elevator stopped on the ninth floor, she walked them down the very luxurious blue carpeted floors to the big double wood doors, of the CEO's office as she told them to have a seat, and Mr. Byrne would be right with them.

As only a few minutes went by, a man slender and medium height walked out of his double doors, and into the lobby of his office. Mr. Byrne, was medium height with gray hair and glasses, as he shook all the Detectives hands and introductions were made. As he showed them into his office, he had them seated at the round oval table in his office, as he already had an employee file on the table, the file of Dr. Nathan Malcolm. As he then asked the three detectives, how can he assist them now?  As Ed, speaks first for his team, as they go over the history of Malcolm's work with the company and how he began to make large profits from his illegal steroid and other drug dealings. As then they went over, who might have known any insights to his doings, or if he told someone he had indeed gone off the deep end, and made him want to turn to murder. As Mr. Byrne looked through some of the pages in the file, he took out one sheet from the others, and handed it to Ed. As Ed, looked it over Byrne began to explain this person to him.

"Nathan Malcolm, worked closely with this man and former employee of ours; Fred Young. He was Malcolm's chief assistant in his pharmaceutical department here. It was Fred Young, who noticed shipping labels to countries outside of the registered countries we are approved by the Food and Drug Administration, to ship legal pharmaceuticals to. He found out what he was doing and, then reported it to our internal security who followed up by gathering all the known evidence on who and where he was distributing these drugs to. Then we brought in the DEA, to take over the case as the arrested Malcolm and seized all his materials to get ready to start the trial against him. Fred Young never mentioned to me or anyone in our personnel department; about Malcolm making threats against anyone or if he had homicidal tendencies against anyone. He did give the appearance, to not be taking care of himself his final weeks here. He looked very drained in the face, as it was obvious he was smoking and drinking heavily. But that is all that I am aware of, until he was terminated by myself and the board of directors, and then of course he did the unthinkable as to what lead to his death four years ago." Byrne went over all that he knew, Malcolm was involved with at his company. As Stephanie, asked him where is Fred Young now? That they needed to talk to him, as Byrne told them on the very bottom of the sheet, was Young's address and home number.

Ed and his partners rose from their seats, as they thanked Mr. Byrne for his time and cooperation into this case. As they stated, if they need any more help from him in the future, they will contact him as Ed gave him his business card. The trio left the office and walked to the elevators to return to the ground floor, as Ed asked Stephanie what did she think about Fred Young? "Well look, we have the statements he gave to the police four years ago still in files. You said, he didn't mention ever hearing that Malcolm was going to hurt anyone. But that still doesn't mean, he knew something and didn't tell you guys at the time. So I say let's go pay him a visit if we can today". Stephanie suggests to them, as they all get into Rob's four door sedan, as Stephanie calls Young's home number. As Ed and Rob listen to her talk to someone, and it seems she is having a pleasant conversation as she told the person who she was, and what this call was all about. As Stephanie thanked the voice at the other end of her cell phone, as she looked at Ed and Rob from the backseat and smiled at them, as Rob asked her, so what did the person say?

"I spoke with Fred Young, told him what this was all about as he asked me if the recent murder is somehow connected with the past murders, and I told him maybe. As he agreed to meet with us this evening at his home in Sorrento Valley," she told them, as Ed smiled and said he and Stephanie will meet with him. As they agreed to head back to Central Division and make log entries on what they just found out and to brief Rick and the others. As Rob pulled out of the parking lot, and passed a string of parked vehicles on the service road as they headed for the Interstate. A pair of eyes that were concealed behind a dark pair of sunglasses followed the vehicle, as the watcher sat in their vehicle and thought of what do to next. As the watcher pondered on what to do; "I will follow them for now, as I can imagine what their next move might be, but I will have something in store for them, that they will not expect!" The watcher said coldly, as the dark Ford SUV that the watcher drove, eased out of the space slowly, and began to pick up speed to follow the trio to their next destination.

As Ed and Stephanie briefed Rick and the team on what they found out earlier in the day; they were now heading to one of the elegant neighborhoods in the Sorrento Valley, to meet with Fred Young. As Ed had picked up Stephanie an was now driving on the 805 Freeway North; as Ed remarked to her, that she was wearing dark jeans along with a sweater. That she still looked very attractive but he would like to see her again in that elegant dress soon. As Stephanie winked to him and said, maybe if they get done soon with interviewing Mr. Young. She would consider spending some quite time alone with Ed at her place, as Ed smiled and said let's get there fast. As he asked her, if Young was married and had a family. Stephanie answered him, he told her his wife would be home to meet them, and she didn't know if he had any children. As they both searched for the home address as they came up the very nice large homes of the valley. As Stephanie told him, this is the house. The one that had a very ling driveway and stucco sandstone design on the outside, as Ed pulled into the long driveway and parked his Envoy. He and Stephanie walked to the front door, and rang the doorbell. As they waited a few seconds, there was no response from within the house. As they looked at one another, Ed told her there are lights on inside the home, as he will go around the back and see if there is another door. As Ed walked down the path of the home, Stephanie again rang the bell of the house as she then took out her cell phone and called the home's phone. To see if she would get a response that way, as Ed called to her; with a low faint voice from the side entrance. Stephanie quickly went to him, as she saw Ed with his gun draw in his hand. As she is pointing to the door that was forced open. He motioned for her to stay outside, as he went into the home to investigate what has happened.

Ed moved slowly down the tiled hallway, as he peered into the first room. That was the laundry room, as he saw the home was kept nice and neat, he moved again slowly to where lights were left on as he suddenly slipped on the ceramic tile, with his rubber souled shoes. Ed was able to catch his balance, as he looked down and saw he had slipped on red blood. That had started to where he was standing, all the way it led a track to the large living room, as Ed called to Stephanie to call 911 right away. As Ed held his gun out ahead of him, he came up the opening to the living room as he quickly turned his body to face whoever might be there. As Ed only saw two bodies lying in a pool of blood, as he scanned the room, he saw that a struggle had taken place there as there were many items thrown from the walls and tables broken in the living room. As Ed turned and called for Stephanie to come inside, he was violently hit from behind by a blunt object, and again as he was falling to the floor. As the intruder dropped the object and ran down the hallway to exit the house, Stephanie was pushed to the floor with a hard elbow thrown into her chest by the intruder. As she fell on her back, she looked back to see a person wearing black running out the door. As she took a breath she was able to get to her feet, and see Ed on the floor hold the back of his neck, that was bleeding. She quickly took some tissues and covered his wound as she helped him to his feet, as she yelled to him; "Ed! Are you all right?" As Ed got to his feet, he looked at her and nodded to indicate he was fine, as they then looked at the bodies on the floor, a male and female who were covered in blood that looked like tremendous stab wounds. As Stephanie helped Ed to sit back on the sofa, as they would wait for the police to come.

Sometime had passed since the police arrived on the scene, as the whole task force was called to the residence along with Rick, as the forensic team had removed the bodies and was now combing the home for evidence as both Ed and Stephanie were outside being treated, by the paramedics. Stephanie was fine; she just had a slight bruise to her left elbow when she hit the floor. As Ed had a gash, just behind his left ear, that was caused from a blow from a wooden log, the assailant used from the fireplace. Ed was lucky, as he was told he didn't need stiches and the wound was dressed and bandaged. As Rick and the whole team were talking to Detectives and to uniformed police of the areas division. Stephanie came over and sat with Ed, on the back step of the ambulance and asked him if he was all right. Ed told her he was okay just shaken up, as she told him she felt the same way. As Rick and the team came over to them.

"So this is what we can tell from the forensic team so far. It seems the suspect, forced their way into the side door by forcing a screwdriver or long steel device into the door jam, and forcing it open. Upon hearing the noise, Fed Young encountered the intruder in the hallway. As he tried to fight him off, as his hands had knife wounds inflicted on them. As he was stabbed multiple times in the chest and neck, as he was forced into the living room. His wife, Clare Young tried to call for help from the landline phone. As the killer then turned his attention to her, and slit her throat from behind left to right. As he then stabbed her once deep into the chest, as he then turned his attention back to Fred Young, who was on the floor covered in blood, as he then slit his throat from left to right. And stabbed him again in the chest, multiple times when he was suddenly stopped presumably, when you two rang the doorbell, as Ed, then entered and you were hit with the wood log, and Stephanie pushed to the floor as the suspect fled." Rick recounts all the details he was given by the Detectives and forensic team. As Stephanie asked him, if the was any witnesses outside who saw the suspect flee?

"The detectives asked the neighbors within the two block radius if they saw anything or anyone in the last two hours, but they all said no. As we feel, he parked his vehicle on the street behind the home. And cut through the home that is connected by the backyard, to make his way to the side entrance and follow the same route to make his escape. There are signs of foot marks made in the blood, but it seems he had his feet covered with sterile shoe coverings and so he left no foot impressions in the house or outside in the dirt and pavement". Rick tells them, as he ask Ed and Stephanie, could they make out anything about the killer? Ed stated that all he saw was the blood on the floor and the bodies, then he felt like someone broke a bat on his neck and he saw stars. As Rick then asked Stephanie, what she saw?

"I came inside once Ed yelled to me, I rushed in the hallway as a figure in black threw his elbow into me, and I fell to the floor. As I looked up, I only saw the dark outline of what look like a hooded black jacket man running out the door." Stephanie recanted what had happened, as Rick just shook his head.

"So the killer knew you two were coming here to meet with young, and he planned this out very well to keep him silenced forever. Seem like the same patterns used by Nathan Malcolm", Jack Kerns stated to them. As some of the group agreed with him, as Julie said that it has to be a new killer being Malcolm is dead. As Rob looked at her, and suggested, what if Nathan Malcolm is still alive? Then who was it that died in the fire, that night at his home? Skip Jones answered him back. As Rick told everyone to calm down now; that he didn't want his team to start jumping to conclusions. As he then gave out the orders on how to handle this now.

"Julie and Skip; you two follow this up with forensics and witnesses being this happened in your division's jurisdiction. Rob, you get back to Aaron Byrne at Quasar, and find out if he mentioned to anyone else, that Ed and Stephanie planned on meeting with him tonight. Ken and Jack, I want you two to go talk to Dr. Diana Farrell, she is the one who did the autopsy on Nathan Malcolm the following day, after his death. I want everything from her, detailing what she did to that body to confirm it was him before they cremated it. Let's get a move on this people!" Rick tells them, as they move out with their assignments as Rick turns his attention to Ed and Stephanie.

"You two, take it easy for the rest of the night and tomorrow morning too. I will call you both once we know something about this. Stephanie, you drive Ed home for me please." Rick asks her, as Stephanie says she would, as Ed thanks Rick. Stephanie tells Ed she will drive his Envoy, and then make him some hot coco to cheer him up. As Ed informs her, he doesn't have any hot coco at home. Just good old instant coffee, as they drive off to his apartment in Lower Hermosa.

Stephanie helped Ed up the stairs as she parked his SUV, next to his motorcycle in his garage. As they entered Ed's condo, that was right on the edge of the beach. Stephanie looked around the apartment as she got a feel for what kind of likes Ed had, as he had many pictures of Jimi Hendrix, hanging on his walls. Along with his many weights, in the center of his living room that seemed out of place to her, as she asked Ed why he didn't have them set up in the spare bedroom? As Ed, told her he has his computer and other files that he made into an office in the other room. As Stephanie made, two cups of coffee for them as she handed him his mug, Ed suggested they walk out onto his deck; he wanted to show her the nice view of the Pacific Ocean at night. As they walked outside, as the wind from the ocean's current picked up, and blew Stephanie's long hair back. She told Ed, what a breathtaking view he has from his deck. As Ed smiled at her, and held her hand. As Stephanie smiled back at him, as Ed spoke softly to her.

"I'm sorry I couldn't protect you in time, as I had lost my attention for that once split second and we both could have been killed tonight". Ed told her, as he was sorry she got hurt.

"Ed, I'm just thankful we didn't get killed, you did everything you could as we were taken by surprise by this new killer. Don't blame yourself for this; it was going to happen even if we didn't go to meet with the Young's tonight. We are faced with a killer, who has knowledge and insight that might be ahead of even me, to be a step ahead of him." Stephanie, told him softly as she took a sip of her hot coffee.

"You know I'm not going to let anyone hurt you, I care about you Stephanie." Ed tells her, as he brings his mouth to hers and they share a soft kiss together. As Ed pulls away, Stephanie asks him what's wrong. He tells her, she has coffee breath. As they laugh, she tells him she has to go now that it's getting late. As Stephanie and Ed walk back inside his living room, Ed secured the glass door to the deck. As he was watching her, put on her short jacket. She came back over to him and asked if he was going to be all right? Ed, told her he would take some Advil for the pain, and then call her in the morning to pick her up. As he walked her to the door, Ed opened it for her, and asked how was she going to get home? As Stephanie smiled and said that he was right. She would have to borrow his truck to drive home and then pick him up, in the morning. As Ed, softly touched her face, as they kissed again passionately as he closed and locked the door; as he pulled Stephanie into his chest, he broke their kiss and whispered to her, that he wanted her to stay with him tonight. Stephanie, pulled her head back so she could look into his eyes, as she whispered, "Yes, I want to stay with you Ed". As they kissed again softly, Ed then picked Stephanie up in his arms, and carried her to his bedroom as he closed the door with his foot, and laid Stephanie down in his bed gently.

The Entity, watched from inside his dark vehicle that was concealed in the shadows of the adjoining alley way to Ed's apartment house. The Entity, knew his main adversary has a new love in his life. The Entity smiled to himself, as he knew he could use Stephanie's love for Ed to trap him. He knew this was his way of a plan, to get back at Ed Brooks for he was able to stop Nathan before. But he will fail to stop, the Entity and his vengeance now. As he started his vehicle up, and drove slowly away into the night.

As Stephanie awoke slowly in bed, she saw the very bright sun shining through the window, as she knew it was early morning. She sat up in bed and noticed Ed wasn't next to her, as she then heard heavy breathing coming from the living room. She knew Ed was lifting heavy weights, as she found his dress shirt and put it on, as she went to see him. As she stood in the doorway, she saw Ed bench-pressing heavy weights as he was sweating, that was a sign he was working out a while now. As Ed finished his last repetition, he placed the barbell, back in place on the bench as he sat up taking heavy breaths. As Stephanie came over and handed him a glass of water, as Ed thanked her and they kissed gently. As Stephanie thanked him for last night, and making her feel safe. As they got up and sat on the sofa together, Ed was going to suggest something to her now.

"I want to ask you this, not only the way we feel about each other but I know you will be a lot safer too. Do you want to move in with me, so I can make sure your safe?" Ed questions her, as Stephanie holds his face gently and whispers; "yes Ed, I would like that". As he smiles and tells her;" great", as they both admit they have fallen in love with one another, Ed's home phone is going off as he answers it. Rick had called to inform him, they made some headway into the murders last night, and they also have the detailed autopsy report from; Dr. Farrell. As Rick tells him the task force will be ready for a noon briefing, Ed tells him he and Stephanie will be there. As Ed informs her, of the briefing, they have four hours to get ready till they need to be at Central division. As Stephanie suggests, they take a shower together and for Ed to stop by her apartment so she can change into fresh clothes. As Ed agrees they again kiss, as Ed removes his tank top, Stephanie notices the deep scare Ed has to his left abdomen from the deadly encounter he had with Malcolm. She didn't notice last night, in the dark as they turned out the lights. But as they headed into the shower, Stephanie touched Ed's side softly and told him she was very sorry for him. Ed just smiled and told her he was all right now, that this case did bring some comfort to him. It brought her into his life, as Stephanie smiled and said he was right. As Ed turned on the water and very cold water rained down on their naked bodies in the marble enclosed shower. As Stephanie screamed that it was too cold, as Ed laughed and told her it was only water. As he turned the handle to the left to make it warmer, they kissed gently as the water splashed down on their faces.

As they just left Stephanie's apartment; she looked at Ed who was silent as he was driving with his eyes hidden behind his sunglasses. She knew something again was on his mind as he was thinking about the case and will not open up to her about what it was, she wanted to know what it was or else now. As she would be out right blunt with him about it' "Ed! I want to know what you have been hiding from me about this case now; I want you to tell me because maybe I can help you piece it all together. Haven't you earned my trust yet, and my love for you? Please talk to me; I'm frustrated that you will not open up to me about this." Stephanie trying to plead to Ed for him to trust her, as he turned his head to face her, he saw the look of hurt and concern on her face as he just turned back to look at the road.

"Please Stephanie; I'm not trying to hold anything back from you or Rick and the others. I have been looking at a theory of mine for some time now. And before I know for certain of what it all is and who may be involved, I can't tell you just yet, so please. Don't ask me this again, okay?" Ed tells her, as Stephanie disappointed just puts on her sunglasses and looks out the side window and whispers back; "fine Ed". As they enter the parking lot of Central Division.

As they enter the conference room together, Stephanie very abruptly was walking ahead of Ed as if she was upset with him. As she took her seat at the head of the table next to Rick, and Ed took his same seat next to Rob Cullen. As everyone knew she was upset with him, Rob whispered to Ed, "there isn't trouble with you and your new profiler friend? Is there Ed?" Rob asks him, as Ed just shakes his head and says; "she has a woman's insight, beyond a profiler's intuition." Ed tells his partner, as Rob just smiles as Rick begins to talk.

"Okay, we made some progress with the head of Quasar, as he gave Ed and Stephanie information that lead them to Fred Young. As someone killed him and his wife last night to conceal that information he was going to give them on Nathan Malcolm. But Rob visited with Aaron Byrne, late last night as he told Rob. Except for his secretary knowing he talked to us about Mr. Young. No one knew the police were going to visit with him at his residence last night. So my guess is, the new Entity killer is tracking our movements into the investigation, or unless someone in this very room is either A, feeding the killer our information, or B, the Entity killer is among us right now!" Rick tells them, as they all look at one another shocked. As he continues to talk.

"I had Ken and Jack, meet with Dr. Diana Farrell early this morning and release the autopsy report she completed on Nathan Malcolm, the very next day after his death. And after reading her full report twice, unless Malcolm is now a ghost, we have a brand new killer on our hands who has knowledge of our investigations and is now, moving at a faster rate of killing his victims and at random. Unlike Malcolm, who just prayed on prostitutes? So we are now at a standstill I believe in this new case, as I will ask Stephanie to give us her opinion on where we can begin to focus our investigation now". As Stephanie takes the podium, and opens her folder and begins to talk to the group.

"The most important thing I can suggest is that, this new killer is trying to mimic the Nathan Malcolm murders. Just as where he left Ashley Cook's body and the same remorseless way he killed Fred Young and his wife. But the main thing for us to be ready for his next move is to trust one another here! Because a certain lead Detective who I have been assigned to work with is holding back information from me, that maybe be very detrimental to us all. This person who is now my boyfriend, and who I have had passionate sex with last night and this morning! Is being a stubborn asshole! So my biggest advice is now, we need to trust one another if we are to solve this case! Thank you!" Stephanie thanks the task force, as she closes her folder and gathers her things and storms out of the conference room. As the whole group is left with their mouths wide open and in shock, as they stare at Ed Brooks who is beyond embarrassed now. As Rick gets up slowly from his seat, and says he thanks Stephanie Morgan for her honest opinions and advice to us. As Rick stares at Ed and tells everyone to work with their partners and decide amongst themselves how they want to work this now. As Ed, just gets up in an angry manner, and storms out the door.

"Rob, leave him alone for now. Stephanie is the only one he will open up to about what he believes. Hopefully her little mind blowing scheme, has worked to get him to trust her." Rick tells Rob, as Rob agrees with his Lieutenant, as he suggests he will talk to Ed. As Rob heads out the door to catch up to Ed. Stephanie was walking back to the conference room; as Rob told her Ed being embarrassed stormed out. As he was going to look for him; "Rob, I just saw Ed pull out of the parking lot. Let him go cool off, I did what I did in order for him to not only trust me but the whole task force. Can we go talk alone please? Being you're his partner, maybe you can share with me what Ed knows." Stephanie asks Rob, as Rob agrees to talk to her, but suggests they go somewhere alone to talk. As they head for Rob's car, they head to the diner for some lunch.

Rob finished his sandwich and fries, but Stephanie barely touched her salad, as they were now talking about Ed. As Stephanie came out and just asked Rob, what is it that he is holding back from her? "Look, you have to understand Stephanie. You're the first woman he has really been with since his divorce. Even though he was able to stop Nathan Malcolm that case has never left his soul. As Ed was convinced Malcolm has a deep connection to a passed serial killer, and Ed was bound to find out what it was. He has studied and researched this going on four years now. Ever since the first murders ended, but now with these recent new killings, Ed is more convinced than ever. The Malcolm murders along with these murders are connected, along with a certain case he believes happened a very long time ago." Rob tells her, as Stephanie presses for Rob to tell her what cases is he referring to? Rob just looks around the diner, and knows he can't mention the name here; she will have to find out for herself.

"You know behind Ed's computer desk in his office, he has the enclosed marker board on the wall?" Stephanie answered," yes" to Rob.

"Open the doors to the board, and you will not only find notes Ed has made himself, but pictures and dates with names of suspects and victims of this person, who Ed believes is connected to these cases now. I'm sorry Stephanie, but I can't tell you any more than this." Rob tells her, as Stephanie thanks him, and just asks if he could take her back to her apartment and help her pack her things. As she will be moving in with Ed this evening, as Rob agrees to help her move.

Ed was lifting weights, as he had the stereo playing the song; "Burning Desire", by Jimi Hendrix. As he heard the door unlocks and opens slowly, as he stops what he's doing and sits up to see who it is. Stephanie and Rob, enter the apartment as Rob is holding all her large bags and she tells him to set them down by the sofa, that her strong new boyfriend will kindly help her with them now. As Ed just makes a smile, and Rob tells them to have a good night, that he needs to get home now, as he leaves. Stephanie just stares at Ed with a sad look on her face, as she goes over and shuts off the CD player. As Ed, remarks thanks for doing that, he was enjoying that song along with his workout. As he takes a towel and wipes the sweat from his face, and heads into the bathroom to shower. As Stephanie makes a mean look on her face, because he is ignoring her again, she runs into the bathroom before Ed can lock the door, as he is naked.

"I hope I really embarrassed you this afternoon, because you needed a wakeup call from me! To make you understand you can trust me fully! Stephanie yells at him, as Ed just goes over and turns the water to start his shower, as he just calmly asks Stephanie to give him an hour to shower, and then they can talk like rational adults. As Ed steps into the shower, Stephanie steps out of her slacks and blouse and follows him in, as she screams again that the water is ice cold. Ed just smiles, at her as they start to kiss each other, as Stephanie whispers to him she is sorry for what she did, but if he could please tell her what's going on with this case. Ed tells her, after the shower and they relax for a short time, he will tell her. As Stephanie, starts to cry, they again kiss one another.

Stephanie awoke, in Ed's bed very slowly as she was able to glimpse the moon's rays coming through the bedroom window. She was surprised that after Ed and her, finished their shower together. He carried her to the bedroom, where they made love and then she fell asleep. Stephanie turned her head and looked at the digital clock on the side table; as the time was 2:36 AM. Stephanie very slowly, turned to her left side where Ed was lying next to her, sound asleep. She remembered what Rob, told her about; the whiteboard in Ed's office. Stephanie very slowly, glided herself out from under the sheets and comforter of the bed. As she put on Ed's pajama top and very quietly opened the bedroom door and closed it behind her. As she walked down the short hallway to Ed's office, as she opened the door and went inside and closed the door partially behind her. She turned on the room's lights, as she walked behind the desk to the large whiteboard that was enclosed by two side by side wood doors. Stephanie looked behind her, and then very slowly opened the left door first. As her eyes were shocked at what she was looking at, with an appalled look on her face, she slowly opened the right side door. As she then noticed more shocking pictures and notes, as she looked back at the left side again, as there were many brutal and even scary crime photos of victims, they looked very old. As Stephanie looked at the pictures of several men's faces, as Ed had written above their pictures; "Jack the Ripper, suspects". Stephanie took a step back, as she said to herself; "my God". As she then took another step back, and felt someone was standing behind her, she turned around and screamed loudly. As Ed was there, facing her now; as he reached out and held her hands. Stephanie said his name softly, as she began to cry. Ed hugged her tight to comfort her.

"I'm sorry I didn't tell you this before, I didn't want to scare you about this, and I wanted to dig up more information about him. Before I knew for sure there was a connection to our crimes now, and to the Ripper murders." Ed whispers to her, as Stephanie was shaking in his arms, very upset over seeing the graphic crime scene photographs, of the Ripper's victims. As she calmed herself down, she looked into Ed's eyes and spoke to him.

"You really think, Nathan Malcolm is somehow connected to Jack the Ripper?" She asks him softly, as Ed replied to her; "yes I do". As Stephanie asks him to explain it to her all that she needs to understand why Ed thinks there is a possible connection with these crimes. As Ed hugs her warmly again, he looks up at the many photographs and written notes he has made on the Ripper murders. Ed just whispers in her ear softly, that he will explain it all to her in the morning. As Ed closes the doors to the whiteboard, and hugs Stephanie as he leads her back to his bedroom.

# Chapter 6

At 7:00 AM, Ed and Stephanie were having coffee in the kitchen, as Ed had brought out some books and notes on; Jack the Ripper. He was explaining it all to Stephanie, that even before they knew Nathan Malcolm was the serial killer them, Ed felt there was a connection between him and the Ripper murders. As Ed was showing her, the crime scene photos of the five known female victims and their names, as Ed told Stephanie; like Malcolm's first three victims. The five women Jack the Ripper killed, were all prostitutes themselves. As Stephanie read off their names; Ed told her the dates of the murders and the last victim; Mary Jane Kelly. Was brutally mutilated from her face, to her legs, as Ed warned Stephanie, the crime scene photo was very graphic to look at, but Stephanie prepared herself and looked at the horrific picture. As Ed told her, he read the crime scene of this murder even shocked the lead investigator from Scotland Yard; Frederick Abberline, and his investigators. As Mary Kelly's, remains were scattered about a bedside table, as her body was laid out in her bed. As he face was completely hacked off. Stephanie then asked Ed, what suspect did he feel; Nathan Malcolm was related to? And besides Rob, did he tell Rick of this theory of his? As Ed, took out a book and a list of names to show her.

"This book was written in the 1990's by two, former British police officers, who found an amazing letter written by; Detective

Chief Inspector John George Littlechild, of the Metropolitan Police Service. Who at the time of the Ripper murders was the Detective Chief Inspector of the case. He wrote a letter in 1913. To author and journalist; George R. Sims, detailing how an American born doctor, by the name of Francis Tumblety. Was one of their main suspects; as the two authors wrote how he would travel to Europe and England frequently; to sell his self-made, Indian Herb medicines and remedies? That he made a fortune on. "As Ed, explained that he was considered a quack doctor, at the time. As Tumblety, was never really identified to be a true doctor. As he was married at a very young age, and he found out his wife was a prostitute. As to why he would have a lot of hatred towards them, and women in general. As Ed went on to explain, he was also considered to me a homosexual, that he was arrested during the time of the Ripper murders, for gross indecency with young men. As he was released in time to commit the final murder, of Mary Jane Kelly, on the ninth of November 1888. As he then fled to France, and then by ship to America, as Scotland Yard, has sent two agents to New York, to detain him and bring him back to England for questioning for his possible connections to the murders in Whitechaple. As Ed, shows her only the two known, photographs of Dr. Francis Tumblety. Showing a man, stocky in appearance with a very ling mustache, as Stephanie looked at the pictures, and thought about everything that Ed was filling her in on. As she took a very long deep breath, and looked up at him.

"Look Ed, you have done a lot of research here, and maybe those two former British police officers and that lead inspector at the time. Did indeed, find this man; Dr. Tumblety to be; Jack the Ripper himself. But there was no DNA evidence back then, and there was no real evidence or even witnesses to tie any suspect they thought at the time, to be the Ripper. I studied the case a while back in college, and I know the FBI, even did a profile of the Ripper back in the eighties or nineties. Let me check, with the head office in Washington D.C. and see, if they can fax me anything they have from that profile match that they did on him. Now let's keep this between us for now, and head to your office before we are late."

Ed, tells her okay. As they gather all the notes and books together.

As they head out to Ed's SUV and drive to Central Division. As Ed was driving, Stephanie took out the crime photos again of the women, the Ripper killed. As she then looked at one of the photos of Francis Tumblety; she thought to herself, "What kind of an evil man could have done this to a human being?" As she knew, even if Tumbelty didn't do these murders, there was a sense of evil in his photograph. That he just had the aurora about himself, of a man that did evil things in his lifetime. As Ed, looked over at Stephanie, and saw the upset look on her face. But he didn't want to say a word about this anymore, until they got to his office.

As they entered the building, Ed and Stephanie met with Rob at his desk. Ed told him he told Stephanie all about his, Jack the Ripper connection to these cases. As they will now tell Rick, if they can formally investigate this possible connection into the case, as the three of them entered Rick's office.

"Hey boss, the three of us got something to tell you, and then we need your permission to follow up on it." Ed tells Rick, as he is sitting behind his desk, listening to what they have to tell them. "I told Stephanie, about my belief these murders now, along with the Malcolm murders are somehow related to, the Ripper case way back when in England." Rick, just made a long stare at Ed, and then at Rob and Stephanie, knowing if he lets them investigate this angle, it could be more harm than good for not only the task force. But the whole police force of San Diego. As Ed, told him he explained it all to Stephanie, and she could use the FBI's main contacts in Washington, to help them profile and even analyze any evidence they have to tie all the cases together. As Rick, looks down at his own files of the murders. He knows they brought Stephanie into this case, to make headway into it. He looks back up at them and says; "okay". As Ed and his partners smile that he has given them permission.

"But look, we keep this quiet between the four of us for now. And you guys use the research office that is secured away from all the other cops we have in this building. As I don't want this to get out starting panic amongst cops and civilians at this point, let me brief the others now and have them follow up on the murders of the Young's. You three, work inside on this today." As Rick tells them his orders, the trio heads to the office, which has two desk top computers and a fax machine. Along with an LCD projector, to help them get started.

As Rob and Ed, set up the projector and posted the crime scene pictures on the whiteboard. Stephanie called the FBI office in Washington DC, to ask permission to fax them everything they had on the, Jack the Ripper case. Along with the profile, they made of him years before. As it took some time, to get this all together to them in California, Ed began to brief them on the dates and the names of the victims who were killed in order, Martha Tabram, Tuesday August seven. Mary Ann Nichols, Friday August 31. Annie Chapman, Saturday September 8. Elizabeth Stride and Catherine Eddowes; both killed the same night. Known as the double event on, Sunday September 30, as Mary Jane Kelly was his final victim. Her remains were discovered on, Friday November the ninth. As Rob stared at the, ghastly crime scene photo of Mary Jane Kelly, he felt the same way Stephanie did when she first saw it, horrified and shocked. As Ed, began to tell them the women were all known prostitutes, but the police and Ripper experts. Can't say for certain, if the first victim Martha Tabram, was a victim of the Ripper. Or was she the victim of a gang killing. Being she was stabbed thirty nine times, but she wasn't slashed or her body mutilated like four of the other victims were, as Stephanie was looking at their faces. She saw these first five women, were all in their forties and not very attractive in appearance as was the last victim. Mary Jane Kelly, who was only twenty five years old. Stephanie looked at an artist's drawing of what Kelly, would have looked like before her murder. As Stephanie felt very bad for this young woman, who was very pretty and didn't deserve to die like this.

As they were now and hour into the investigation, the fax machine was beeping as they were now receiving the incoming faxes on the case. As Rob, took them from the machine and handed them to Stephanie. She was looking through them, as Ed was explaining to them why he thought, Francis Tumblety was the killer.

"He was living at a lodging house in the center of Whitechaple, twenty two Batty Street. Just a ten minute walking distance from where all the victims were found. The police had this lodging house under surveillance then, as they knew an American doctor was living there. As one of the cities nearby museums, had stated an American doctor was interested in buying preserved female wombs. As he collected them in glass jars as a collection for himself", Ed described in detail from the book he was getting all his information from on, Dr. Tumblety. As Rob was shaking his head yes, thinking he was living in close distance to the murders at the lodging house. And he could commit a murder, and escape back to his loft unseen. As Ed, had a map of the Whitechaple district taped to the whiteboard, with all the crime scenes pegged. To show a short distance, Dr. Tumblety would have to travel to from each block back to twenty two Batty Street. As Stephanie, was reading the FBI's profile on the Ripper. Ed continued to explain away, details that would no doubt time Tumblety to the murders.

"So he collected and wanted female wombs and uteruses, two of the victims had their wombs removed. What average killer, would have known to extract a person's organs if he did not in fact have, medical and anatomical knowledge. And don't forget, there was no electricity back then. The street lights were gas lamps, and rooms were kept lit with candles and fire places. I bet my money, the Ripper did have a satchel bag with him when he committed each murder. Not only to carry his sharp knives, but also to carry a bullseye lantern. Just like the police constables carried with them, to eliminate enough light for him to see what he was doing, in the dark night and early mornings in the crowded areas of Whitechaple." Ed continued, to brief them. As Rob believed everything he was saying, as Stephanie kept reading about the Ripper's profile. As Ed looked at her and said her name loud to get her attention.

"Stephanie! Are you going to say anything here, or are you just going to sit there with your legs crossed and keep reading what you're so called experts in Washington D.C. think?" Stephanie gave him a deep stare, as she put down the papers and looked at the map of Whitechaple, that was detailed to 1888, period of the time the crimes happened. As she then, told them what the profiler believed he found to be the characteristics of; Jack the Ripper.

"Ed look, lead FBI profiler John Douglas, made this profile of the Ripper. Let me read to you some of the qualities he believed the Ripper had. A male, with average height and weight. Was never married, or maybe a very short marriage with a profound hatred for women, he was a loner with very little social contact. He was very familiar to the area of Whitechaple, believing he always lived there. With the skill and profession of a butcher or mortician's assistant," Stephanie reads to him aloud, the profile of Jack the Ripper. As Ed, agrees and disagrees with some of the profile's findings.

"Well I don't agree that a plain butcher or mortician's assistant, had the medical know how to remove these kinds of organs from a female, in the dark of night and very quickly. He had to carry a bag or some kind of box, to place the organs and preserve them in jars, as Tumblety is said to have done. Did you read and compare the two letters, which were said to have been written by the Ripper to the police? The Dear Boss, and the Letter From Hell. Both signed by; Jack the Ripper." As Ed hands Stephanie copies of both letters as she reads them aloud to them. She lets them know first, there are many typing errors and punctuation errors as she begins to read it;

"Dear Boss,

I keep on hearing the police have caught me but they wont fix me just yet. I have laughed when they look so clever and talk about being on the right track. That joke about Leather Apron gave me real fits. I am down on whores and I shant quit ripping them till I do get buckled. Grand work the last job was. I gave the lady no time to squeal. How can they catch me now. I love my work and want to start again. You will soon hear of me with my funny little games. I saved some of the proper red stuff in a ginger beer bottle over the last job to write with but it went thick like glue and I can't use it. Red ink is fit enough I hope ha. ha. The next job I do I shall clip the ladys ears off and send to the police officers just for jolly wouldn't you. Keep this letter back till I do a bit more work, then give it out straight. My knife's so nice and sharp I want to get to work right away if I get a chance. Good Luck. Yours truly

Jack the Ripper

Dont mind me giving the trade name

PS Wasnt good enough to post this before I got all the red ink off my hands curse it No luck yet. They say I'm a doctor now. ha ha"

"So he is denying he's a doctor, in the letter. But Ed, I myself have read and believe this letter was a forgery made by one of the local journalists who worked at one of the papers in London at the time; just to draw attention and controversy to the case and sell papers. Even back then, bad news and controversial stories that were said and involved the Royal Monarchy, was an open field day for tabloid papers and it got the whole world talking." Stephanie told him, as Rob agreed with her, that most experts then and now believe the" Dear Boss" letter, to be a fake. As Ed agrees with them, he then asks her to read the, "From Hell" letter. As Stephanie clears her throat, and makes a face she begins to read the letter. The letter was addressed to, and sent to George Lusk, head of the Whitechaple Vigilance Committee at the time, being he owned a small business in the area.

From hell

Mr Lusk

Sor

I send you half the Kidne I took from one women prasarved it for you tother piece I fried and ate it was very nise. I may send you the bloody knif that took it out if you only wate a whil longer

signed

Catch me when you Can Mishter Lusk

Stephanie again, pointed out the errors in typing and punctuation. As Ed told her and Rob, this letter was sent to Lusk, in a box that contained half a human kidney, as just around the time he received it. Victim, Catherine Eddowes, had one of her kidneys removed, as the letter was covered in blood and thought to have been written in blood itself, by some researchers. As Ed, told them, the two writers of the book, who state that Francis Tumblety, is the Ripper. Had a hand writing expert compare this letter and copies of letters that

Tumblety wrote, and the expert came to the conclusion that he did in fact write the; "From Hell", letter to George Lusk. As Stephanie shakes her head in both disbelief and in amazement at what Ed is complying with her.

"Fuck the movie with Johnny Depp! And the stupid theory that the Royal physician, Sir William Gull, was Jack the Ripper. You convinced me Ed, Francis Tumblety, is the Ripper! I have no doubts about it!" Rob agrees with him, as Stephanie looks into Ed's eyes, as he is waiting to hear what her opinion is.

"Ed, you make great points along with these experts about Tumblety. So even if he is Jack the Ripper, what does he have to do with our cases now, besides the victims being mutilated, we have to find out if Dr. Nathan Malcolm is somehow related to him. Tell me everything you know about him, up until his death and then let me check with the head office in D.C. if we can find a link between him and Malcolm." Stephanie tells him, as Ed smiles and then fills her in with everything he has found on Tumblety.

"He might have been born in Ireland in 1833, but we know he was raised in upstate Rochester, New York. He was known to move around from state to state and to Europe, selling his Indian Herb remedies and posing as a Doctor. He was known to use many alias names, and used the one; Dr. Frank Townsend, as he arrived in New York. December third, as Scotland Yard sent agents to New York to look for him, and bring him back to London in connection with the murders, but he gave them the slip. As again he moved around America, till he died on May 28, 1903. In a hospital in St. Louis, of heart failure, it was reported that among the things he was found to have. Was a box containing two cheap brass female rings, identical to the ones that victim, Annie Chapman was known to have been wearing the night she was murdered, but were found missing from her middle finger by the police when her body was discovered." Ed, details everything to her, as Stephanie and Rob are both busy taking notes down, as there was a knock on the door, as Rob goes over and opens it. Rick comes in and is amazed at all the paperwork, documents and books they have compiled all over the table. As he sees Stephanie wipe sweat from her forehead and the signs of exhaustion on her face, as he looks at the clock on the wall, and tells them. They have been locked in here for three hours now, as it was going on four PM.

"Well, looks like to me you guys are really getting Stephanie involved in this opinion of Ed's. But I think you guys need to call it quits for today, and my advice to you all go out and celebrate with each other tonight." Rick suggests to them, as Stephanie agrees and admits that she is tired now, as Ed states they will stop and head home for the day. Rick tells them to have a good night, and will see them in the morning. As he closes the door and leaves, as they start to clean up their notes and books together. Stephanie tells them, before they leave she will fax everything they have found on Francis Tumblety to, Washington D.C. and ask for all they have on Nathan Malcolm. Hoping by this time tomorrow they can find ties that bind them together. As Rob has a suggestion for them, as he has a smile on his face.

"Hey while it's still early in the afternoon, and I think Stephanie needs a nap now. Rick was right about celebrating, how about we all get together tonight at my house for dinner. So my wife the great Italian cook that she is, can make you two a nice home cooked meal, what do you both say?" rob asks them, as Ed smiles and says it's up to Stephanie.

"That sounds very sweet Rob, Ed and I will be more than happy to have dinner at your home. As I am interested in meeting you're lovely wife". She tells him, as Rob looks at his watch and suggests around eight PM, to come to his house. As Ed thanks him and says see you then.

As Ed was getting dressed in the bedroom, he was using his lint brush as he was dusting off the lint from his expensive black slacks, as he then looked at himself in the mirror, dressed with his tan button down dress shirt and black tie. He thought to himself, "Ed, you are one bad stud!" As he laughed, and then thought what was taking Stephanie so long in the bathroom, that it was going on 7:30 PM, he didn't want to be late for dinner at Rob's house. As Ed remembered, even Kayla took her time to get ready too. "It must be a female complex with them". Ed said to himself, as he saw Stephanie standing behind him in the mirror. As Ed was floored by the way she was dressed, and looked so beautiful, as she wore an elegant black dress. That was just below her knees, with spaghetti string shoulder ties. As her hair was soft and wavy, as she only had some lipstick and blush to her cheeks. As the two hour nap she took when they got home, seems to bring her back to life. As she saw the smile on Ed's face, she spun around for him. And asked, what did he think of the dress?

"It's not the dress that's catching my eye right now, it's the very beautiful woman who is wearing it that I love very much, that has caught my eyes and heart." As Stephanie walks slowly to him, as they share a passionate kiss gently. As Ed, gently brushes his hand on her face softly, he tells her they need to get going now. As Stephanie tells him she knows, as they kiss again she whispers to Ed; "I love you to".

Ed and Stephanie arrived at Rob's house shortly after eight PM. As Rob lived in the North Clairemont area, as Rob and his wife, Antonella who were also both dressed elegantly. Took Stephanie on a small tour of the house, as Ed has been a guest of theirs many times before, as Ed and Rob both sat in the living room sharing drink. Antonella told Stephanie, their daughter Megan, was sound to sleep in her room, as she took her around the two level Spanish style home. Rob, admitted to him that Stephanie is a very beautiful woman for an FBI profiler. As Ed thanks his partner, and states that he is very blessed to have met her, and have her in his life now. As the women came into the living room and Antonella announced that dinner was ready, that she prepared stuffed shells to start, and then she made veal with vegetables and salad. As they all sat in the dining room, to enjoy dinner, Antonella asked Stephanie what did she think of San Diego, and her thoughts of maybe moving here?

"Oh I really love it here in San Diego, just a more relaxed feel of a lifestyle very different that we have in Los Angeles. I would look to move here after this case is over, if a certain someone would like me to?" She said, as she smiled at Ed. Who reached over and held her hand, as he said he would be more than happy to have her here with him. As Antonella, asked them all how was the investigation into the case going so far? As Rob, looked at Stephanie and Ed. With the look as to who should answer that question. Stephanie, answered her.

"I feel the three of us, along with the other good Detectives who make up the task force. Are heading to a big lead into the cases soon, but we don't know anything about this new suspect just yet." Stephanie says softly, knowing she would not mention nothing about; "Jack the Ripper", to Rob's wife. As Stephanie says no matter what, this case has brought her and Ed together now. As both Rob and his wife, admit they are happy that Ed has another woman in his life now. As he kisses Stephanie on the cheek, Rob's home phone was going off. As he told them he will answer it, Stephanie was telling Antonella. What a nice guy and great Detective Ed is, and besides he is very handsome just like Rob is. As Antonella thanks her for the nice comment about her husband, they overhear Rob talking on the phone. As he said to the caller, Ed and Stephanie are here at his house having dinner with him. As they all stare at each other, knowing something has happened, as Rob hangs up the phone and walks back to the table. As his wife asks him; "what's wrong Rob?" As he looks at Ed, and tells them that was Rick who had just called.

"They found another body of a young female, on the banks of the beach right near the Coronado Bridge, and she has been badly mutilated. Rick and the task force are on their way there now." As Ed takes a deep breath, he and Stephanie rise from their seats as they get ready to go. Rob, says he will drive them in his car, as they all get to the door, they say thank you to Antonella for dinner, as she tells them all to be careful.

As Rob was driving on route 75, as he drove over the San Diego Bay, and into Coronado. They saw the many flashing lights of emergency service vehicles, coming from beneath the bridge of the banks of the beach below. As Rob took the first off ramp, as police from Coronado stopped his vehicle but Ed and Rob showed them their badges and the vehicle was cleared to move on. As Ed looked down at Stephanie's feet, he told her the sandy and many stoned riddled beach would ruin her nice black heel shoes. As the car came to a stop, Stephanie made a face at Ed, and told him not to open the door just yet. As she kicked off her heels and left them in car, she then crossed her legs. As she pushed her dress up to her thigh, as Ed was staring at her amazing legs. Rob also had his eyes glued to the rear view mirror, as they watched Stephanie, glide down the thigh high stalking's from both her legs. As she left them next to her shoes on the floorboard of the car, she then smiled and said; "we can go see what this is all about now". As Ed smiled back at her, Rob just made a big grin on his face as they exited to car.

Ed and Rob saw Rick talking with the task force team. As Stephanie walked gingerly on the sharp rocks and sand, as a male uniformed officer took her hand and helped her to peer at the body closer. Stephanie bent down to look at the fatal wound that was a slash across the throat once. Plus there was a major gash in the head, and heavy bruising on one said of the body, one of the forensic team members told her. As she also had her breasts removed, as they were found to be with her. As the body was incased in a large clear plastic bag, that was very bloody. As Stephanie looked up at the bridge and then down at the body. She used the forensic team member's flashlight to look at the gash in the victim's head on the right side, and the bruising. As Stephanie stated to the forensic team; "the murder happened somewhere else, and then the body was flung from the bridge above. As to why there is no vehicle, tire impressions in the sand." Stephanie stated, as they heard a woman screaming. The team looked up as a woman was trying to make her way to the body, as Rick stepped forward and caught her in his arms. As the woman started to cry as Rick hugged her, he then called for Julie O'Keefe, to come and help comfort the mother of the victim. As Ed looked on, he felt the pain this poor woman must be going through now, as she has just found out her daughter has been murdered. As Rick, calls the task force together. Stephanie watches as Rick, brings the team around the body. As Ed holds her hand, Rick begins to brief them about this victim.

"This young ladies name was, Jackie Mays. Twenty six years old, she worked at nearby Hotel Del Coronado. As a waitress at one of the hotel's restaurants, as her purse was found inside the large plastic bag that contained the body, as we found her identification and traced it back to her home address, as to why her mother is here now whom she lived with." As the entire team, had a feeling of sorrow over them, in having to deal with another young life taken away for no reason.

"Besides the body being thrown from the bridge, any other signals for us to go on here?" Detective Ken Rogers asks Rick, as Rick goes over the mutilation wounds made, and the sharp knife wound to the throat. Rick then asks Stephanie, what information she gathered from examining the body closely.

"We know she worked at the hotel, I say the killer was probably driving a cargo van or minivan. As he was watching her leave in the parking lot, he then must have known her vehicle and parked right next to her vehicle. As he slowly opened the door to his vehicle, clamped his hand over her mouth and pulled her inside, as he already had this plastic bag laid out inside his vehicle for her, as he slit her throat and then cut her breasts off. Her fingernails were not removed like the other victims, being he did this so fast, this young woman didn't have a chance to fight him off." As Stephanie finishes her statement in anger, as she looks at the very pretty face of; Jackie Mays.

"So any surveillance cameras catch anything in the parking lot or witnesses?" Detective Skip Jones asks Rick, as Rick replied, the Coronado Police checked the hotels security cameras. As they were roving and panning around, they didn't catch the incident as it happened. As there was only one witness, another female employee who heard a female scream, and then a few seconds later a vehicle drive off in the distance. But she didn't see what kind of vehicle it was, or anything else at the time.

"He stalked her out; he had to be a patron of the restaurant or even a guest at the hotel. For him to know where she worked, and what time she got off work, and where her vehicle was parked in the employee parking lot," Stephanie tells them, as Rick is helpless again, with few leads and witnesses to go on. As he says he hopes forensics and Dr. Adams may find something, but if the killer was again methodical to use sterile clothing and gloves, very little forensic evidence would be found. As they watch the body of the young woman, being placed into the body bag and then into the county coroner's van. As Rick tells his team, to gather back at Central Division very early in the morning, that they can't find anything else out now, as they say their goodnights to one another, the trio heads to Rob's car as Ed is holding Stephanie's hand he hears her crying softly, "are you all right?" He asks her.

"No I'm not, let's just go right home, and please Ed?" Stephanie asks him, as Ed tells her yes.

As they arrived back home, Stephanie went right into the bedroom and closed the door to change. As Ed, went into his office, and made another entry into his file of the; "Entity Murders". As he added this latest woman's name and age, he then heard the kettle pot whistling, as he knew Stephanie was making herself either tea or coffee. As Ed, was finishing up he would go join her now. As Ed logs off his computer and turns off the light in his office, he goes into the living room where he sees Stephanie sitting on the sofa. With her knees in her chest clutching a cup of hot tea in her hands, as Ed sits with her on the couch and holds one of her hands softly.

"Too late for coffee?" He asks her, as Stephanie breaks a smile at him, and just said tea helped calm her down right now. As Ed asked her, if she was all right?

"Ed, when I bent down and I saw the look on that poor girl's face. It wasn't only that she was too young and didn't deserve this. But to think as her mother thought she would be happy to see her daughter come home, after a night at work and then to be called to a crime scene and find out she was murdered by some creep. This one really hit me hard unlike the other victims. Being this girl was innocent and for the most part lived a good life. I don't know if I want to continue on in this case any longer Ed, I'm scared now for some reason. And I have never been scared before in all the cases I have worked on, and I saw the anger you have every time we are called to a new crime scene. Because you want not only catch this guy, but you want to kill him yourself. Don't you Ed?" Stephanie questions him, as Ed knows he can't lie to her, or try to word his answer to her in any other fashion but the truth.

"Your right, I want to kill him myself for what he has done. And I know he is going to come after me soon, as to why I'm going to ask you to tell Rick and Chief Chase, that you want to be released from this case in the morning. Please Stephanie; I don't want you to be harmed in any way because of me. You know I love you, and I can't live with myself if something happened to you now." As Stephanie starts to cry, she just rests her head in Ed's chest as he holds her warmly.

"Ed, I care for you so much, and I know if I asked you to resign from this case you will not. And I know if I resign from the case, I don't know if I'm ever going to see you alive again if I go back to L.A. So then I want to stay here with you, and just strive on together so we can catch this son of a bitch!" Stephanie yells out, with anger in her voice. As Ed feels her spirit drives on hard, wanting to catch the Entity and also be with Ed. As they kiss each other softly, Stephanie starts to undo the buttons to Ed's shirt. As Ed does the same to her top, Ed glides his fingers down the bare back of Stephanie's soft skin. As they slide gently to the soft carpeting of the floor together.

As Rick had gathered the task force in the conference room, they were just waiting for Ed Rob and Stephanie to come join them. But Rick had already had other plans for the three of them as they just entered through the door, and they greeted everyone as they took their seats. Rick was going to be very fast now, in handing out their assignments in looking into the new murder of, Jackie Mays.

"So I got a call this morning from the Coronado Police Detective, who is handling the case of Jackie Mays. It seems a white cargo van, was seen by at least four witnesses driving away from the hotel, around 10:15 PM last night. I want Ken and Jack to go interview the witnesses, go back to the hotel and crime scene and get everything you can about a possible make and model. As you can tie it into the crime, and see if maybe the hotel had any outside contractors with a need for a van like this to be on site last night. Julie and Skip, I want you two to go interview this girl's mother again, along with her friends and co-workers. See if she mentioned to them about a possible ex-boyfriend a worker she maybe complained about, or maybe a person who she felt was following her. We need to try and fine something.

As I myself am now getting involved here, my wife and I are going to go over the DNA evidence of all the victims together and I will talk with Dr. Diana Farrell who did the autopsy on Nathan Malcolm. She may provide some answers to why we have so little forensics to go on here." As Rick then tells them to get a move on, the others leave as Ed and his partners look at him wondering what Rick wants to have them do this morning. As he was waiting for the others to leave, they see him produce a large folder of paperwork with a serious stare in his eyes, as he is about to explain what it's all about.

"Just about an hour ago, the FBI office in D.C. faxed all this over here that was for Stephanie only. I didn't look at it and made certain no one else looked at it here, to keep your side investigation quiet for now. I will leave you guys alone and suggest you work in the same secured office again. I'm going to go meet with Cate now, as you can reach me on my cell phone if something turns up." Rick tells them, as he hands the folder to Stephanie. She looks through it quickly, as she see's something that catches her eyes. She smiles at Rick and thanks him, as she tells Ed and Rob to hurry into the secured office.

As Ed locks the door behind them and Rob turns on the computers; Ed asks her what did she find that is standing out?

"Listen to this, Dr. Francis Tumblety, whom was married but is not known to have had any children of his own, did have up to eleven siblings who some of in turn. Got married and had families of their own, who like Francis Tumblety. Moved away from Rochester New York, and settled down around the country. One of the last few surviving relatives of Francis Tumblety, was a younger brother named Jessup Tumblety. Who was married and had children as he lived in the small town of Marion Iowa. He was contacted by the hospital in St. Louis, in 1903. Where Francis Tumblety passed away; Jessup Tumblety ventured to the hospital where he claimed his brother's body and had it brought back to Rochester New York, for burial in the families plot. As he then took possession of Francis Tumblety's all belongings he had with him when he passed away, from a small house he was staying at the time of his passing." Stephanie reads from a document the FBI investigative team has found out, as Ed just shrugs his shoulders and asks her; "what is so significant about that to this case now?" He questions her, as Stephanie smiles at him and answers.

"Soon after the funeral of Francis Tumblety in Rochester New York, Jessup Tumblety returned to Marion Iowa and legally changed the family's last name from Tumblety to Malcolm, in 1903." As Ed and Rob raise their eyebrows and look at one another.

"So his brother Jessup had to find something that belonged to Francis that caused him not only to change his family's name; but also prove that he was Jack the Ripper". Ed says with heated eyes, knowing now they are on to something that can finally tie Francis Tumblety, as being Jack the Ripper.

"We need to maybe go to Marion Iowa and search for any family records of the Malcolm's, and see if there is any known next of kin still living there now." Rob suggests to them, as Stephanie agrees with him. As she looks at Ed, on what he wants to do being he is the lead Detective into the case.

"Rob, Stephanie and I will head to Marion Iowa to check this all out. You team up with Rick and work on any leads that come up into the May's girl's death. As Stephanie and I need to go home and pack, as we have a plane to catch to good old Iowa." As Stephanie, smiles at him as she says she is ready to see the good old heartland of America.

Rick and his wife, Dr. Cate Adams agreed to meet with Dr. Diana Farrell as she agreed to show him all her findings in the autopsy she done, four years ago the day after, Nathan Malcolm died in his own home in the fire. As Cate and Diana were talking, Rick was very intense as he was reading off the cause of death, and the areas of the body that was outlined in the autopsy report by Dr. Farrell. She was in her late thirties, a very educated and accomplished biologist and criminologist forensic scientists. She held degrees from MIT University, along with her medical education at Duke University School of medicine. Cate had praised her work to Rick on a few occasions, as Dr. Farrell was even consulted by law enforcement agencies around the country, to work with them on complex cases.

Dr. Farrell, like Stephanie was also an accomplished athlete in college, in swimming and track. As she still would jog up to two miles every morning, along with yoga and weight lifting routines. As she even had a picture of herself, in her office of her completing a long distance marathon held recently in San Diego. She was about 5 foot 5. With shoulder length blonde hair, and crisp hazel eyes. Rick found her to be very attractive, but knew to keep his eyes glued to work only, in the presence of his own beautiful wife. As he then questioned Dr. Farrell.

"Diana, you state here in the autopsy that Malcolm died of a result of the massive burns he sustained in the fire, as well as smoke inhalation. Was there any other sufficient injuries he could have sustained when he had that, violent encounter with Detective Ed Brooks, right before the fire broke out in the house"? Rick asks her, as she looks at the autopsy results she made, and answers him.

"As I can recall, the body was so badly burned and charred. If there were any signs of open wounds or even broken bones, I couldn't physically see any on him. The smell of burnt flesh was so hideous; Cate and I couldn't even get close enough to the body to take the forensic photographs as you see in the report. His flesh and hair was badly singed, and he even had several teeth, that decayed and fell out of the gum line, because the fire had decayed the flesh and bone to the point, not even cells could live." As Rick looks at another photograph of the body, even Malcolm's eyeballs melted out of their eye sockets, from the intense heat.

"Rick don't forget, he was using alcohol as an accelerant to start the blaze, and when the gas line ruptured and caused the huge explosion in the house. That added to the tremendous heat that would have taken a toll of the human flesh, which is very fragile to begin with." Cate adds, as Diana nods to him.

"He may have a child from his previous marriage, but we were unable to confirm that and his ex-wife passed away in 1988, as a result of Alzheimer's disease, and no next of kin claimed the body. So the judge ordered it to be cremated once you signed off on the final results of the autopsy." Rick asks Diana, as she tells him; "correct".

"May I take the autopsy report? I feel it may help us in our investigations now, into these recent murders." Rick asks Diana, as she tells him of course, but she doesn't know hot it may help them now, as she asks Dr. Adams if she made any progress with the recent body now. As Cate tells her, so far no but she hasn't completed the autopsy just yet, as Diana offers to help her, if she would like the assistance?

"Sure, that would be great. A second pair of eyes to help me, from the great Dr. Farrell." Cate praises her counterpart, as they agree to work on the autopsy together. Rick then receives a call from Ed, as he informs his boss of what they found. Rick walks to the side to be away from the women, not wanting them to hear his very confidential call with Ed.

"Ed this is great news you and Stephanie have found, Dr. Farrell is going to assist Cate with the autopsy on Jackie Mays. I'm sure they will find a flaw this killer has made in his crimes, as Rob and I will go over Nathan Malcolm's known contacts with a fine toothed comb, while you're in Iowa with Stephanie."

As Ed tells Rick, he and Stephanie will book a flight to leave for Iowa this evening. Rob will meet up with Rick as he was about to leave with Cate and Dr. Farrell now. As Rick rejoined the two doctors, Cate agreed to have Dr. Farrell drive her back to the county coroner's facility to begin work, on the autopsy. As the three of them head to the parking lot, eyes from afar watch as Rick gets into his car as he waves goodbye to his wife and drives off. Cate gets into Diana's, Lincoln SUV. As they drive off together. The watcher starts up his vehicle, and decides to follow the women, and try and find out what they are working on together.

As the two doctors had changed into their scrubs and foo sterile attire, they began the slow and very detailed autopsy of Jackie Mays. As Cate was filling Dr. Farrell in on the details of the murder, that she was pulled inside a white cargo van and then had her throat slit, and then the killer removed her breasts. As to why her fingernails were not removed, like the other victims, as Dr. Farrell listened to Cate talk. She was shining a sharp blue florescent beam of light on the body, in the dark as the lab lights were turned off. The very bright light will pick up spots of blood that are invisible to the naked eyes. As Dr. Farrell did spot something in one of her right fingernails, as the light had shown a spot that they did not see before. Cate asked her if it was blood. But Dr. Farrell answered; it didn't appear to be blood. As she used a pair of metal tweezers, to grasp the unknown material from the victim's right index fingernail. As Diana held the light to the material very close, she said it was a piece of carpeting, possibly from inside the cargo van. As Diana, went over the entire body twice with the blue light, she did not see any other unknown evidence and asked Cate to turn the lights back on.

"It looks like a piece of light gray carpeting; that is used to line the bed floor and inside wall panels of the van. Jackie must have torn a piece of the right side panel off, when the killer forced her into the van." Diana suggested to Cate, who was astonished by this find.

"So if the killer, rented a cargo van that has now physical damage to it. If he doesn't know about it, before he returns it to the rental company. Rick and his team have an opportunity here, to track down the person who rented it!" Cate says very quickly, as Diana tells her to call him quickly to inform him of this.

Rick and Rob were going over Nathan Malcolm's personal records. They read Malcolm's medical background and the schools he attended. He graduated from UCSF, medical school of California in 1982, at the age of 28. He divorced his wife, Jane Malcolm in 1984, just two years later. As there was a mention of a child in his personal records, but no known existing records ever since, to declare his child's whereabouts since 1984. As Rob comments to Rick, "he was born in Marion Iowa, as he then came to San Francisco to attend school in the 1970's. So he settled out here and married his wife in 1978, as she was from San Diego. It doesn't tell us, if they met in medical school but we can assume that. As she passed away from a rare form of; Familial Alzheimer disease, a person between the ages of 30 and 60 can be diagnosed with this rare form of Alzheimer's." Rob read, off to Rick. As his cell phone was ringing, it was Cate telling him the evidence they have found, as Rick informed her they would come right over. He told Rob of their find, as the two men hurried to meet them at the county coroner's facility.

The watcher saw the approaching headlights coming toward his direction in the dark parking lot, as it was now 10:00 PM at night. He saw the two policemen get out of their car quickly and go in the main doors, as the security guard buzzed them through the secured double doors. The watcher knew they were cops, because he knew the taller one was Ed Brook's partner. He concluded that the two doctors had to have come up with a certain piece of evidence, for them to still be working this late into the night. The watcher knew, he had to get it away from them somehow now. He needed to stop watching and become the Entity now. For he paused and waited for a moment, as he needed to come up with a silent and stealth way of getting into the facility, that had security in the main entrance. But he looked at the back loading dock, and saw a surveillance monitor pointed to the incoming traffic lane. He knew this would be his way into the complex, as he was hidden in his black mask and hooded long black coat. He had his tools in his pocket, as he looked around the area and didn't see a soul. He made his way slowly to the back door, that was secured as it needed an access badge of an employee to open the door. The Entity, took from his pocked a very this piece of metal, as he placed it in between the door latch and its lock. As he took out a made up identification badge, that he modified with a magnetized access swipe, as he swiped it against the square panel on the wall, the latch unlocked itself. As he slid the metal strip in between the latch, to keep the door open. As he made his way upstairs to the second floor, where the lights were still on in the three story building.

"Hey guys, look at what Diana found." Cate was telling Rick and Rob, as they showed them the piece of material found in the victim's finger. Diana explained what it was and how it was lodged in Jackie's fingernail. As Rick was telling Rob, they now can check on this lead about white cargo vans, with a light gray interior that has been damaged. As suddenly they all hear the sound of glass shattering from the outside hallway, as they all look up at once. Rob tells them he will go and see what that noise was, as he walks out of the lab and makes a right turn down the hallway. He doesn't see anything at first, but at the end of the corridor, he spots the outside light reflecting from the floor. As he knows the large window glass, has been shattered as he walks over to investigate what caused it to break.

From inside the lab room, there was an eerie feeling that something didn't feel right here. As Rick called out to Rob, and Cate said softly to them, if they heard that noise coming from inside the room. As all of a sudden, the labs lights were turned off and the room was cast into darkness. As Rick told the women to get behind him, as he took out his gun from his side holster. As Diana grabbed the blue light from the table next to her, and turned the beam on as she flashed it to her left and then to her right. As she then flashed the blue beam in front of her, the bright face of a masked hooded figure was cast in front of her. As the Entity hit the light from her hand, and then slashed Diana, across her left forearm with a sharp knife. As she screamed in pain, she fell to the floor. As Rick pushed his wife to the floor, and started to shoot in that direction from where the Entity stood.

As Rick screamed to the women to stay on the floor, he cautiously looked for the light on the wall as he was hit hard from behind; Rick discharged a shot as he dropped his gun. As the Entity kicked him in his back, while he was on the floor. The Entity, didn't find anything useful to himself here. As he started to run down the hallway, Rob was running full speed in his direction. As the two men collided on impact, Rob was thrown off his feet backward, as the Entity staggered as he hit the wall to his left. But he was able to regain his balance and kick Rob hard in his chest. As he ran down the corridor full speed, As Cate turned the lights on. She saw Dr. Farrell crying in pain, as blood was coming out of the open wound on her left arm. Rick got to his feet as he ran out into the hallway, as he found Rob struggling to get up. They heard the sound again of glass breaking. As Rick ran down the hallway, as the building's security team was coming up the stairwell. The men then began to look around the rooms of the floor, as they heard the sound of a vehicle driving out of the parking lot at high speed. As Rick took a deep breath, he ordered one of the guards to call the police right away, as Rob came running toward him, with blood coming out of his mouth. The two policemen returned to the lab, as

Cate had fixed a sterile dressing on Diana's arm. As the security guard informed him, he also called for an ambulance to come as well.

Rick re-holstered his sidearm as Rob was cleaning his face with tissues; they looked around to see if anything was taken, as Cate informed them that the piece of gray material was still in its plastic on the table. As Rick just wondered to himself, why would the killer go to this great length of risk, if he didn't accomplish anything here? Except to expose himself to the police, and maybe he could have gotten killed or apprehended. Rick just leaned on the table to regain his composure from all the excitement. As he thought of the scenario in his head, he then went over and hugged his wife, as he asked Dr. Farrell if she was all right?

"I'm fine thank you; but I am very scared now. He knows who we are; and he could be watching us still at this very moment." She tells them, as Rob tells her to relax, as he applies pressure to the knife wound to try and stop the bleeding, as they hear the sounds of sirens approaching.

Rick was talking to the uniformed officers who were going take make the report, as Rob was huddled with the task force. As he told them what happened here and that Dr. Farrell had a deep laceration to her left forearm that required stitches, as Rick's wife accompanied here with a police escort to the hospital. As the fellow detectives asked Rob, if he or Rick could make out a description of the assailant? Rob just told them, "The guy was tall, strong as hell and dressed in all black. None of us could make out anything about him, when he shut the lights off. But as I ran into him head on in the hallway. I knew he was wearing some kind of jacket, from the nylon material I felt on my skin." Rob briefed them all he could remember, as the team took their notes and Rick came over to them.

"Well I just talked to the forensic team here; I took four shots at the suspect in the dark here in the lab. Two shots hit the far wall and were lodged in there still. My other two shots hit the glass enclosed medicine cabinet over there, shattering the glass and breaking some expensive medical stuff, that will be replaced. I just called Cate at the hospital; she said Dr. Farrell received sixteen stiches to her injured forearm, and she is shaken up a bit. As she will be staying with some relatives, of hers for the night." Rick explains, as he also adds they don't know what the Entity was looking for, as the only find the two doctors discovered was the small piece of fiber carpeting in the cargo van, stuck in the girl's fingernail.

"Look guys, I know it's late but we have to get a move on this lead now. All of you are going to call each rental agency all around western San Diego, and find out who they rented a white cargo van to. Within the last three or four days, and if it returned with any damage to its right panel covered in a light gray carpeting. Let's move on this people!" Rick shouts at them, as the team goes to research all they can find on the computer and make phone calls, at 11:30 PM.

"Do you think any of them will find out anything by the morning?" Rob asks Rick, as Rick suggests if the rental companies have the name of the person who rented the van still in their system, they can track him down easily because car rental agencies only accept credit cards, as cash payments. So they can track him down that way, even if he used a stolen credit card. As Rob told his boss, just like the CSI shows. Rick smiled at him as he took out his cell phone, he told Rob he was going to call Ed now and tell him what happened. Rob stated that he and Stephanie might be sleeping now, as Rick looked up at Rob and said; "believe me, Ed and his new lady friend are not sleeping right now."

Ed and Stephanie had checked into the Days Inn of Marion Iowa, around 9:35 PM central time. As they went out for dinner and noted where the town library and town hall were located, so they can begin their search of the Tumblety and Malcolm family history, early the next day, as the television was on very softly in their room. Ed was on top of Stephanie, as they were making passionate love together, as Ed's cell phone began to ring. As he looked up at it, next to them on the side table, Stephanie tried to pull his attention back to her.

"Ed, don't answer it just yet. Let it go to voicemail first, come on now". She said softly, as they kissed one another deeply. Ed, reached over and held his phone to his left ear and said; "Hello?" As Stephanie made a face, and just closed her eyes as she was disappointed they were being disturbed at this very moment. As Ed's demeanor became very serious, as Stephanie heard Ed, ask Rick if he was all right? She sat up next to him on the bed, as she covered herself with her pajama top. As Ed, was telling Rick, thank goodness none of them were hurt, as he and Stephanie will try to finish up their investigation in one day in Marion, and try to be back in San Diego late tomorrow night. As Ed hangs up with Rick, he looks over at Stephanie and tells her what happened with them tonight.

Stephanie makes a sad look into Ed's eyes, as a somber feeling has taken over her. "Ed, this person no matter who he is wants to kill your friends now. I'm surprised he didn't kill Rick or Rob, or even one forensic doctors. I have a feeling he knows we are here, and he will strike at you or me, when the timing is right for him." Stephanie tells him softly, as Ed just touches her face with his right hand.

"Hey, I told you I'm not going to let anything happen to you or anyone in my team got it. So we finish up here early tomorrow and get back to San Diego, as I want to teach you a few things when we get home all right?" Ed, tells her as Stephanie just smiles at him and says; "okay". As they kiss gently, Ed shuts off the LCD television with the remote, as he tells her they need to get some sleep now, as they lie back in the bed together as Stephanie rests her head on Ed's strong chest. Feeling she is very safe with him, as Ed shuts off the lights and hold her in his arms. He prays to God, for him to keep his word and make sure he can keep Stephanie and his friends safe from harm.

While Ed and Stephanie were sound asleep in Iowa, as Rick and the task force were busy late into the night investigating what happened at the county coroner's facility, it was now just passed midnight; California time. As Charles Neast, and his wife Kayla, were just relaxing at home in their large bedroom, just about to get ready for bed. John was lying in bed watching the late news, on their large LCD television, as Kayla walked into the bedroom from the bathroom holding a jar of Ponds cold cream. Kayla was wearing lingerie, under her short silver silk robe, as she sat on the edge of the bed; Charles leaned over and kissed her on the back of the neck gently. As Kayla kissed his lips, she then crossed her legs as she started to apply the cold cream to her bare legs, to sooth them after she just shaved them during her shower. As Charles was flirting with the idea they should have sex, Kayla told him no. That she needed to be at school early tomorrow for a teacher's conference as Charles can get to work whenever he wanted, being he was one of the head lawyers in his firm. As they heard their dog "Shadow"; repeatedly barking from the backyard where he was restrained by a twelve foot chain, mounted into the ground deep next to his doghouse. As Kayla questioned her husband what was he barking at?

"I don't know, German Shepard's don't usually bark unless there is a reason. Let me go find out what's wrong with him. I might have to bring him inside for the rest of the night if it's going to keep him quiet."

"Chuck just do whatever it takes, we don't want the neighbors complaining about our dog now." Kayla tells her husband, as Charles puts on his long plain bathrobe over his pajamas, as he heads downstairs towards the back door, which leads to the backyard. As Kayla finishes applying the cream to her left leg, she crosses her right leg and starts to spread the cream up and down her ankle to her inner thigh and softly to her upper thigh. As she massages it in deeply, she adores the thought of how good it feels. As she then hears "Shadow"; make a crying yelp sound, and then he begins to howl. Kayla looks up and wonders what is taking Chuck so long, as she then feels a hand on her right shoulder.

"What took you so long, and what was wrong with the dog?" She questions him, as the voice from behind her says; "so pretty you are, Mrs. Brooks". Kayla stunned by the unfamiliar soft raspy voice, starts to turn her head around to see who the intruder is, as the hand shoves her done to the bead very hard. Kayla was about to scream, but the gloved hand covers her mouth up very strong. As the intruder covered all in black, just makes a soft; shoosh sound for her to be quiet. As Kayla relaxes a little bit, hoping if she does what he wants, he will not harm her. As the Entity, begins to talk to her very softly.

"It's a shame Kayla Brooks, you are so pretty indeed. Too bad because of your ex-husband, you have to die now; just like your present husband did." As Kayla tried to scream under his gloved hand, he just slit her throat very fast and then again from the opposite direction, as the wet blood just gushed all over her neck and onto the bed, Kayla was coughing and gasping for air, as she just took her last breath and closed her eyes and her head fell the side. As the killer kept his hand over her mouth a few seconds longer, to make certain she was dead. As he thought to himself, he would not mutilate this body but he would leave Ed Brooks. A very different calling card instead, as he dipped his gloved finger in her own blood, and wrote out a message on the large mirror on the wall; "Just for you Ed Brooks; we will meet again soon my friend." Was what he wrote in blood, as he quickly ran down the stairs and out the back door that he forced opened, passing over the dead body of Charles Neast. As Shadow, started to bark again very loud; as the Entity jumped over the back wall of the house, and disappeared into the night. Shadow fought hard as he pulled and tugged on the chain, as he was able to break free of the collar that it was latched to around his neck, he quickly ran into the house. As he stopped and licked Charles's face, as he barked again, as he got no response from his master. He then ran up the stairs and into the master bedroom, as he jumped on the bed and licked Kayla's face. As her blood, was washed up by shadow's long wet tongue. He then began to cry and howl again, knowing his masters were dead.

The couple who lived right next door to the Neast's, heard Shadows continues barks and howls. As they put on the homes lights as; Bruce Feldman sat up in bed and told his wife this is annoying him now. As his wife asked him what she wanted to do, he just picked up the phone and dialed 911. He told his wife he is calling them to look into a noise complaint from the Neast's home, as well as a motorcycle driving around their quiet neighborhood, very fast at this time of night. As Mr. Feldman was done talking to the dispatch officer on the phone, he thanked him for his cooperation as he hung up the phone. He told his wife, the police are sending out a squad car to the Neast's house, to see what the problem is. As he shut off the light, and then covered his head with his pillow and went back to sleep.

# Chapter 7

E d instructed Stephanie not to unpack their two suitcases
because; he wanted to be ready in a hurry once they were
done here in Marion. As they had a quick breakfast together
at a local diner, they then took a taxi over to the Marion Library, as
they were given access to the film files of the city of Marion, once
Ed and Stephanie proved to them to the librarian on duty, that they
were law enforcement officers investigating the Entity murders in
San Diego. The librarian gave them access to all the films from 1903,
and to the present day. Regarding anything from the Tumblety
and Malcolm family histories in the town of Marion, as Ed and
Stephanie received the discs that were converted recently from the
film strips, as they sat at a desk top computer together and started
to view the earliest disc from 1903. As Stephanie was reading and
quickly making notes in her pad, of what she was reading from the
local paper from July 1903, as she read aloud softly to Ed.

"Local farmer Jessup Tumblety, changed his families last name to
Malcolm today, just two months after he saw to the burial of his older
brother Francis Tumblety. In the families plot in Rochester's Holy
Sepulchre Cemetery, in May 1903. No reason was ever given why
Jessup Tumblety changed the family name, as his only son, Jessup Jr.
Malcolm. Remained in the town of Marion, as he then married and
stayed at the family ranch farm, along with his wife and two young
sons, Nathan and Peter," Stephanie finishes reading as Ed tells her to

THE RECKONING  OF JACK THE RIPPER

hurry, as he takes out that old disc and puts in a disc, title Marion town history, September 1962. As Stephanie begins to read the third disc of three that was given to them by the librarian.

"On September 4, 1962, tragedy struck the small family of Jessup Malcolm Jr. As his youngest son Peter, drowned to death as he fell into the farm's 30 feet deep well. As he was playing with his older brother Nathan. As tragedy has hit the family two years earlier in 1960, when Marjorie Malcolm succumbed to cancer at age 47." Was all this entire disc contained on the family, as they put in the last and most recent disc, as they read this new article was from four years ago in in 2008. As the article described in detail about how, former childhood resident Dr. Nathan Malcolm, was named in the Quasar Pharmaceutical company scandal, as he then was killed during the San Diego police connections into the Entity murders of three prostitutes. Stephanie just read the Ed the dates and names of the victims that they already had on their files back in San Diego.

"So except, Jessup changing the family name two months after he buried his brother Francis back home in Rochester New York, we still don't have anything officially here to tell us why he did that." Ed tells Stephanie as she agrees with him, as they go and return the discs to the librarian. As they get ready to go to town hall for more information, but before they leave. Stephanie asks the elderly lady, where they could find some good information about residents from Marion in the early to mid-twentieth century. As the old lady smiles and advises them to seek information from the caretaker of the town's historic museum for information, as she tells them him name; Joel Quinn, she tells them he will be more than happy to help them. As Ed and Stephanie thank her, as they called another taxi from the library to take them to the town museum.

Rick was in shock as he received the call early this morning, to notify his task force along with his wife, as they were assembled at the home of lawyer Charles Neast. As when they found out he was married to Ed's ex-wife Kayla. There was no doubt about it now; the killer did this as an act of retribution to Ed Brooks. As

Rob and Rick spoke softly to Dr. Adams, away from the others as they were questioning her autopsy on Nathan Malcolm again, four years ago.

"Rick as God as my witness, and along with dental records and a conformation of DNA analysis done by Dr. Farrell. Unless Nathan Malcolm rose up from the dead, had his whole body of newly reformed skin, and a new pair of eyeballs. That man was diseased when Diana and I did the autopsy on him. As in the new victim's I told you the knife wounds and slashes are in different and sporadic patterns then the wounds Malcolm inflicted on his victims." Cate angrily yells at both Rick and Rob, as they question her autopsy. As Rob just rolls his eyes.

"So then the only other possible motive we have here is either a close friend or relative of Nathan Malcolm. Who not only is committing these new murders but has also now targeted Ed and his family. As Stephanie maybe in danger too," Rob tells them as Rick shakes his head yes.

"We have the team and forensics does their work here, as I will call Ed now and tell him as soon as he gets back here to San Diego. Come directly to headquarters along with Stephanie, as Chief Chase and I will tell him about Kayla and her husband.  As we will place them in guarded protection round the clock and moved to a safe unknown location for their safety." Rick instructs Rob, as he takes out his cell phone and calls Ed in Iowa.

As Ed just finishes his conversation with Rick on his cell phone, Stephanie asks him who called him. "That was Rick, he wants us to go to directly to Central Division command. As soon as we get back tonight, no matter how late it is. Another murder happened late last night there, and he wants to fill us in on it right away." Ed tells her, as they walk into the town's small museum. As Stephanie saw an elderly old man, cleaning the glass showcase that contained some historic items and books, detailing the towns historic history. As Stephanie asked him if he was Mr. Quinn, and he politely said he was. As Ed asked him if he had any knowledge of Jessup Malcolm, and the name Tumblety, as it pertained to their history here in Marion, Iowa. As

Mr. Quinn saw the serious looks on their faces, as they then told him they were law enforcement officers. He smiled and said he would help them as much as he could, as he told them to sit down at the small square table in the middle of the museum. As he took an old book from one of the bookshelves and sat with them.

"I do stay up late at night and watch cable news, as I hear you have a new series of murders in San Diego now. So may I ask has it to do with that fellow, Nathan Malcolm from four years ago?" Quinn questions them, as Ed responded that they know Nathan Malcolm is deceased now, but could there be other family members related to him, who also knew of some certain family relatives and secrets of Jessup Tumblety. Ed asks Quinn, who just opens the old book and reads from one page, as the book is an old scrap book of very old articles of very old events that took place here in Marion. As Quinn begins to explain the change of the family name to Malcolm in 1903 to them.

"My grandfather towards the end of his retirement from town hall, where he worked as the county clerk, recanted the event on why Jessup Tumblety came back from his brother's funeral in Rochester that year. My father told me the story, that Jessup showed up to town hall requesting documents to change their name from Tumblety to Malcolm. As he also brought back with him certain items in an old box, which belonged to his brother. My father told me, the story my grandfather recounted to him was, he questioned Jessup about changing his last name, as Jessup showed him this box, and said all the proof he needed was what it contained for him to rid the evil atrocities' his brother Francis had done while he was alive. As Jessup, would not want to his children and their future children to be outcast for whatever Francis had done. So he filed for the courts in Des Moines, to have their last name changed as the court granted his wish, as Jessup and his family were regarded as a good church going and hardworking family." As Quinn told them the story he was told by his grandfather, as he then showed them the article on the story, as the mention of the antique box.

"Jessup returned from Rochester with a Calamander wood box, which was locked. As its contents belonged to Francis Tumblety, I am certain, whoever that box was passed down to, knows what it contains and the answers to your questions Detective Brooks. Quinn tells him, as Ed looks at Stephanie and she nods her head.

"So Jessup Tumblety; knew the truth about his brother and being a good person and Christian, he distanced himself and family from what he found out about his brother." Stephanie answered as Quinn told her; "correct".

"Now we have to find what that box contained, a journal a map or maybe a news article about what we think he did." Ed tells them, as Quinn asks them.

"If I may ask, what is still so important now, that can tie Francis Tumblety and his great nephew to his crimes and these recent crimes you have in your city, Detective Brooks?" Joel Quinn asks, wanting to know the answer to this century old mystery that has been kept here in the museum and his family.

"All we can say for now is, if we are correct on our theory. This will be the answer and the closure to one of the biggest mysteries of all time." Ed tells the old man, as he and Stephanie thank him for his time and help. As they get ready to return to their hotel and pack their things for the most recent flight, back to San Diego.

Rick just got off the phone with Ed, as he told Rob who was seated in front of him in his office. That Ed and Stephanie were in the air as they spoke, and will be landing in two hours or so. As Rick looked at the clock on the wall and told Rob, just around 11:30 or so they should be here at headquarters.

"Rob we take Ed and Stephanie into the conference room and tell him about Kayla and her husband. As I'm pretty sure he will be stricken with grief and then rage, as Chief Chase will also advise him to be removed from this case for his safety and placed under protection." Rick tells Rob, as Rick sits back down behind his desk and looks over the records of all the known rented white cargo vans. From all the various car rental agencies around the city, as none of the team members could come up with any vehicle that received interior damage, or returned the very next day after the murder of

Jackie Mays. Rick just takes the file and flings it to the ground, as Rob walks over to it and picks it up slowly.

"It's been almost a month now since the first murder happened, and all we know so far that Cate and Dr. Farrell both agree, the killer is copying the same patterns and wound inflictions as Nathan Malcolm. But we know for a fact, that it's not Malcolm because we have positive DNA evidence that he died four years ago." Rob says to Rick, as Rick just rubs his right hand straight back through his short hair. As Julie O'Keefe, knocked on his door and said Chief Chase was here along with his staff members. Rick thanked her, as he instructed for his team to gather in the conference room, as Rick took out his small brush from his desk and brushed his hair back as he said they need to make a press conference tonight, and now ask for Chief Chase, to appeal to the citizens of San Diego to come forward and help break this case. As they will be offering a huge reward, leading to any information possible on the killer.

The late unscheduled press conference ended about forty minutes ago, as it was cast on the late evening local and cable news outlets. As in the conference room, Rick along with Rob and Police Chief; John Chase, broke the news to Ed of the murders of Kayla and her husband Charles Neast. Ed just sat in the chair at first stunned, as he broke a tear for Kayla. As he soon became enraged and angered now that the Entity has singled him and his family out as he stood up and threw a chair against the wall, breaking it to pieces. As Stephanie, came over to him and hugged him to console him. As Ed hugged her back, as she whispered to him she was very sorry. As Rob told Rick he would take Stephanie to his office and talk to her, so Rick and Chief Chase can talk to Ed alone. As Rob holds Stephanie's hand, and asks her to come with him, she nods and tells Ed she will be right back.

As Rob closes the door behind them, Stephanie wipes the tears from her eyes as she can't explain the amount of grief and sadness she feels for Ed right now. As she also knows, she could have been the intended victim, instead of Kayla as she just sits down as Rob hands her a cup of coffee and sits next to her. "Stephanie, the Chief and Rick are going to suggest to Ed, you both are placed under round the clock watch for your safety. And they are going to suggest you both are removed from this case now, as the killer knows everything personally about you both now." Rob tells her, as Stephanie just looks into his eyes as she takes a sip of the hot coffee.

"Rob, we were getting closer on this. We just need to find some certain items that Malcolm passed onto a family member or close friend, to tie him to his Grandfather's brother, Francis Tumblety. Ed was right all along, and at first we doubted him but he proved even I was wrong. We can't give up now; I know we can close this case within a few days' time. Please Rob, try and convince Rick and the Chief to let us continue. Because now more than ever, I want to see this Bastard burn for everything he has done." Stephanie quietly tells Rob, as Ed and Rick come into his office together. Stephanie hands the cup of coffee back to Rob as she and Ed kiss and hug each other warmly. As Rick gives Rob some instructions now, as the task force is outside Rick's office waiting to hear what the Chief's decision was.

"Rob, you along with the team and eight uniformed officers are to escort Ed and Stephanie to a disclosed safehouse in Ocean Beach. The house is three stories and it's used for witness protection so it's already fortified for us with communications and computers so we can stay in constant contact." Rob agrees with Rick's orders, as Ed and Stephanie thank Rick as Ed holds her hand and they walk out into the hallway, as four uniformed officers are holding twelve gauge shotguns at their ready, as they lead the couple out the back doors and into the parking lot, where four patrol cars with the drivers were ready to move them out. Ed and Stephanie got into the middle squad car. As Rob told his team members to follow them, in their unmarked vehicles as the convoy of vehicles headed out to their disclosed location. As they were driving, Ed just looked out the window to his right and remembered the happy times he shared with Kayla, as she was his first love. Stephanie still had a hold of his hand as she wanted to still comfort him; she just laid her head on his left shoulder. As Ed kissed her cheek, "I'm so sorry Ed, Kayla and he husband didn't deserve to die like this." Stephanie whispered to him, as Ed just kept staring out the window.

Once the team had them inside the large house, Rob explained to them all that the first floor was living quarters for the uniformed officers and communication's room. The second level was for Ed and Stephanie that was equipped with a large master bedroom a bathroom and a gym and living room. As the third level was living quarters for the task force, as two partners would be assigned with eight different officers to watch them round the clock, on eight hour shift per day. Till this was all over with, as Ed and Stephanie looked around their living area, as Ed didn't care for the idea of being contained when he wanted to be out there tracking the Entity down. As Rob told them, they had spare clothes for them in the closets, as new clothes will be brought for them tomorrow. As it was now late at night, Rob informed them that Ken and Jack would take the first shit together. As Julie and Skip will relieve them in the morning, as Ed and Stephanie thanked the whole crew as they all hugged Ed and gave him their condolences for Kayla and her husband. Ed watched as Stephanie walked them to the door, and closed and locked it. As she looked back at Ed, he was just peering out the living room window, as he was lost in deep thought. Stephanie didn't want to bother him right now, she just picked up her bags that Rob and the other brought with them, she just went into the bathroom to freshen up and shower. As Ed walked into the weight room, as he picked up a 35 pound dumbbell and started to curl it in his right hand. He thought about Nathan Malcolm, and Jack the Ripper. He thought how all these innocent lives were taken away for no Damn reason. He knew he had to stop this new killer just like he killed Nathan Malcolm four years ago. Ed wanted to take the dumbbell, and hurl it through the glass window with a vengeance. But he just kept curling the weight in his hand; "you stole a precious person from my life, now I'm going to send you to Hell with the rest of your family, you bloody bastard," Ed whispered to himself as he continued to work out.

Stephanie feeling refreshed from her shower, as she was lying in bed watching the late news as the time was 3:30 AM. Stephanie heard the water from the bathroom running, as Ed was taking a shower after his long work out. Stephanie and he didn't talk yet since they arrived at the safehouse over four hours ago, as Ed came out of the bathroom. He was bare-chested, just wearing his striped pajama bottoms. As Stephanie smiled at him, he came over to the bed and lied down next to her, as she moved closer to him. He wrapped his strong arms around her from behind, as they kissed gently.

"Thank you for helping me through this tonight. I don't think I can handle it without you being here for me Stephanie." Ed tells her, as she just holds his hands in hers gently as Stephanie sheds a tear for him.

"Ed, please don't let your anger get in the way of what you know is the best for us. Regardless of what happens from this point, he wants to either kill you or make you suffer very much." Stephanie tells him, as Ed lays her back on the bed so he can face her, as Stephanie softly touches his massive scared wound on his left side with her fingertips.

"He is going to try and hurt me, if not kill me to get back at you. You know that Ed?" She tells him softly, as Ed just covers her lips with a finger, wishing she didn't think of that right now.

"He can think that way all he wants Stephanie, but the reality is I'm not going to let him hurt you or anyone else who is close to me. Because I'm going to kill him, I swear it." Ed tells her, as he kisses Stephanie deeply, as he undoes the buttons to her top as the lights go out in the bedroom.

Stephanie's eyes slowly fluttered open as she heard music, coming from the other room. She saw the sunlight streaming through the long drapes of the bedrooms window, as she knew now it was early morning. As she then heard footsteps above them, and below as there were the sounds of car doors opening and closing outside. She just remembered now, she and Ed were guarded at the safe-house on the beach. She knew she had to get up and get changed, in case Rick and Rob along with the others came by. As Stephanie put on her top and long bathrobe, she then recognized the guitarist whom Ed was listening to; "Jimi Hendrix, Ed's favorite." She smiled to the thought, as she went into the bathroom, and closed the door behind her. Stephanie turned on the hot water in the sink, as she bent down to the sink and splashed the warm water on her face to wake herself up, as she thought that this whole ordeal seems like it has been going on for a year all ready. As she looked, up she saw Ed standing behind her in the mirror as she screamed as she was startled by his silent approach from behind. As Ed grabbed her around the waist, as she relaxed in his arms. As they shared a deep kiss together, as Ed smiled and motioned to her with a glance of his eyes to his right side. As Stephanie looked over and saw the shower, she knew what was on his mind. "Well it has to be a fast shower, since we are not alone here anymore." She tells him, as Ed opens the glass door and they both enter the marble tiled shower. As Stephanie turns on the water, as she screams out loud that the water is cold again.

Just after 11:00 AM, Rick and Rob were meeting with Ed and Stephanie along with Skip and Julie who were on duty now, along with eight new uniformed cops for their safety. As they were all seated in the living room, Rick and the others again expressed their condolences to Ed. As he then began to brief them about what happened at the county medical examiner's office, where they discovered the gray piece of material, belonging to the cargo van, but they have no records of any type of van being rented that day or prior day to the murder.

"So after all this, we are back to square one again. We have six victims this copycat killer has murdered. We asked the FBI for help, as to why Stephanie joined our team for detailed profiles of the killer. No DNA evidence, no use of undercover female officers can be used. As he has now moved away from killing escorts, as he is killing random civilians. But the only thing we have to go on, is a piece of an inch of gray material, that we can't track down from what vehicle it came out of stuck in the victim's fingernail. I say if there was ever a perfect killer, we are up against him right now." Rick tells them, as the team's mood is somber and it's like their spirit has been broken by the killer.

Stephanie thinking to herself, she feels if this killer is a step ahead of them all the time and he found out where Kayla lived with her new husband. He has to be getting inside information on Ed and the others during their investigation, as she thinks to herself again. "The cargo van, medical examiner's cargo van is white. No DNA evidence of the victims, an inside medical person whom Cate Adams works with," she thinks to herself. As she raises her voice and tell the all what she was just thinking. Ed and Rick just stare at her, as Ed then realizes she's on to something here.

"If not a person who works with Cate, how about one her forensic crew who gather up the crime scene's evidence after a murder. The person acts like he is doing a thorough search as they gather all trace evidence, then instead of bagging it and labeling it they discard it without any ones knowledge." Ed suggests, as all eyes fall on Rick, being Cate is his wife and he should be the one to confront her with this theory.

"Okay look, let's not jump ahead of ourselves now. Let me talk to Cate and interview her staff along with Rob. Maybe we can be finally on to something here. Skip and Julie, keep them company and safe." Rick tells them, as she smiles and tells Rob to come with him now. As Ed just thinks to himself, they get to work on his case that he's in charge of. As he has to stay here and just sit back for something to happen, as he sits next to Stephanie on the couch and turns on the television with the remote.

"Cable news or soap operas, take your pick guys." Ed tells them, feeling bored already.

Rick and Rob were both taking different parts of the investigation at the county medical examiner's facility. Rick along with Cate were questioning her three man team of crime scene technicians, as Rob was outside with the lead analyst as they were looking at the two white vans they use. They were both white, with gray carpeting lined floors and side panels. As there were side draws to contain evidence gathering equipment, but there was still room enough for the van to hold a body on its inside floor. Rob searched both vans inside door, and wall panels. As he was looking for signs of any damage or perhaps the carpet liner had been fix or replaced. But both vans seemed to be fine to him, as he closed the back doors of the van he was looking in. He then looked at the outside of the van, as both vans had painted on either side of them in black lettering; "County Examiners Office". He looked for any signs for the letterings to be covered over by a taped on covering or sorts, being these vans would have stood out for any witness to remember the wording on them. Rob took a deep breath of disgust, as he knew even with this good theory of Stephanie's, they again hit another brick wall. As he told the technician that's all for now, as they went back inside to Cate's office.

As Rob opened the door to Cate's office, Rick was talking to the other forensic team members as he looked at Rob, but Rob shook his head no to his boss. To let him know they have no leads here either. Rick thanks the men for their time, as they say they were happy to cooperate in any way possible with their investigation. As the men leave the office, and Rob closes the door behind them as Rick flings his clipboard of notes on Cate's desk in anger.

"Nothing, no torn material from the vans they are perfect inside and out. So I guess, the crew's alibies checks out too huh?'" Rob questions Rick, as he tells him yes.

"The men all recanted the same thing; they gathered the DNA swabs of the victim's. Labeled them and placed them inside the brown paper bags for either Cate or Diana to work on. Everything they logged corresponds with Cate's and Dr. Farrell's autopsy works, so there are no leads here either." Rick tells Rob, as Cate smiles at her husband and tells him; "told you so!"

"I have been working with this crew for almost twelve years now, and I have known Diana for eight years. Do you think we would expect if something was wrong with the people who we worked with? Women's intuition Rick, we know when something is wrong." She tells him with a smile, as Rick smiles back at her.

"Well you know what, since I'm mentally exhausted from this whole case right now, at the whole day has gone one without incidents. I say Rob and Antonella, join us out for dinner tonight at Clover's restaurant. We all deserve a break from this case now, what do you say Rob?" Rick suggests to him, to go one a double dinner date with Cate and himself.

"Only if we can bring Megan along, my mother-in-law doesn't like the baby sitting duties dumped on her at the last minute." Rob tells them, as Rick says that's fine to bring his daughter with them. That they needed to get out and have fun finally during all this hard work.

At the house in Ocean Beach, Ed was fulfilling his promise to Stephanie as they were in the gym room together. Ed had made room by pushing some of the equipment out of the way, as he laid out one of the thick large mats on the floor, to fall upon and not cause them injuries. Ed was showing her some self-defense moves and counter holds, if she found herself cornered or if the killer, had a knife or other sharp weapon he intended to use on her. Ed used a plastic fake knife, as he pulled her around the waist from behind and had the plastic blade to her throat. Ed instructed her, to hold his hand tight into her chest. Then bend down and twist out of his grasp, buy by the whole time, holding onto his hand to control the knife and either take it away from the attacker or throw the knife far beyond his reach. As Stephanie understood his instructions, they then went into full exercise of motions as Stephanie surprised Ed and took him down to the mat. As Ed was surprised, he started to get up as Stephanie took hold of his right arm, stepped into Ed closely and then flipped him over her should. As Ed was flat on his back, angry now he started to get up fast as he got to his feet, Stephanie bent down low and she swept her right foot into Ed's left foot, and pulled his foot out from under him as he fell to the mat again on his back. As she quickly picked up the fake knife, and sat on top of his chest and held the knife to his neck, as she smiled at him. Ed just raised his hands up and said; "okay I give up now". Stephanie smiled at him, as she threw the knife to the side and then kissed Ed gently on his lips.

"You didn't ask me if I had any martial art's training there Mr. Ed, I'm a first degree brown belt in Kenpo karate. I have been taking it for the last few years, but because I have been busy with various cases I haven't been able to reach my black belt status just yet". She tells him, as Ed tells her, she will reach it in no time. As he smiles back at her, he slides his hands up and down her bare thighs softly, as Stephanie is wearing white shorts and a sweatshirt with sneakers, as Ed is wearing a full jogging suit and sneakers. As Ed pulls her all the way to the floor with him, as they kiss one another deeply.

"Ed, we are not alone hear remember, we can't be acting like this right now." Stephanie tells him softly, as they hear Skip and Julie on the top floor, and the policeman from the floor below them. As they ordered pizza, and now were making noise as they were watching the Padre's baseball game. Stephanie suggested to him, they go upstairs and see what plans Julie and Skip made for dinner, with intentions to join them. As Ed, made a face saying he felt safe here but he wanted to get out if not only for a few hours to be alone with Stephanie. As he reminded her, that Rick and Rob were having a dinner date together with their wives, as Ed suggested the thought to her, to sneak away and have dinner together.

"Ed! We can't do that, what if something happens tonight and God forbid he comes looking for us. We need to be here right now for our protection." She tells him, as Ed protests to her.

"Stephanie first, we are right on Ocean Beach here, even though this house is set far away from the others, there are so many civilians around here, he would be crazy to come here and try anything. Even if he did know we were here, secondly I don't like it being kept watched over when this is our case and now it's a personal vendetta between him and me now. And it's a Friday evening just after 5:00 PM. I want us to try that new Italian restaurant in Little Italy, called Carmine's. Rob told me they have the best, brick oven pizza there and it's very close by. We shower and change real fast zip there and zip back in Julie's car. Because I know she will do it for me and you, and we come right back before 10:00 PM, for some final desert together. So what do you say, karate girl?" Stephanie smiles at Ed, as she also wants to be alone with him tonight, as she says to him dinner only and right back here for desert. As Ed tells her that's his plan. She tells him let's do it, as Ed tells her to start the shower with warm water, as he will tell Julie and Skip, and get Julie's car keys from her. As they get up and Stephanie starts to run into the restroom, Ed tells her there is a present hanging in her closet; he wants her to wear it tonight for them. She smiles and tells him she will, as Ed heads up stairs to make plans for them to sneak away for a few hours.

Ed got Julie's car keys to her Mazda 6, as Julie felt bad for them and agreed they needed to get out for a while to be alone, as Skip at first was very against the idea, as he felt for their safety was in peril, and what would happen if something happened and Rick or Chief Chase found out about this. But they both changed their minds, when Ed told them her had big question to ask Stephanie tonight, as Julie surmised what it was, and then Skip gave into Ed's plan, but they both agreed they needed to be back here at the safe house by 10:00 PM sharp. As Skip suggested they use the disabled ramp, which connects to each outside terrace of the house. As they can access Julie's car parked in the back, so the team of cops on the first floor will not spot them leave. As Ed tells them, they will be so focused on the ball game they will not see them or hear them leave. As Ed kisses Julie on the cheek, and hurries back downstairs.

As he walks into the bathroom, Stephanie had herself covered up with a white towel. As she told him to hurry now she was going to get changed now, as she went into their bedroom he opened the closet and saw a black garment bag from Nordstrom's Department store, hanging on the clothes line. She removed it off the hanger and laid it out on the bed, as she unzipped the long zipper she was stunned at the beautiful royal blue, V-neck dress with matching blue heeled pumps. Ed had left in a shoebox on the bed. As Stephanie quickly dried and fixed her hair up nice, she then slipped on the dress that with off the shoulder style with an open back. As Stephanie stepped into the heel shoes, she looked at herself in the mirror and adored the dress and shoes, as she placed her hand on her hips and smiled, that the dress was about five inches above her knees; "Ed's definitely a man who love's women's legs". She says to herself, as Ed whistles behind her. As he is already dressed in a black and blue stripped dress shirt and black slacks and shoes. As he smiles at her and compliments her on looking so fine, as he jokes and then asks Stephanie; "now where do you suppose you are going to hide your gun on you now?" Ed asks her, as Stephanie winks at him and comes over to him as they kiss softly.

"Ed, you didn't need to do all this for me, I feel bad now because since we have been together, I haven't had a chance to get you any gifts as of yet." She tells him, as Ed tells her not to worry about it. That he printed out the dress from the computer and Rick had one of the oncoming cops, pass buy the mall and get it for him. As she asked him, what was the occasion for them to get all dressed up just to have pizza for dinner? As Ed told her it was just to make them enjoy a very special evening together, as Ed put on his shoulder holster as he checked is silver, Smith and Wesson 45. He knew it was fully loaded as he had another two full clips inserted on the holster. As he picked up the car keys and told Stephanie; "now let's sneak out of the house." As Ed opened the sliding door, as they walked down the ramp quickly but very quietly. As they got into the black Mazda, and drove off to the Expressway.

Ed and Stephanie were seated in a cozy booth together, in the back of "Carmine's", Stephanie expressed to Ed felling a bit over dressed for this family style restaurant, as their plain pizza and ice teas were just brought out to them by their waiter. Ed told her not to worry, that people here in San Diego love to dress up on a Friday evening and spend a lot of time here in the Downtown district and being the very nice and lavish Westfield Mall was close by. As Stephanie asked him if that's where he purchased the dress and shoes for her. As he told her yes, as she asked him if it they cost him a fortune, she would feel very bad that he spent that kind of money on her. As Ed looked around the restaurant and saw there weren't that many people sitting near them. He reached into his jacket pocket and handed her a small black gift box, with a very small red bow attached to it. Stephanie looked at him puzzled and took the box, as she began to undo the gift wrapping, and told Ed that this wasn't necessary for him to do. As Ed just smiled and said; "Well the dress and shoes were a lot cheaper than this little gift, I got for you." As she smiled at him, she removed the paper and saw it was a velvet enclosed box, as she opened the top cover, her mouth dropped open as her eyes were gleaming at a breathtaking engagement ring. With a small note set in the inside cover that read; "Stephanie will you marry me."

"Well will you?" Ed asks here, as Stephanie removes the ring from the box that was a 1-1/2 ct. Princess three cut diamond ring, set in 14K white gold, with two rows of smaller diamonds on either sides of them. As Ed told her to hurry up and try it on for size, as she slipped in on her left ring finger and held it out for him to see. As Ed smiled at her, Stephanie had tears in her eyes but also a look of over well-meant. As if she didn't know how to respond to this as Ed asked her; "Well I do need an answer now from you. As Ed held her hand and asked her himself; "Stephanie Morgan, will you marry me?" As she looked at him with a full smile on her face as she yelled; "Yes!" As Ed reached over and kissed her gently, as a few people in Carmine's saw them embracing together, they started to clap for the happy couple.

"So now, we should wait for the case to be over with and then we can break the news to all our friends on the force and family." Ed suggests as Stephanie takes out her cell phone from her purse, as Ed looks on and says to himself; "Oh women just can't hold good news in". As Stephanie calls her mother at home and tells her the news while she is crying, that Ed proposed to her and she accepted. As Ed instructs her now, not to tell the whole world just yet, as they hold hands as Ed can hear Stephanie's mother is elated for her daughter.

He watched from the rooftop of the apartment house twenty yards away, he was looking at the three level beach house through his night scope binoculars. He was looking for Ed and Stephanie on the second level, but didn't see any signs of them being there. Just the television was left on in the living room, as he knew they went out for the night. He then looked at the top floor, and was able to see partially the first floor. As he saw Skip watching the ball game and Julie was in her bedroom, on her lap top. As he peered into a window on the first floor, which had its curtain drawn back, the Entity knew where to start his point of attack into the house. He had with his a large black duffle bag, as he opened it up. He took out a black carbon bow, as he assembled it together with a steel tipped black arrow. He looked around as he aimed and fired the arrow into the home's rooftop, as the steel found its target and became strongly lodged into the stucco wall. He then anchored the steel wire very tightly around the chimney of the rooftop he was standing on, as he pulled and tugged on it hard. He knew it was secure and able to support his weight, as he then took out a small black pulley wheel and placed it on the cable. As he looked across the way, he will sail about 60 feet high and the reach home's rooftop that was not as high as the building he was standing on. This would be perfect for him as he will be coming over the sand and the back of the house disguised by the night, and able to take them by surprise. As he flung the bag over his shoulder, he stepped up on the roof's retaining wall. As he cast himself down on the cable, as the wheel was oiled and didn't whistle as he sailed in the wind so fast he felt it against his face through the dark black sterile hood. That had no slits for the mouth and nose, just cut outs for the eyes to see. As he wore night vision goggles to see in the dark, as this was another method of his to take them by surprise. As he was over the homes roof, he quickly jumped down from the wheel before he collided into the wall. As the wheel hit the wall hard and made a thud, Julie looked up from her computer screen as she heard the sudden noise. As she just shrugged it off and continued to work, Skip didn't hear a sound as he was glued to the baseball game just like the cops below them.

He was all dressed in black ninja style outfit, as he even wore the shoes of the ninja uniform. That had a rubber souled bottom and was colored black and able to step into. They were made of thin black polyester and were high to his ankles. He took out a pair of wire cutters and went over to the fuse box and cut the power of the house and then the phone line. As he quickly went into the duffle bag, and took out two samurai short swords and placed them in his black sash belt. As he then equipped his black cross bow with an arrow, and then holstered many more arrows in his belt. As he waited near the door, he heard talking coming up from the stairs as Skip was talking to the lead officer in charge of the homes security. They would go and investigate the cause of the power outage, as the roof door opened up slowly. Both men had their guns in hand, as Skip told Julie to call Rick and tell him about the home losing power and phone service on her cell phone.

As the men split up, Skip took out his small flashlight and was looking at the circuit breaker and saw its door was open. As the lead sergeant moved around the roof very cautiously with his gun and flashlight in either hand, as Skip yelled over to him and said the power line had been cut, but before the sergeant could respond to Skip, an arrow shot in through his left eye as he sailed off his feet and hit the ground hard. Skip stood up as he heard the sound of something sailing from above his head as he stood up and flashed his light at the body of the policeman, and saw the arrow protruding out of his eye. He was about to yell, when a hand from behind him covered his mouth as the blade from the short sword came across his neck deep, and then he let his hand go of Skip's mouth and used both hands to quip the sword as he slashed his neck from behind deep. As he saw the blood jet out of his neck, as he fell to the rooftop dead.

He quickly rearmed another arrow, as he made his way to the door and down the stairwell. He knew Julie was there alone, and he will leave her for last as he knew he had seven men left to kill. As he stopped on the top floor, he heard voices of men coming up the stairs yelling with the light of their flashlights, making the hallway brighter he had to kill them now before they saw him. He took a knee and aimed the crossbow, as he fired up even before the first man came around the corner as the bow was shot deep into his neck, as the force knocked him backward into his partner and the fell to the floor. The Entity jumped on top of the helpless man, as he took out and short steel dagger and stabbed him in the throat hard, as he left it imbedded in his throat he stood up and then slashed his neck with his sword as his head, was decapitated from his body. Julie heard the noise as Rick was questioning her, what was happening there. As she saw the man in black standing outside her door, she slammed it shut and locked it.

"Rick, he's here! The Entity is here!" She screams into her phone as she runs into her bedroom to get her firearm. As Rick just yells to Rob they have to go now, as both men just shoot out of their seats leaving their wives stunned at what is happening, as they run to Rick's car in the parking lot of the restaurant and drive off to Ocean Beach. As Rick is telling Rob what's happening he uses his phone to call Western Division and instruct them to get as many officers over there as soon as possible. As Rob takes out his cell phone and calls Ed, to see if he is all right.

As Ed is eating is slice of pizza, Stephanie called her brother and her close female cousin to tell them she just got engaged and she is still on the phone with her, as Ed just felt to let Stephanie be happy and enjoy this moment as he said they will be taking home the rest of her pizza, as his phone was ringing as Ed answered it.

"Ed! Are you all right?" Rob asked him.

"I'm fine, I'm with Stephanie in little Italy having dinner, I sneaked her out to pop the question to her Rob, she said yes!" Stephanie smiled as she knew he was talking to Rob, as Ed's face then went from happy to very serious. As Rob, told him the Entity was in the beach house killing their team, and Julie is trapped. Ed just put his phone down, dropped his pizza and got up and grabbed his leather jacket. As he grabbed Stephanie's hand and pulled her hard as he screamed to her; "Come on! He's at the house now!" As Stephanie got her purse and shawl, she ran with Ed to the Mazda as everyone looked at them stunned in the restaurant. As Ed fired up the engine and pulled out of the parking lot at high speed, as Stephanie fastened her seatbelt tight, as she was questioning Ed to what was happening.

"Rob just called me; the Bastard is at the house killing our men off! He no doubt came to kill us too! But tonight it's him that's going to die!" Ed screams as he makes a hard right onto the San Diego freeway and floors the gas pedal to reach speeds exceeding 80 MPH. As he holds the wheel in one hand and keeps talking to Rob with his cell phone, Rob says there about fifteen miles hour as they are on the freeway themselves as the patrol cars should be getting there soon.

He kicked open the door to Julie's apartment as she heard him from her locked bedroom. She had her 9 MM, ready in her right hand as she screamed to Rick in her cell phone; "Please get here Rick! He's in the house now!" As Julie hears gunshots from outside her bedroom, two more men came into the apartment as one was stabbed behind in his back, as the blade came out through his chest as he screamed in pain. As his partner turned to shoot, the Entity took out his other sword and slashed his right hand off, as the hand still holding the gun fell to the floor firing rounds. As he was then slashed across his neck, as the remaining three cops came into the room. They opened fire in all directions as they flashed their flashlights all over the room. Till there was a pitch of silence, Julie crouched down behind her bed as listened as she heard the men speak, as they said to one another did they get him.

"Please, kill him. Please God, I don't want to die". Julie said to herself, as Rick was screaming at her into the cell phone, asking what's happening there. As the men move inside the apartment deeper, they see the bodies of their friends on the ground, as an arrow is shot across the room and finds its mark hitting the cop in the middle right in his forehead. As he fly's back off his feet to the floor, the Entity rises from the floor, slashes one cop across the neck with his sword, ducks down to avoid the gunshots from the other policeman who fires at him. As he stand up and stabs him from under his jaw and into his skull with a short steel dagger, as she then slashes him in the neck, and does the same to the other policeman who was still standing, as he knows he has killed all nine men. As he places both swords in this backside sheaths, he holds the steel dagger as he makes a running leap and kicks open the bedroom door, as Julie stands up and fires her gun. As the Entity, fell to the floor and jumped and rolled on top of the bed as he kicked the gun out of Julie's hand. As he flung her hard to the bed, and jumped on top of her as he covered her mouth with his gloved hand.

"Quiet please my dear Julie, only four years ago in another capacity you lived. This time you don't have that chance from me." The Entity spoke to her; Julie was stunned by the words from the voice. As he used the dagger to slash her throat deep, and then again, as he watches her gasp and choke on her blood as she falls silently dead. He quickly gathers his weapons up and returns to the roof, and places the swords and crossbow in the duffle bag. As he hears the sirens of the police cruisers coming closer, as he stands up and sees their flashing lights in the distance. He takes hold of the steel wire that he used to make his way onto the roof. As he stands to the edge of the roof, he cuts the wire with his sharp blade, as he sails across the air as he comes back to the apartment house as he drops himself down on the wire to the ground. As he braces his legs up and his feet hit the side of the building to stop himself. He replaces his soft shoes with black sneakers, as he places a black motorcycle helmet, which was painted plain black over his head. As he placed his night vision goggles in the duffle bag, and flings it over his shoulder, he runs to his. Suzuki Hayabusa, a black sport motorcycle and fires it up and heads out into the night. He kick starts the motor, and cranks the throttle and steps on the gas he speeds off into the night.

Rick and Rob were coming up on the exit to Ocean Beach, as they both saw the streaming lights coming from a mile ahead to there right hand side, as in the opposite lane they spotted a black sports bike whiz by in very fast speed. As both men commented on the bike, Rick made the statement; "The rider is in black, the bike is black, that's got to be him!" Rick makes a fast hard right turn onto the off ramp, as he guns their vehicle through a red light and makes a left hand turn onto the ramp to get back onto the Freeway and follow the motorcycle. As Rob calls Ed on his cell phone to alert him they are following the black bike. Ed who is busy driving as a high rate of speed, just hands his phone to Stephanie for her to answer. As Rob instructs her, they are following the presumed suspect on a black sports motorcycle. Stephanie tells Ed, as he looks to his left in the southbound traffic, as he sees the bike passing them at least 80 MPH. Ed notices a break in the freeway above, as he speeds up and just glides over from the right lane to the middle and left lanes cutting off a few vehicles. He makes a hard left turn into the southbound freeway, and hits the gas hard as he and Stephanie fly back into their seats. As Ed takes the cell phone from her, to give advice to Rick on how to box in and stop the suspect.

"Rick, get a hold of dispatch and advise them to have multiple cruisers box in the cross points at Martin Luther King Freeway. And John Montgomery Freeway, we can stop him there, along with spotlight helicopters!" Ed shouts the instructions to Rick, as he tells Rob to call Western Division dispatch and get the vehicles at the cross intersection right away.

Ed guns the gas pedal all the way down, as his Mazda is keeping pace with the motorcycle. As Ed watches him dip very close behind the cars and trucks as he passes them very close, and zigzags in and out of all three lanes. Ed having experience riding motorcycles knows, the driver can't make a fast break on a turn or he will fly off the bike. Especially riding a bike that has six speeds, for him to shift on, Ed knows the intersection will be the point of impact for them to stop him. As he tells Stephanie the plan he and Rick have set for the suspect. Stephanie's phone was going off, as she answered it. Ken Rogers had just called her to alert them he was at the beach house along with Jack Kerns and multiple uniformed officers. As he told her, all eight officers were dead along with Skip Jones and Julie O'Keefe. As he said the crime scene was a bloody massacre here, as they searched every floor and room with their flashlights. As Stephanie told Ed, softly about their friends and the eight cops. Ed looked over at her and then back at the bike ahead, and cursed to himself. "You son of a bitch bastard, what the hell do you want!" Ed yells, to himself as they are coming up fast at the cross intersection, as the police cruisers are just now getting on to all three freeways, to box in and divert civilian vehicles away from harm's way.

Rob calls Ed again on the cell phone, as he got word from dispatch they have cruisers on every main freeway and intersections. As they also have two helicopters in the air, that should pick up the motorcycle with moments. As Ed acknowledges Rick on the phone, Ed spots them in back of him speeding up to his position in the middle lane. As Ed looks ahead as they are approaching the three way highway junction, Rick asks him how they are going to do this. Ed thinks of a quick plan, as he notices the flashing lights of the police cruisers in all directions up ahead; "Rick close in tight on my left side now, we will give him no shot of escape. Tell Rob to tell dispatch to have all the cruisers on John Montgomery freeway, came straight at him and the other bound cruisers combine and form a roadblock to keep him, from exiting the off ramps!" Ed yells the plan over to Rick, as he tells Rob and conveys the plan of interception to the dispatch office on his cell phone.

The black motorcycle now reaching speeds of 90 MPH, squeezing right in between two SUV's in the middle and right lane. As the Entity looks back and sees the fast Mazda and another car close in tight together behind him, as he sees the lights of the police cruisers coming straight ahead as the intersection is blocked off on the east and west bound off ramps. He has no choice but to go straight ahead, being he can't stop or slow down knowing he will be caught. He cranks the throttle and changes gear, as he gives more gas getting up to 100 MPH. As Ed and Rick are just fifteen yards behind him, the cruisers in all three lanes converge together to box him in, as Chief Chase was now at Western Division's dispatch desk, he screams to Rob on the phone to take the suspect out now. The Entity stays straight in the center lane as all vehicles are about to converge on the black bike, he waits to the last split second, as he banks to his left just a few feet. As the driver in the oncoming lane doesn't want a head on impact with the bike, he steers his wheel hard to his left. Creating a gap for the bike to maneuver into as he passes them, as Stephanie screams to Ed to watch out, he steers hard to his left hitting the concrete center divider hard. As Rick yells to Rob to brace himself and he slams on the breaks and steers hard to his right, all four vehicles collide with one another.

Rick's vehicle is hit right into the driver's side and rear side doors, by the middle bound cruiser as both cars make a complete 180 degree spin around, as the finally come to a stop as their airbags deploy for their safety. The left lane bound cruiser caught the tail end of the middle cruiser and flipped into the air as massive speed and height, as the vehicle came down on its topside and skidded to a halt against the medium. As the right bound cruiser, hit a large SUV that was stopped in its lane as the vehicles exploded on impact. Ed was able to regain control of the Mazda, as he bounced off the barrier very hard. Stephanie told him to suspect took the second off ramp to their right. As Ed gunned the black Mazda down the ramp, he told Stephanie to call dispatch and tell them the Entity was now in the downtown district of San Diego.

The Entity was now southbound on Park Blvd, as the helicopter above picked him up in the darkness of night with its blue beamed searchlight. The bike's driver weaved in and out of traffic as he saw the oncoming squad cars, coming in the wrong direction on the boulevard to again box him in. He saw something up ahead, as he changed gears and eased up on the gas as he arched himself back and steered his hi right side. As he tugged hard on the handlebars and propelled the bike high into the air, jumping over the right medium and landing softly on his rear wheel, as the front wheel came down hard to the pavement. As he shifted his body upward on the seat, to regain control of the bike, he heard the loud collision of the cruisers behind him smashing into one another. As they were unable to stop at their high speeds, as they hit the medium.

Ed who just got on Park Blvd. Slows his speed down as he lost sight of the fast bike, as he comes up on the accident of the police vehicles. As one officer was standing pointing to Ed, in the direction of the street to his left, Ed knew what he was saying as he floored the gas pedal again as he yelled instructions over to Stephanie; "tell them he's on 11th Avenue now! He is heading right for the mall!" Ed screams over to her, as Stephanie relays the information to dispatch on her cell phone.

Chief Chase hears the conversation the dispatch officer is saying with Stephanie and all the other police cruisers. As he has them on speaker phone, so the control room can hear what is happening at once. As Chief Chase goes over to the large map of downtown San Diego, he looks at where the motorcycle is heading. He says to the other Captain and Lieutenants that he is heading to the large Westfield outdoor mall. As he looks at the time on the wall, it reads 8:30 PM. The mall just closed a half hour ago, but there will still be shoppers and employees just about leaving the five story mall and its large parking garage. As the Chief orders to have one helicopter position it right over the mall, and the other to monitor East Harbor Drive. Being that is the only other highway he can get to, if he gets by their cruisers.

The Entity makes a fast right turn onto First Avenue, as he watches the crowds of people exiting the mall. He slows down to avoid hitting them, as he notices more police cruisers coming at him from the opposite direction as he hears a car's tires shrieking behind him. As Ed and Stephanie come around the corner behind him, as Ed slams on the breaks to avoid hitting civilians as the cruisers also stop ahead of them. The Entity, stares back at Ed through is dark smoked visor.

As Ed knows he's staring at him, Ed knows he is going to try and lose them in the five story mall. That has a long strip running though the center and on either side, there are five tiers of stores lined with stairs and escalators. That is enclosed by the parking garages on the outside of the stores on either side. A very upscale and different design is the Horton Mall. Ed watches as the Entity cranks up the shit handle and the gas. As he yells to Stephanie, "Tell them he's going into the mall, and have them enclose both sides of the parking garages to block his escape!" Ed yells as the Entity, makes a right turn through the open doors as Ed guns the gas pedal and follows after him.

Stephanie relays the instructions over the phone, as she screams at Ed not to follow him inside the mall. Ed ignores her pleas as their car, narrowly is able to squeeze through the wide open double doors. The motorcycle and its rider stream fast all the way down the main floor, as he dodges by shoppers and just avoids hitting a mother who is with her infant in a stroller. As people curse and yell at the driver of the bike, as Ed slows down and hunks his car horn repeatedly to clear the way for himself. As the people unknowingly don't know what this situation is all about, start cursing at Ed and Stephanie. As uniformed police officers, file into the mall on foot with their weapons in hand. As they hurry to clear out the mall, and keep all persons safe from harm.

The bike makes its way to the very end of the first floor, as there are no exits in sight for him to escape unless he turns around and takes on the Mazda head on, as it comes toward him from behind. The Entity notices the flight of stairs to his right side. He makes a circle around the water fountain in the middle of the floor, as the car comes full speed at the bike as Stephanie screams for Ed to stop. The motorcycle avoids the collision as the Mazda runs straight into the marble water fountain damaging both the car and the nice statue. As the Entity races up the stairs, Ed quickly moves the deployed airbag out of his way, as the passenger side airbag also deployed to shield both Ed and Stephanie from the hard impact. Ed asks her is she is all right, as Stephanie told him yes. Ed just takes out his gun in hand, and leaps out of the car as he watches the motorcycle now on the second floor. Ed runs up the stairs very fast, as he tries to keep pace with the bike in hopes of getting off a clear shot at him.

The policemen run up to Stephanie who is holding her head, from the impact with the airbag. As she tells the officers who she is, and that Detective Brooks is in pursuit of the suspect on foot. As four of the six officers run up the stairs to assist Ed, the two others remain behind to assist Stephanie. Ed knows he can't keep up with the very fast sport bike, he just keeps running as hard as he can breathing very hard ignoring the pain in his legs, as he spots the black bike just a few yards ahead of him. Ed hears the rotor blades of the helicopter overhead, as its light shines down into the mall searching for the suspect. Ed watches as the bike, races up the escalator's steps as the Entity makes his path for the third floor. Ed takes aim and fires repeatedly at the rider in black, as his rounds barely miss him striking the acrylic glass of the escalator, shattering it on the spot of impact. The rider reaches the top of the floor, and guns his way down the opposite position away from Ed and the police. Ed curses to himself, as he notices the elevator behind him. Ed runs into the open door of the elevator, and presses the number five to take him to the fifth floor. As Ed ejects the empty clip and replaces it with a full clip, he knows he is making his way to the top floor to get away.

The elevator car comes to a stop on the floor, as the doors open and Ed runs out. He watches as the bike is coming around the corner fast at him, as Ed takes aim and shoots directly at the rider in black. As his first three rounds miss their target, the Entity looks at Ed as he takes aim for a direct shot. The Entity leans back as he stand up on the bikes seat, as Ed is about to fire his gun. The Entity pulls up hard on the handle bars and hits the break hard. As the motorcycle is propelled through the air, directly at Ed who within seconds leaps to his left side to avoid impact. As the motorcycle crashes into the wall behind him, the Entity flipped backwards off the bike, and summersaulted himself to a stop on the floor. As he took out one of his sharp samurai swords to confront Ed, as Ed got to his feet. He noticed he lost his gone as he leaped to avoid the motorcycle. Ed braces himself as the man in black runs fast at him with the steel sword, swinging the blade at him. Ed jumps to the floor to miss the swing of the blade, as he spins on the ground and jumps to his feet as he is able to catch the hands of his opponent. Right before he was to swing the blade at him again, as both men push hard against one another to control the sword. Ed with his left hand forces the blade down and with his right hand makes a first and hits the Entity with all his might square in the chest. As he falls backward, as Ed makes a running jump and kicks the Entity in the chest as he flies backward off his feet and hits the floor hard. As he loses the sword as he falls to the floor, along with the black duffle bag. Ed screams to him as he looks down at the person who took Kayla's life away from her; "You Son Of A Bitch!" Ed screams, as he rushes his foe who barely made it to his feet, as Ed is about to hit him with a roundhouse right fist. The Entity bends down to avoid the blow, as he takes out a sharp dagger from his inside jacket pocket and slashes Ed in his thigh. As Ed falls to the floor, the Entity then kicks him in the face.

Ed coughs for air as the hard blow stunned him, as the Entity reclaims his sword he hides behind the pillar. As three armed cops come rushing towards Ed, but before he can warn them. The Entity slashes and hacks at them from behind in a fury of speed, his sword slashed through their necks and he finished them off with fatal deep stab sounds to their hearts, as they lay helpless on the floor. Ed crawls on his back trying to reach his gun that's only a few feet from his grasp, as the Entity comes over and kicks it well beyond his reach as he holds a foot on Ed's chest pinning him hard to the floor. Ed looks at the man in black, holding the sword in his right hand knowing he is about to end his life now, as they both hear the loud voices of the many oncoming cops running up the stairs. The Entity looks back at the policeman, and then stares at Ed on the ground as he points to him with his left index finger without saying a word. A short stare and point that lasted a few seconds as the man in black ran to the side wall and leaped up to grab hold of one of the stores draping signs. As he was able to climb up to the roof of the mall, and run down the opposite side. As Ed took a deep breath, and covered the gash his left thigh that was bleeding heavily. As the policeman reached him, Ed told them were the suspect was going as the lead officer radioed to the helicopter to look for the suspect on the roof.

The man in black ran very fast, as he tried to avoid the search light from the helicopter above him. He ran full speed and he leaped down to a lower rooftop of the mall, as he knew he was now on top of the parking garage. He looked down and saw one of the streets below him, as squad cars kept converging in from every side of the surrounding streets. The Entity ran down to the far side of the malls rooftop, as he leaped again down on top of the last low rooftop, but yet it was still too high for him to leap to the streets below or he would get seriously injured. He ran inside the parking garage as he saw he was on level three. He quickly looked around and thought of a way to escape, as he saw a large dumpster to the side elevator and stairwell. He quickly jumped inside the dumpster and closed the lid, as he lit his flashlight inside to give him light; he started to remove his black ninja outfit and helmet.

Stephanie made her way up to Ed on the top floor, as they were flanked with many policeman as the head Captain of the Swat team unit, ordered the, to sweep the parking garage levels from top to bottom. As he ordered another heavily armed team, to sweep the interior of the mall from the ground floor up, as the two helicopters above and the units who had the entire mall surrounded from street level, did not pick up the suspect. Leaving the grounds of the mall as of yet, as Rick and Rob had just reached the mall at that very moment. As Ed and Stephanie were taken to a waiting ambulance, to receive medical treatment, as Rick and Rob had bruises and cuts from their tremendous vehicle accident. Ed's knife wound was being cleaned and dressed, as Stephanie was holding and ice pack on her bruised left shoulder. Rick was in constant contact with the Swat team's Captain as his men continued to search the entire mall for suspect. As Rick had now gone to the mall's security office, as Detectives searched the surveillance monitors for the suspect from.

"Are you all right?" Stephanie asked Ed, as the paramedic finished dressing up the knife wound to his left thigh, that didn't require any stiches. Ed smiled at her and said, except for running a good pair of pants, and his pride being hurt a little, he was all right. Rob made a call to his wife, and told her what had happened at the safe house and at the mall. Antonella along with their daughter and Cate were taken from the restaurant, by a police escort to Central Division headquarters. Where they would all wait for them to come, as soon as the search was over with at the mall, as the time was now 10:30 PM, it had been nearly an hour and a half since the Entity was last seen on the mall's roof, as no sign of him has turned up since.

In the darkness of the stairwell he waited for a while, as he had stepped out of his ninja outfit and was now wearing a black sweatshirt and black sweatpants and a ski mask. That covered his whole face and neck, as he positioned himself up on two large lead pipes that carried water for the fire sprinkler system of the parking garage. He was turned on his side, as his slender body was covered just right as he was concealed way up on the ceiling of the stairwell, as he was waiting for the right moment to make his escape. As he hard their footsteps approaching and soft voices getting closer, as the mag-flashlights attached to their machineguns, illuminated the stairwell brightly. As the Swat team of five men, walked right under his position as the team leader radioed to his superior saying, the ground floor was all clear. As he heard their superior tell the team; "Ten-Four," the team leader told his men to move straight forward. As he waited till he knew they were well enough away from his area, the Entity very quietly lowered himself to the floor as he looked around the garage and saw no signs of policeman or civilians. But two security surveillance cameras, positioned up high on the ceiling. One was pointed in the other direction away from him, as the other was pointed in the area where he needed to make his escape. He saw the grand opportunity he needed, as he low crawled on his hands and knees quickly. He was able to crawl behind a large SUV, which was parked directly in the cameras point of view. As it gave him cover as he pulled open the steel grate of the sew cover, and lowered himself inside as he stepped down on the fixed ladder on the wall. He closed the grate quietly, as he stepped down all the way to where his feet touched the dirty water of the saw. He took out his small flashlight, and looked around to see if he can get a bearing of his position, he knew he had to be right under the main part of the mall that was on 1st Ave. He then walked to the three way corners of the saw system, and figured if he traveled along the right tunnel, it would take him due east and he would be able to find a manhole cover under 4th Ave. He quickly but very quietly walked fast down in that direction as he knew, once again he out smarted the Police force.

He climbed up on the steel steps of the ladder, as he heard the rushing sounds of vehicles over him. He looked up as he used enough strength to push up the steel cover, and see he was on 4th Ave. Besides the rush of cars, he didn't see or hear any people passing by as he was right under a pedestrian sidewalk. He pushed away the steel cover and climbed out of the manhole, as he rolled to his left side, and placed the cover back into place. He again stayed low to the ground and rolled to his left, as he found himself hidden behind a group of planted tall bushes, in front of a tall commercial building. He took off his ski mask and placed his flashlight in his back pocket and dusted himself off. As he calmly strolled out from behind the bushes and started to walk in a slow pace, as two police cruisers whisked right by him in the direction of the mall, he laughed at himself as he saw a yellow taxi parked on the side of the street. He very politely asked the driver if he can be taken to National Ave. As the driver obliged his request, he sat in the back seat and just smiled again to himself; "The fools, I evaded them again as I took out so many of their elite team members. But I didn't get to kill you just yet Brooks! But I will wait for the right moment; I want to face you in person alone. So I can kill you along with your precious Stephanie." He said to himself, as the taxi made its way to the address he requested.

# Chapter 8

At 1:00 AM, when all the teams had completed the search of the Westfield Mall and the only items that were found at a garbage dumpster, that was on the top level of the parking garage. Was the Entity's ninja like uniform that he wore, and both of his swords that he used on the fatal attacks of his victims. Any other small daggers or tools that he used, he took with him as he made his escape Chief Chase briefed Rick and the others, as they were in Rick's office. As Chief Chase asked Rick, if the team was assembled in the conference room now, as Rick picked up the phone and called the rooms extension, as Rob answered the phone, and told him the team was present now. Waiting for the Chief and his staff to brief them on the bloody night of, Friday August 19, 2012, a date that will now go down as marked by a massacre by murder and other fatal accidents that took the lives of 16 Policemen and civilians in the city of San Diego, as Rick and Chief John Chase entered the conference room. Rick closed the door behind him, as his Deputy Chief was already present along with the remaining members of the task force and Stephanie. As Chief Chase glanced, a dirty look over at Ed and Stephanie who were seated next to one another. The entire room was dead silent, as there was a feeling of just shock and sadness among the remaining team members, but they knew the mood was now going to turn to heated anger. As Chief Chase was about to speak; "I want to first say, I thank God that my remaining team members were not killed or seriously hurt here. But we lost our fellow good friends and exceptional team members; Julie O'Keefe and Skip Jones. Along with thirteen other policemen and one civilian who were killed on the freeway, during the vehicle chase of the suspect while he was on his motorcycle". The Chief told them as he was reading from his briefing report, as he threw the folder down on the table.

"So now we are over a months' time into these new serial slayings, and from what Rick has told me now. We are no closer to solving this case on forensic evidence or even naming any suspect at this time, which has resulted in a total of twenty three victims here in my city. The largest number of serial slayings involving men and women and police officers in the shortest amount of time in the history of not only our country, but the whole Damn world! Even with the help of the FBI, who gave us the assistance of Miss Stephanie Morgan, their best west coast profiler here in California? The only thing we accomplished so far was a nice love matching between Miss Morgan and Mr. Ed Brooks, who are now engaged to be married. Well that's Fuckin impressive Brooks! Congratulations to you both, because you can now spend as much time with one another as you want! You're both removed from this case along with this entire team, as I am letting the FBI now lead this investigation into this whole case. Rick will be the only member staying on to assist the FBI, with a whole new team of lead Detectives that I will pick myself." Chief Chase yells at them, as he finishes off his statement with a clam voice, letting the team know they have been replaced, without making any useful leads or evidence to follow up on, only Ed's theory that the murders are tied to the suspect in the Ripper murders.

Both Ed and Stephanie glared back at Chief Chase with dirty looks after hearing his remarks about them, Ed slowly rose from his seat to stand up. Stephanie gently reached out and held his left arm to try and persuade Ed, not to confront the Chief. But Ed just pulled away from her grasp as his eyes darted with burning rage at their boss; "you know something John, out of all those victims you just mentioned. I think you forgot this guy killed my ex-wife and her husband, and he was truly out to kill Stephanie and me tonight at your so called safehouse. How did he know we were staying there? And you think we have no new leads or connections or evidence, your wrong! Because Rob, Stephanie and I think there is a link here to this killer and the Nathan Malcolm killings, four years ago along with another big link. No one has put together, except for the three of us." Ed tells the Chief, as he mentions the connection to the; "Jack the Ripper" murders over a century ago. Ed goes into gory details about how those five victims were mutilated then, and how the similarities of these recent murders four years ago and now. Are tied to the main suspect; Francis Tumblety and his supposed family relations to, Nathan Malcolm, the Chief just stands in place with a stare of disbelief, as he turns and looks at Rick who admits to him, he knew about Ed's theory from the beginning. But they decided to keep it classified, not to leak it out to any fellow officers and mostly the media to break this story, until they were absolutely certain they were right about this.

Both Ken Rogers and Jack Kerns turn and look at one another, as for four years they were kept in the dark about this from Ed and Rob. As Chief Chase is still mystified about what he just heard, he orders Rick to have them bring all their files into the room now. And for Rick to arrange for, food and coffee to be sent for them now, as the Chief says this is going to be a long night and very late morning till the team goes all these files and evidence now.

For four and a half hours, Ed and Stephanie went over everything they uncovered about Nathan Malcolm, growing up in Marion. Iowa. As his Grandfather claimed his brother's body in 1903, in St. Louis, the body of Francis Tumblety, as he changed his family name to Malcolm, a short time later as he saw to the burial of his brother in Rochester, New York. As Chief Chase read all about Francis Tumblety, as not only Ed, but other "Jack the Ripper"; historians believe he was the Ripper. As Chase can't believe what he is reading, that he is a blood relative to Nathan Malcolm, and this is what put him over the edge to murder those poor women. As all the men kept on talking about the case, with their sleeves rolled up and drinking the freshly made coffee, Stephanie who was still wearing her elegant royal blue dress placed her hand over her mouth as she yawned softly. As Ed looked up and noticed how tired she was, he got up from where he was sitting and came over to her as they held hands, and started to talk to her softly; "hey, why don't we get a large number of cops together and have them escort you back to my house, so you can get some sleep. I know it's been a very traumatic and sad night for all of us." Ed tells her, as Stephanie holds his face and says, it started out as a happy night for them as they got engaged. As Rick heard them talking, and he told Stephanie that Ed is right. They will finish up here soon, and then they will break for a few hours and then convene again by early afternoon.

The Chief gives Rick the permission to have ten officers escort Stephanie back home, and he wants them all heavily armed and in constant contact with them at all times. As Ed places his blazer jacket, over his fiancée's shoulders, he walks out the door and into the hallway. As five heavily armed cops are ready to escort Stephanie to the parking lot, and the awaiting unmarked vehicles, as she hugs and kisses Ed gently, he tells her not to worry she is safe, and he will be home very soon. As the cops walk her out the back exit doors, and Ed looks on as he watches Stephanie get into one of the vehicles, as they all drive off together. Ed over hears Rick telling Rob, he has two units of cops looking after his wife and daughter at his home, as they speak. They will take every precaution necessary to maintain their safety, until this whole ordeal is over with.

"So we were able to recover the suspect's duffle bag, which contained two short samurai swords, one black crossbow with arrows. A pair of short steel pliers, and this whole black ninja outfit made of black sterile cloth, we had all the items shipped over to Dr. Farrell's office. So she can test all the items for any DNA matches and for fingerprints. But my guess is, we will not find anything if he used gloves and cleaned all his weapons good before he used them tonight." Rick tells John Chase, who just nods his head to him. As he looks at the gruesome crime scene photos from the supposed safe house, where his men were to keep Ed and Stephanie safe, Chase now feeling sorry for the way he snapped at ED before, wanted to say he was sorry to him.

"Look Ed, I'm sorry I lost my temper before with you and Stephanie. I was just so mad we lost so many good men and women tonight, and now their families have lost them forever. I know this piece of crap killed Kayla and her husband just to get back at you, and he was after you two tonight. So being as it was, you saved Stephanie's life by taking her out for the evening, and that was really a brave thing you did. Confront the Entity in the mall all alone before backup got there to assist you, just like you did when you went after Malcolm the first time." Chase tells him, as Ed breaks a smile and thanks him. As they turn their attention back to the case again, they are still frustrated they can't find any connecting evidence or suspects who may be related or connected to Nathan Malcolm in any capacity. As Chief Chase looks at the time, which is now 8:30 AM.

"All right, we have been going over this all night and now its morning. Let's all break for a while as Dr. Farrell and Dr. Adams does their jobs and I will have Western Division's detectives check and see on the sport bike the suspect was using, as we know it came up stolen from a civilian the other day. Maybe some witnesses saw the suspect take it from the beach, where it was last parked by its owner. We will need to be back here by 2:00 PM, and Ed and Rob will be escorted to their homes." Chase orders, as everyone felt a bit of relief so they can break for a shower and some good sleep finally.

Ed arrived home shortly after 9:00 AM; there were six police cruisers parked outside his housing complex. As he entered his door, he was met by the lead Swat team commander assigned to his protection. He explained to Ed, he and his four five man team will stay inside the apartment with him, as there will be a change of shifts of uniformed officers stationed outside the homes perimeter. As even the uniformed cops, or heavily armed with M-4 machines guns. Ed thanks him and his men, as he tells them to make themselves comfortable. But for no one to touch any of his Jim Hendrix, CD's and his LP collection, as Ed opens the door to his bedroom quietly. He notices Stephanie asleep in bed, as he walks over to his dresser and takes off his shoulder holster and gun. As he undressed himself and just gets into bed, beside Stephanie trying not to awaken her. As Ed faces up at the ceiling, he thinks of Kayla, Julie and Skip. The people whom he knew the best, along with all the other cops who were killed, Ed closes his eyes not because he is tired. But because now more than ever, he wants to kill this new murderer, for he has made this a personal vendetta against Ed Brooks. As he still is searching for the reason why? As Stephanie reaches over and holds Ed's hand under the covers, Ed looks over as he sees her smiling at him.

"Please promise me you're not going to do anything crazy to stop this guy Ed. Because you may walk right into his trap, if you go out on your own to stop him, I can't lose you now after you just asked me to be your wife. Please think of the life we can share together before you go back to headquarters later." Stephanie pleads to him, as Ed reaches over and pulls her to him. As Stephanie rests her head on his chest and closes her eyes.

"I promise you, I will be all right and make sure no harm comes to you and the rest of our friends, as I also promise you. We will get married shortly after this is all over with." Ed promises her, as Stephanie feels safer and content being held in Ed's arms. As she drifts back to sleep, Ed softly glides his hands up and down her smooth bare skin, as he closes his eyes and dreams of a new happy life with Stephanie.

At 2:00 PM, Ed and Stephanie were back at Division's conference room, as Dr. Diana Farrell passed along her DNA findings of the recovered weapons and pair of pliers, used by the suspect. As Rick read off the findings from the printed out report, he then passed the folder for Ed and Stephanie to look over. As Ed again, became very mad and frustrated that the suspect left no DNA evidence behind.

"Dr. Farrell found no human DNA of fingerprints, blood or animal hair on all the weapons and the pair of pliers. Along with no DNA evidence in or the outside of the black duffle bag, and the ninja costume that he wore, as latent fingerprint experts went over the motorcycle inch by inch and found the only fingerprint's on the bike were that of the owner's on the handlebars and the rest of motorcycle. As both Farrell and the fingerprint expert believe, the suspect wears either sterile cloth gloves or latex gloves before he touches all his weapons and clothes. As the swords and knives, did show they were all cleaned with honing oil before they were used last night." As Ed reads both Farrell's findings and the handprint examiners findings, as he tells Rick and Stephanie that by the killer cleaning his weapons in honing oil. He keeps them free of rust and dirt, besides being very difficult to leave any DNA behind. As Rick confesses, they are dealing with a smart, inelegant person here. Who is very aware of DNA and forensic works, as he is able not to leave any traces of himself behind?

"Well I say the killer has medical knowledge and means of medical equipment to carry out his work, what if we searched local hospitals and even medical colleges for any potential suspects." Stephanie suggest to them, as Ed raises his eyebrows at the idea.

"That's one thing we haven't looked into yet, being the he would have access to a hospital's medical equipment and the white van. There is white cargo vans used at medical schools to teach students, of what they would expect from crime scenes as a medical examiner." Ed suggests, as Rick picks up the phone and calls Ken Rogers and Jack Kerns on one of their cell phones, to get them back to Central Division as soon as they are done with all the leads into the stolen motorcycle.

"Once they get here, we brief them on this new possible lead. As the three of us are going to look in the computer at all the medical staff of doctors and nurses at all the area county hospitals. There has to be at least one person with medical knowledge who has broken the law in some fashion that we can point a finger at." Rick tells them, as the three of them agree to begin searching hospitals in the area, as they work on separate computers to save some time.

As Ken and Jack, made their way into the homicide division's office, they told the others they had no luck with any prints or witnesses who saw the suspect steal the motorcycle. As another good lead turned into a dead end for the team, as Rick and Ed briefed them that they are now looking at medical personnel in the areas eight main hospitals, mainly physicians who may have criminal pasts that can tie their medical knowledge into the crimes as Ken and Jack take seats and start to look up names and hospitals for any leads to help them. For the time was now going on 4:30 PM, as they were hoping to find a good suspect this evening to perhaps investigate, as the FBI informed Chief Chase, they will be sending six top agents to take over the lead of the investigations. As Ed and his team did not like losing control as the lead team, but they all knew they had no choice in that decision.

For four hours they went over all established Doctors, Nurse Practitioners and student residents. As they eliminated the smaller hospitals, they were now looking at the last two major hospitals in the city. As both hospitals were medical centers and Universities for student doctors to work on their internships. As Ed had a feeling they may be on to something here, but time was against them as Ed kept encouraging the team to work till 9:00 PM, before they would break for dinner. As Ken Rogers was looking through the last names that began with the letter P; he clicked the mouse on the next name; Alan Pace. As he leaned back in his chair to stretch his arms and legs out, he hoped Ed would let them break for dinner soon as he was starving for food. As he was about to let out a big yawn, the screen brought up Alan Pace's driver's license picture along with a felony record of the medical resident. As Rogers held his yawn in, his eyes were now locked on the computer screen as he yelled for Ed and the others; "hey guys! I think we got something here." He yelled to them, as Ed and the others all came over to Ken's desk to look at what he found. As Ed was the first one there, he began to read about Alan Pace.

"Alan Pace; 27 years old born 8/22/1985. Was arrested while in college with others while they were interns at, California Medical College, as Pace was the lead suspect in an attempted gang rape of a fellow female student as they attended a frat party two years ago. Pace had planned with two other males to lace the alleged victim's drink with sedatives and move her to a secluded location where they were to take turns raping her. As the men were stopped by the victim's friends, before they could move her out of the house and into his vehicle. As the police were called to the scene, but after Pace and his other two accomplices were arrested. They were released for lack of evidence, as his high powered attorney claimed the female was just drunk, and not having any outside narcotics in her system, as found in her urine test." Ed read the whole police report on Pace, as he continued to read that Pace is a resident currently at Regional Medical Center for general surgery. As Ed looks at Stephanie, Ken continued to read more about Alan Pace.

"Hey Ed, according to this, Alan Pace's father is Dr. Albert Pace. A head member of Quasar Pharmaceuticals here in San Diego," Rogers told Ed, as the whole team just looked at him, knowing that's were Nathan Malcolm worked. As his father might have been a close colleague of Malcolm and this guy Alan Pace, may have some knowledge of that connection and a link into these murders now.

"Okay, Ed you and Rob along with Ken and Jack, go locate where Alan Pace is now. Stephanie and I will go locate his father, and find out whatever he knows about Nathan Malcolm and his son. I'm not telling the Chief or anyone else about this yet, because we are merely going to question these men once we find them, understood people?" Rick tells his teams, as they all comply with his orders. They head out to their vehicles, as Rob and Stephanie both know, Ed wants to do more than just talk chat with Mr. Pace.

As Rick and Stephanie, went to the listed home address of Dr. Albert Pace in one of the very affluent neighborhoods in San Diego, his wife invited them in being very cordial to the two law enforcement officers, being they didn't call beforehand and the time was getting late into the evening. As Ed and his men, went to Regional Medical Center, to see if they locate and question the younger Alan Pace. As the four Detectives walked into the hospital, after parking their unmarked vehicles in the front drive of the large hospital, Ed and the others had their badges out to identify themselves as policemen. As the volunteer at the desk, paged one of the nursing administrator's to come assist Ed's investigation.

A female Nursing Administrator come to the main lobby, as Ed briefed her to why he and his team were on the premises, as she started to make phone calls to the different departments of the hospital to try and locate Mr. Pace for them. After a brief time, she was able to find out that. He was working alongside a surgical team, as they were performing minor surgery in one the O.R. units upstairs.

She escorted Ed and Rob up to the fifth floor, as Ed instructed Ken and Jack to stay in the lobby. As Rob told them, he would call them on the main lobby desks extension, right away if there was trouble dealing with their suspect. Both Ken and Jack stated to Ed they would remain in the lobby as they had a printed out picture of Alan Pace, in case he tried to make his way passed them.

Ed and Rob both posted themselves right outside the two metal doors, which led into the unit's O.R. wing. As Ed went over to the desks landline phone, he called Stephanie on her cell phone to see if she and Rick made any progress with Dr. Albert Pace. As Stephanie answered her phone, she whispered to Ed as Rick was interviewing the older Doctor and his wife.

"Ed we just got here, and Rick has been asking him if he had any deep knowledge on Nathan Malcolm, we didn't get to ask him any questions about his son just yet. He told us, as the news broke that Malcolm was about to be inedited on the illegal steroid charges, he just flipped out. As he was making statements he wanted to hurt those who were against him, and how his wife Jane, destroyed his life and relationship with their child. As he wished he could have killed Jane himself, and how women in general were the cause of all the problems in the world." Ed was listening to her, as he saw the doors open and Alan Pace come out in his blue hospital scrubs, as Rob pulled him to the side and started to talk to him. Ed looked back down as he continued his conversation with Stephanie, to try and make her push Dr. Pace, if his son followed the case of Nathan Malcolm.

As Ed was about to say goodbye to Stephanie, he heard Rob scream his name out as he looked up and saw; Alan Pace running away from them down the hallway; "shit". Ed yelled as he hung up on Stephanie and called Ken and Jack on the lobbies' extension, to warn them he is running from them. As Jack said he would go cover the back exits in case he tries to flee to his vehicle. Ed starts to run in the direction of the opposite hallway along with Rob, as they spot Pace running up the stairwell to the top floors. Ed and Rob run right behind him, as they know the hospital has eight regular floors and the ninth and tenth floors are mechanical rooms for the elevators and the roof access doors. As Ed calls out for Pace to stop running, he passed the ninth floor landing, as he made his way up the last flight of stairs to the roof. As Pace opened the door and ran into the top floors mechanical room, Rob reached the door, but waited for Ed before they proceeded inside together. As Rob took out his small flashlight, and they both armed themselves with their guns, they went in very cautiously to the very dark and large room. As the mechanical units for the elevators, were in operation with their cables and mechanics functioning. As Ed and Rob passed the units, Ed motioned to Rob to go check the right side of the floor as Ed stayed to the left side of the room.

The room was very dirty and had the smell of oil in the air, as Ed noticed the door in the back of the room, which he thought led out to the roof. As he moved very slowly along the wet stained floor, as Rob held his flashlight out, to peak around the corners he came upon. He knew Pace was still lurking on this floor, as he didn't get by he and Ed, as Rob came around the corner of a large metal cabinet. His hand hold out the flashlight was struck hard with a metal crowbar. As Rob dropped the flashlight, he looked up and was struck in the left side of his ribs hard again, as he hit the cabinet and was struck with a punch to the face, as he fell to the floor. Ed hearing the commotion ran over to Rob as he looked up and saw Pace darting for the roof's door, as Ed screamed for him to stop running. Pace threw open the door, as it's alarm went off very loud to let the security personnel know the roof door was open.

Ed bent down to Rob, who stated he was fine to go after their man. Ed ran full speed out the door as his feet felt the large gravel rocks of the roof; he looked around the large roof top, and saw many air condition units and alcoves that Pace could be hiding behind. As Rob made his way to the doorway, Ed instructed him to stay there, that it was the only way for him to make his escape; as Rob took out his cell phone and called dispatch that they needed assistance here stat. Ed moved with his back against the bricks of the alcove, as the light of the half-moon gave them enough light in the dark to see very well. As Ed kept his finger very gingerly around his gun's trigger, not wanting to kill this young man but in hopes of apprehending him, to question him and gain knowledge for these crimes. As Ed moved to the corner of the alcove now, he was about to peer out and look slowly when Pace came from behind him and wanted to strike Ed in the back of his head with the crowbar, Ed heard his feet scrape on the gravel behind him as he turned quickly and bent down, as he dodged the swing of the crowbar as it hit the bricks very hard. Ed blocked a return swing with his left hand as he kicked Pace right into his stomach and hit him with a left fist, as Alan Pace flew off his feet to the rooftop. As Ed called for Rob who ran with his gun drawn, Pace got up and started to run away from them.

Ed and Rob very slowly followed behind him, knowing he had nowhere to go, as Rob told him units were on the way to assist them. As Pace made his way to the far railing and had no more room to run as he looked back at the two cops who now had Pace cornered, as Ed started to talk to him very calmly; "all right Alan, that's enough. You have nowhere else to run to, drop the crowbar and just surrender to us so we can take you in and talk this all over. No harm will come to you now, I promise you." Ed tells him to assure him, they will take him into custody and he will be treated very well, knowing Alan Pace must be emotionally disturbed. As he drops the crowbar to the graveled rooftop, and throws his hands up into the air, to give them the impression he is about to surrender himself. Ed tells Rob he has him covered with his gun, as Rob holster's his weapon and takes out his handcuffs in order to secure Pace.

"You think you can help me? But you can't! No one can help me, all the best doctors and shrinks have tried but they can't! I don't want to go back to another mental hospital! I want my freedom and continue to do what I love! Ed and Rob just look at one another, as Rob tells him to move away from the edge of the roof, as Rob moved closer to him to place the handcuffs on him. As Ed whispered to Rob they needed to get him very quickly, now as they started to run to subdue him. Pace cursed at them as he smiled and leaped over the metal fence and hurled himself through the air as he fell ten stories to the ground below as he hit head first onto the pavement, killing himself instantly as Ed cursed out loud knowing they lost a key suspect here.

The police had blocked off the area of the back parking lot, where the body of Alan Pace landed from his plunge off the roof of Regional Medical Center. The forensic team was just removing the body as they spoke, as the team had gone through the suspect's pockets and found a set of car keys and a key lock, to his personal locker in the staff locker room. To save time, Ed and Rob went to investigate his locker, as Jack and Ken went to look through his vehicle parked in the staff parking lot, a Mercedes SUV. As Ed and Rob found many Playboy magazines in his locker of issues depicting naked women, they also found the house keys to his apartment at a nearby complex. As the other two detectives looked through the SUV, while wearing latex gloves on their hands, they found some very disturbing items in the center console and glove compartment. As Ken and Jack looked at one another, they said they need to bag these items now and inform Ed about it first. As they then informed the forensic team, they could now two the vehicle to the lab for examinations and print testing to be done.

They met up with Ed and Rob at the Mission Hills Garden apartment complex, as they entered the room equipped with a search warrant. They began to look around for more evidence and more items like the ones found in his vehicle. As Ed and Rob checked the bedroom, Ken and Jack looked through the kitchen cupboards and refrigerator for new evidence, as Rob found a shoe box on the floor of the closet. He opened it to find various styles of knives and duct tape, as Ed called them all together into the bedroom. As Jack and Ken found some key items in the refrigerator as they bagged them and went to see what Ed was calling them for, as they entered the bedroom Ed had turned on the television as it was hooked up to a partible recording system. As they were all watching a very disturbing video, of a naked girl unconscious in bed, as Alan Pace was filming her and they were able to hear him gloat over her, as he was very pleased to have another sexy girl as his victim. Ed quickly turned on the television and instructed Jack to get the camcorder and all the discs together, as Rob found more CD's and pictures of naked women. As Ed informed them they will bring all this evidence back to Central Command for Stephanie and Rick to view, as Ed called Rick on his cell phone, Ken came over to him and showed Ed what items he and Jack had found. As Ed looked into the paper bag, he saw many bottles of liquid ecstasy the date rape drug. Ed just shook his head in disgust, as Rick came on the line as Ed began to brief them on their findings, as Rick told him good job and they will see him soon at the office.

Stephanie was interviewing the parents of Alan Pace, in a small office to get more detailed information about him, as his parents were very distraught over his suicide. As they had no idea their son, had a dark side to him, which was to meet and drug women who would decline his romantic advances on him. So by raping them while they were unconscious, was his way of extracting his revenge on them. As Rick was now getting the full story from his Detectives in the conference room, it does appear to the team and Chief Chase, even if Alan Pace has nothing to do with the serial murders. He was in fact a serial rapist, of at least four women if not more as the forensic team is going through the CD discs they recovered from his home, as Stephanie came into the conference room holding her notepad and ready to brief them on what she was able to find out, as she took her seat next to Ed.

"Well from what I gather from his parents, Alan was very smart and very outgoing from his childhood till he began school and when he started medical school. He was liked by his friends and wanted to follow his father in the medical field and enjoyed sports and traveling, just like any young man his age. But one thing his parents did admit to me, and they didn't feel it was a very big issue as he kept it all a secret from them, was he had no luck with women. From when he was in high school, to even now at his present age, he was never able to have a steady girlfriend and there may have been disturbing reasons behind why women didn't find him attractive. So for him to advance himself on unsuspecting young women, he would meet them in a club or a bar, make small talk with them as he would lace their drinks with the liquid ecstasy, and walk them out of the bar or club with the assumption the female was only drunk, and take them to his apartment and carry out the rape and video record it for him to cherish the act. He was very sick and disturbed indeed, but after watching three of the rapes he recorded. I don't think he ever killed any of his rape victims, as he never stated in his videos he wanted to hurt women, just he found by drugging them, it was his only way to fulfill his sexual desires and fantasies with them." Stephanie tells them, as the men just look at one another and feel sick to their insides as what this up and coming doctor was doing to these poor women.

"This guy had the same MO as the famous Andrew Luster case, another sick Fuck that's imprisoned for life." Ken Rogers's remarks, as Stephanie believes Alan Pace watched the trial of Andrew Luster and got his motivation to act these crimes out from that case.

"So this is great we were able to stop this piece of shit! But is there any connection with this guy to Nathan Malcolm or Francis Tumblety or Jack the Ripper at all here?" Ed blurts out, getting very mad that after almost getting himself and Rob into a violent confrontation with Alan Pace that resulted in his suicide. They are again no closer to breaking open their case, as they are about to lose their investigation to the FBI agents tomorrow.

"Ed if you will let me finish explaining, I did find out a few things from Dr. Albert Pace who knew Nathan Malcolm as they worked together at Quasar Pharmaceuticals. He told me he knew Malcolm would always work late in his office, researching the most potent brands of GHB and anabolic steroids. Not only to make a wealth to distribute them as he did, but he felt if he took them himself, they would make very powerful and even younger in appearance. As we all know, a lot of sports athletes use them to enhance their performance and make them stronger. So in Malcolm's case, he did it to fight off and control physically fit young women, and my guess was able to elude the police as well." Stephanie tells them, as impressive as this all is; Albert Pace had no knowledge that Malcolm was the killer until he was stopped four years ago, as he told Stephanie. Malcolm never told him, if his only child was a boy or a girl and what ever became of his child after his divorce from his wife.

"So what do we do now? All of our solid leads have turned out to be futile; it's obvious the killer has inside knowledge of our doings and investigations, from the safe house attack. To the attack he committed on Dr. Farrell and Dr. Adams, as he tried to retrieve that piece of evidence from the van he used. So what if the killer is one of our own? A cop or another forensic investigator we missed, or even an FBI agent." Rob tells them his beliefs that the killer maybe one of their own investigators, as when he stated and FBI agent as the killer, they all looked at Stephanie as Ed's eyes locked on her. He thought to himself, why couldn't the killer be a female? Stephanie is strong and in great physical shape with martial arts training, could she be the daughter of Nathan Malcolm? As Ed thought of this crazy scenario, Stephanie became all red in the face as she knew what Ed and the other men were thinking,

"What! Are you men crazy to think I'm the killer? Ed what's wrong with you? I was with you the whole time during the murders at the house, and when we chased him into the mall! I'm you're fiancé! How could you all think this about me?" Stephanie screams at them, as she gets up from her seat and storms out of the conference room as she runs down the hall. As Ed runs after her, Rick and the rest of the men now feeling embarrassed at themselves, now feel rotten that they had thought of that idea. Rick tells them to break for the rest of the night, as it was already after 11:00 PM, he instructed them to be back early in the morning.

As Stephanie ran into the parking lot, she saw a team of uniformed cops around their squad cars, as she was going to ask them to take her home. As Ed caught up to her, and told the cops to forget about it, that he will take her home. As Stephanie broke away from his grasp she walked fast towards Ed's SUV, as Ed called to her to wait, as Stephanie yelled for him to open the door. As Ed caught up to her he placed his hands on her shoulders, as Stephanie screamed for him to take her home now, and that she was going to pack her things and book a plane back to L.A. tonight.

"Hey, I'm sorry Stephanie, the guys are sorry. I know you could never hurt anyone, I know how you feel about me." Ed tells her, as Stephanie keeps looking at him with a mean deep stare, still very upset with Ed and his friends.

"What on Earth would make you think that I could be involved with harming any innocent person, or related to Nathan Malcolm? Why, just because I know karate and kicked your ass one night! That makes me a prime suspect for murder? She yells at him, as she starts to cry as she yells at Ed to open the door and take her home now. As Ed, gently holds her in his arms as Stephanie tries to break away from him, he gently kisses her on the lips as she calms down and returns his kiss gently. As Ed breaks their kiss and now holds her tight in his arms, he whispers to her that he's sorry, and he knows he's a jerk for thinking that way about her.

"No Ed you're not a jerk, you're an Asshole like the rest of your friends for thinking that way about me." Stephanie tells him, as Ed breaks a soft laugh, as he asks her if he can take her home now, and if she can forgive him.

"Yes Ed, take me home now, but your sleeping on the couch tonight." She tells him, as Ed tells her fine, as they get into his Envoy and head home escorted by the two squad cars.

Ed had eaten a quick sandwich as Stephanie only had a ready-made salad, as she didn't say a word to him since they got home. Ed had showered and changed into his pajamas as Stephanie waited for him to finish in the bedroom, she left him two blankets and his pillow on the edge of the bed, for him to sleep on the couch in the living room. As Ed noticed the pillow and blankets, he thought she was only kidding but she indeed wasn't. As Ed not wanting to get her more mad, just took the items and walked out to the couch and made himself comfortable, as he used his remote and started to play a Jimi Hendrix CD, on his stereo system. As Ed thought to himself; "well at least I got you Jimi, women! I wish I knew what is about them that make them so sensitive to everything." Ed says to himself, as he turns the television on with his remote control, as he keeps the sound off so he could hear his music play.

Stephanie had finished her shower, and put on an elegant cream silk slip as she put on her long bathrobe to cover herself as she heard the music coming from the living room. She thought about Ed and his favorite musician, as she thought how was she going to get any sleep tonight listening to Jimi Hendrix songs. As she walked to the door and looked out at Ed, watching the late news cast about the death of Alan Pace.

"Ed please, can you turn that music off. I want to try and get some sleep now, if that's all right with you?" She tells him, as Ed just stared at her he was about to say that this is still his house, but knew Stephanie would probably pack her things and walk out this very minute if he said that, so he just shut off the CD player. As she told him thank you, and closed the door to the bedroom. Ed then shut off the television, as he picked up a book that Rob had lend to him. As he was about to read the first chapter, Stephanie opened the door and came out of the bedroom, as she asked Ed if she could sit with him for a minute to talk. As Ed told her of course, Stephanie still wearing her long bathrobe sat next to him on the couch, as she looked at the book, she asked him what he was reading. Ed told her, it was a book that Rob had loaned to him a while back; that he raved it was a very good book. Based on a true UFO case, and that he didn't have a chance to read it yet. As Stephanie smiled at him, Ed held her hand and looked at her engagement ring still on her finger.

"So this must be a good sign that you're still wearing my ring, are we still engaged or are you just going to keep the ring and sell it for the money?" He asks her, as Stephanie shakes her head no.

"Again Ed, you say something that you know is impossible for me to do. I have no plans to end our engagement and I will never sell this ring. As it is my first and will be my only engagement ring, as I still want to be your wife. But I'm still mad at you for thinking that way about me, at headquarters tonight."

"Stephanie I said I'm very sorry, and I know I hurt you, what else I can do to make you forgive me. Let you kick my ass with karate again?" He answers her, as Stephanie starts to laugh and says, "That will be a start". As Ed laughs at her, as he holds her soft hands and pulls her towards him as they kiss each other. As Ed picks her up gently in his arms, he carried her to the bedroom and lays her down gently in his bed. As they kiss passionately as Ed removes her bathrobe, and undoes the straps to her slip. As Stephanie stops him, and asks him what made him think that she would ever be a serial killer?

"Well I did remember the movie, Basic Instinct with Sharon

Stone, so I thought why not the woman you love as the killer." Stephanie called him an Ass, as Ed removed her slip as he started to kiss her deeply, as Stephanie removed his top and bottoms. Unaware they were being watched from afar, as the looker also counted the number of policeman gathered around the house in both marked and unmarked vehicles. As he looked through his night vision scope as he gazed upon Ed and Stephanie through the sheer curtains of their bedroom window, and debated what to do next.

"Twenty cops assigned to protect you two from me, way more than the last time. I can have so much more glory and satisfaction killing all of them now, and then you Ed Brooks. But I'm having such a delight watching you make love to your dear Stephanie, I have elegant plans for this beautiful woman of yours. As I will wait for the right time to kill you Brooks, along with the rest of your friends, the time is sooner than you all expect." As he laughs to himself, as he keeps watching Ed and Stephanie make love as he is positioned on a nearby rooftop, as he watches them with his scope. He becomes very sexually intense, as he gazes at Stephanie's naked body, her figure and breasts along with her very good facial features makes her the most beautiful woman he has ever laid eyes on. He feels he can't kill her, but he now wants her for himself, as he knows she will be his soon enough.

# Chapter 9

As Ed awoke the next morning, he didn't see Stephanie next to him in bed. He got up and places his bathrobe over himself, and went into the living room where he saw Stephanie working on her lap top computer. As Ed walked over to her and kissed her good morning, he fixed them both a cup of coffee each as he asks her, what she's working on. Stephanie tells him, with the amount of known evidence they have gathered now about the suspect, and knowledge of what he knows about the Malcolm killings, and the Jack the Ripper murders, she can now formulate a suspect profile of the killer. She tells Ed she has been working on it for two hours now, as she will print it out and show the whole team the age, height and weight. As well at the ethnicity of the suspect as she explains to Ed, the work of a profiler is not a science but an art, to outline the traits of the suspect and follow this traits path that will lead the police and investigators to their person of choice. But Stephanie cautions him, even profilers can be wrong, as the suspect can turn out to be someone they would never have suspected.

As Ed tried to peer in closer at the monitor, to read at what Stephanie was typing. She pushed his face away gently, and told him at the office she will tell them all what she believes their suspect's characteristics will stand out for them to arrest him finally. As Ed tells her good work and they share a kiss, he tells her they need to hurry to get ready to get to headquarters for the briefing to begin.

Stephanie had completed her detailed profile of the suspect, as she printed out a copy for each team member to carefully look over, as they all sat in the conference room along with Chief John Chase. Who Rick had called to come and view the profile for himself, as Stephanie used the rooms lap top to bring it up on the LCD screen for her to outline key points of the suspect's profile, as the men would read on their own as she spoke.

"Now before I begin to describe how I put this all together about our suspect, let me first say, I can be wrong about this. As I admitted to Ed this morning, a profiler's job is not say definitely if a certain individual is the exact one who committed a crime. But our job is to combine all the evidence, along with the person's patterns of crimes and known movements of behavior to get a matching profile as close as possible." Stephanie explains to them, as the men ask her questions about her profile.

Rick reads the age of the suspect and his physical stature and traits back to Stephanie; "so Stephanie, you conclude our suspect is a white male, between the ages of 34 to 43 years of age. He may have ties to Nathan Malcolm as either a close friend or co-worker from the pharmaceutical company, or he may just be a person who is very interested in both the Nathan Malcolm killings and the Jack the Ripper murders, as he wants to be recognized as an infamous sociopath killer like them." As Stephanie tells Rick, that is precisely what she believes, as there is also the remote chance, that is killer may even be a blood relative of Nathan Malcolm who is out to extract his level of revenge, on both innocent victims and the policemen who stopped Malcolm. As Stephanie brings up the murders of Ed's ex-wife and husband, as Ed just looks up at her.

"So you also believe the killer lives within the exact radius of all the murders and know the city of San Diego very well, as he preselected his victims and the locations to both meet them and murder them. As in the cases of Lauren Morton, Ashley Cook and Jackie Mays, as he abducted and killed them in different locations, and left their bodies in areas that people inhabit and visit often. So he wanted his victims remains to be discovered, and for law enforcement to try and catch him." Rob reads to her, as Stephanie tells Rob, this killer like Malcolm is not afraid of the police or the FBI itself, and he isn't afraid to die. As Rob shakes his head, knowing from all the things the killer has done and the big car chase that he led them on, he has no remorse for people or life itself.

Ed isn't one bit surprised at all the things Stephanie detailed is her profile about the killer, but one thing like the Ripper murders she has stated stood out to him. 'You write that you believe, just like the Jack the Ripper suspect who wrote the From Hell Letter, to taunt George Lusk and the police of Scotland Yard. You think this suspect, is trying to do the same thing to us now. He wants us to piece this all together somehow and you think he may be setting a trap for us, if not to kill a policeman he has singled out?" Ed asks her, as Stephanie makes a sad face at Ed and nods to him, as Rick and the team want her to explain this theory.

"After the murders of Kayla and her husband, and the massacre at the safe-house that we all know was the intent to kill Ed and myself. There has to be a big motivation for this killer to want to kill Ed Brooks and myself, being I am now romantically connected to him. But being we are guarded by the police now 24/7, the killer will now look to extract revenge on our close friends and families if he knows they are being less guarded and easy targets." Stephanie tells them, as Rob and Ed look at one another and then back at Rick.

"Guys call you're families now and find out where they are and ask them to get to a public crowded place or to a friend's home right away if they can". As the men take out their cell phones and begin to contact their loved ones right away, as Rob calls Antonella at home. Rick calls Cate at her office, as Jack and Ken call their wives. Ed picks up the offices landline phone and calls Dr. Diana Farrell, being she was already a victim of the killer's attack before.

While all the men are busy contacting their families, Stephanie tells them the killer will only stick to late hours of darkness, as to continue his patterns of concealing himself and easier for him to escape if he is cornered again. As Rob is still waiting for his wife to pick up the phone, Antonella finally answers, as Rob asks her what is she doing right now and if the two policeman are outside in their vehicle, watching her and their daughter. She told him she just came into the house, as she did some errands before heading to work.

"Rob I just dropped Megan off at my mother's house to baby sit her, for I know you will be working again very late tonight. As I have to get back to work for a busy day and a late meeting;" Antonella tells him, as she talks to Rob on the cordless phone as she looks out the window at the unmarked vehicle. As Antonella , is unable to see the two men in the car, puzzled she tells Rob she doesn't see them.

"Look, lock the doors and stay inside, I'm coming over!" Was all Rob could say to his wife, as the phone line went dead, Antonella quickly dropped the phone and ran to the front door as she made sure the door was locked. As she then hurried to the back door of the house, she was about to pass through the living room, when she stops and screams as she sees a uniformed policeman sitting on her sofa with his throat slashed open, as blood is flowing out from the deep wound. She was about to turn and run through the living room, when she stopped and screamed again. Impaled to the wall with knives in his palms and two knives in driven deep into both his eye's was the other policeman. As Antonella turned around, and standing behind her was the Entity dressed in all back holding a sharp short dagger. He told her with his soft voice, to sit down in the chair. For he was not going to hurt her, as he told Antonella she will not be harmed as long as she did what he said. Antonella knows everything about this killer, from what Ed and Rob have told her. She knows she can't get away from him, as she knows Rob and Ed are coming to save her. So she complies with his instructions, in order to save her time until they come.

She sits in the chair, as he tells her to place her hands behind her cross her wrists. As she crosses her wrists together, he quickly uses duct-tape to bind them tight together, as he then does the same to her feet. As Antonella starts to cry softly, she tells him to please don't hurt her, for she has a young child.

The Entity places his dagger back in its holder, as he then picks up a picture of Megan from a shelf. As he stares at her innocent young smile as he holds the picture next to Antonella's face, and makes a very surprising comment; "you're daughter looks just like you Mrs. Cullen. Very beautiful young child and her very beautiful mother;" he says as he strokes Antonella's cheek with his gloved hand.

"You are different from those other foul women I have disposed of, for you are a mother of a child. I will not harm you my dear, for I need you to deliver a message for me." He tells her, as Antonella listens to him in horror, as he tells her his message.

As Antonella, hears sirens blaring loud and the screeching of tires coming to a stop. The front door was kicked open, as Rob and Ed fly inside the house with their guns drawn in hand, as Rick along with Ken and Jack broke through the back door of the house. As all the men came into the living room, as Antonella yelled for Rob as she was crying. Rob and Ed rushed over to her, as Ed took out his pocket knife and carefully cut through the duct-tape to free her. As she stood up and Rob held her tight in his arms, as he asked her if she was all right. She told him he didn't harm her, but he killed those two poor policemen. As Ed and the others, looked at the way they were killed and posed in a shocking way for the killer, to openly mock the police of how he killed their friends. As Antonella, called for Ed, as he walked over to her and asked if she was all right; she was about to tell him the killer's message.

"Ed, he instructed me to tell you this message. He said not only is he going to kill you, but he is going to take away everything you love and hold dear to you. He said like Kayla, he is going take away the woman you love now." She tells Ed crying hysterically, as Ed knows she means Stephanie. They left her at headquarters with other policemen in the building but Ed just ran out the door followed by Rick.

Outside of the house, Ed called Stephanie on her cell phone as she answered him; he asked her if she was all right and if she was still at headquarters? She replied to him, that she was all right and there were many policemen still with her, as she asked him if Antonella was safe. Ed filled her in on what happened with her, as Rob and his family were now going to be moved to a safe location for their safety. As Stephanie just paused as to hearing what happened to Rob's wife, she knows it's going to be up to her, to come up with a candidate for a lead suspect, if Ed and his fellow cops can't catch him in the act.

Rob and his family were taken out of the city of San Diego for their protection, as Rick and Ed weren't even told of where they were moved to, to keep it secret as possible. As Chief Chase agrees with Stephanie and Ed on one point about the suspect whoever he may be, is that he believes the suspect could be a local medical doctor. Who has superior knowledge of the city, and police procedures? Or the suspect has an inside contact, who is leaking him vital information of the task force members, as for where they live and personal information about their families. Rick and his wife, Dr. Adams were seated with Ed and Stephanie in the conference room. Cate had joined them at Division headquarters as she brought over the latest autopsy results, she and Dr. Diana Farrell had done on the last victim. As the two couples had ordered dinner, and taken a break as it was now 9:00 PM, in the evening.

"So do you think Rob will be rejoining us soon again, or do you think he will want to stay with his family until this is over with?" Ed asks Rick, as he looks over at Cate before he answers Ed.

"I think Rob may want to stay with his wife and daughter and make certain they are safe, I don't blame him one bit. As I talked with Chief Chase a short time ago, Ed he feels you and Stephanie should be placed into full protection and taken out of the city like Rob and his family. We know the killer has now set his intentions on both of you, and it's only a matter of time before he makes an attempt at one of you." Rick tells them, as Ed knows he's right, but he wants to stay on the case until he catches the Entity himself. But Ed wants Stephanie off the case and back home in L.A. by tomorrow.

"Rick you know I'm staying active on this one until it's over, but I agree with you that Stephanie needs to be taken off the case and moved back home by tomorrow." Stephanie made a face at her fiancé as she was about to argue with him, Ed just cut her off and told he how he felt.

"Look Stephanie, this guy wants to not only kill me but you too.

He killed Kayla just to get back at me, and if it wasn't that we went out for dinner that night, away from the safe-house. He would have killed both of us, so please I want you back home in Los Angeles tomorrow and placed in round the clock protection." Ed tells her, as Stephanie was now tired of arguing with him but she knows he is right, as she is now very scared for their safety. As Rick looked at Ed and Ed returned the same stare at him, this was a great way to get their families and close friends away from harm, and hopefully concentrate all their efforts in stopping the Entity.

As Ed and Stephanie returned home by 11:00 PM, escorted by a great number of police cruisers and unmarked vehicles as they entered their condo. Stephanie placed her lap top carry bag and brief case down on the couch, as she made a face of feeling tired but also a feeling of disgust and anger with this whole situation. Ed saw she was upset but he didn't know what she was mad about, as he went into the bedroom and took off his jacket and shoulder holster, as he placed his handgun on the end table next to the bed. As he came back into the living room, he found Stephanie sitting on the couch and with a cup of tea in her hands, as Ed went over and sat with her as he held her hand she smiled at him, as he asked her what was wrong.

"Ed I'm not mad at you or Rick and the cops you work with. I know you are all doing your best to catch this creep and also protect me, but I don't like being watched by men I don't know round the clock even if they are cops and protecting us. Last night when we made love, I did feel a little uncomfortable and felt like we were being watched." Ed wanted to sound encouraging to her, as he tried to assure her that the fellow police would not peer or pry into their personal business.

"Ed I didn't feel it was the police, I feel it's him and he knows all about us and he may be watching us right now." Stephanie tells him, as Ed starts to look around the room and looks at the windows, as the curtains are drawn, but he feels she may be right. The Entity might have the upper hand and know all their movements if he is following Ed and Stephanie when they least expect it. Ed gets on his cell phone and calls down to the shift commander assigned to their protection for the night. As Ed asks him to sweep and look into all the parked vehicles up and down his street, and the nearby rooftops. As they feel they are being watched by the Entity. The commander feels Ed and Stephanie might just have a bit of eerie chills about this guy tonight, but yet he complies with Ed's orders as he will get two teams of four cops to patrol the areas around the complex.

From the same rooftop he occupied his dark surveillance of the couple last night; he couldn't see them with his powerful night-vision scope. But he was able to hear all their conversations with the use of his portable, dish and microphone pointed at the complex as it was so powerful, he could hear them from 300 yards away. As he listened through his earphones, he just heard the squad leader to begin the search of the vehicles below and the spot check of all nearby rooftops. The Entity knew he had to leave now, or risk being spotted by the police. He quickly gather his equipment and placed it back into his black carry bag, as he again was all dressed in his black ninja style outfit with full black mask. He took out his black steel dagger, as he moved to the far side of the roof, away from the stairwell door as he heard voices coming from below him. He expected the police were moving in pairs or teams of four, as he had to get by them to make it to ground level. As he heard footsteps coming up the stairs as the door slowly opened, as he watched them from around a brick corner. The two cops flashed their mag-flashlights around the roof, as they radioed back they were now checking the rooftop of the apartment complex across the street.

He smiled to himself and knew this was a challenge for him, but it will also be another adrenaline rush to kill Ed's friends. As he quipped the handle of the knife harder in his right hand, he waited for the cop closest to him to come into view, as he rose from the ground behind the cop and grabbed his mouth and chin with his gloved left hand, as his blade cut into the man's throat hard and deep as he sliced it open. As the cop yelped in pain as he fired his gun into the air, he was the thrown to the ground as his partner turned around and started to fire into the darkness, not even knowing what he was shooting at. As the Entity charged at him quickly as he viscously made a flying tackle into the cop's chest, throwing him back into the wall. As the Entity pinned his gun holding right hand to the wall as he stabbed him hard repeatedly with his dagger into his chest and stomach, as with the last thrust he slit his throat deep. As his blood poured through his uniform out of his deep wounds, he fell to the ground dead. The Entity the cops screaming below, as the gunshot alerted them to his location on the rooftop. He ran to the edge of the wall, as he leaped down to the fire escape and began to run down the stairs.

Ed hearing the gunshot ring out ran to get his gun as he returned to Stephanie who was standing in the center of the living room, as Ed told her to stay away from the windows. As there was a loud knock on his door, as the voice identified himself as the squad commander. Ed quickly unlocked the door, as the commander entered with five of his heavily armed men. As they secured the apartment, he instructed Ed they will stay with them for their safety as the rest of his team searches for the Entity, as he already called for fellow police to come and aid them. Ed enraged now, he hugged Stephanie and told her he will be back as he told the commander he was coming with him to search for the killer. As the two men ran out the door, as one squad member locked and secured the door behind them. Stephanie didn't even have a chance to tell Ed no to go, as she found herself alone being guarded by men with heavily armed sub-machine guns. As she just crossed her arms over her shoulders and started to cry, as she prayed Ed and his friends could stop the Entity now.

He ran down the fire escape till his feet hit the sidewalk, as he bent down and saw police cruisers going by on the street to the condo. The Entity ran away through the back alley as he heard voices behind him yell for him to stop, he saw the chain link high fence ahead of him, as he jumped to his right side. His feet landed on top of a steel dumpster, as he jumped off the dumpster quickly as shots narrowly missed him as he leaped over the fence and down to the ground. He ran again very fast, as the cops behind him started to climb the fence, and radio back to their fellow squad members their location, and the direction the suspect was running to.

Ed heard the conversation on the team leader's radio, he told all his mobile units and foot patrols officers to set out and search the area of La Jolla Boulevard, as it was the main road in the area of Lower Hermosa. Ed didn't wait, as he charged alone to the back alley way of the last sighting of the Entity. He ran through the back gates of the adjoining apartment complexes, as he ran into the alley to find himself with five armed cops. As Ed asked them, where did the suspect go? As one of the team members explained to Ed, they chased him to this point but he just disappeared from their sights. As they had two groups of five man teams now searching the rooftops of the two buildings on either sides of them. They feel he ran up one of the fire escapes to make his escape, as Ed took a deep breath to control his breathing as he was holding his Glock 45. Tight in his right hand, as he was about to turn and run up the fire escape to his left. A black car crashed through the garage door across from them, as Ed dove to the ground to avoid getting hit. As the vehicle struck three policemen, who tried to fire at the vehicle as they were run over head on. Ed heard their terrifying screams of pain as they were hit; he just got to his feet and ran after the dark older model vehicle, as it drove out of the alley way and onto the boulevard.

Ed tried to steady his right hand as he ran fast after the vehicle; he took aim and fired round after round at the back of the car. One round struck the back window shattering it, as Ed quickly dropped the empty clip to the ground, and took out his last full clip from his pocket and rearmed his gun. As the old Monte Carlo car, made a hard right turn as it was hit from the side by a police cruiser as it spun around fast, but it didn't stop as its driver was able to regain control and drive straight on the main road. But the few seconds it took to stall the vehicle from the impact, Ed was able to gain ground on the car as he leaped from his feet onto the back of the trunk of the Monte Carlo. As Ed grabbed hold of the shattered windowpane as the shards of glass, cut his hand and he tried to aim his gun at the driver, who saw Ed in his review mirror. Ed was about to shoot at the dark figure, as the car made a hard swerve to the left as it hit parked vehicles. Ed quickly braced himself, as he almost lost his quip as he repositioned himself on the trunk again as he fired into the car, but his rounds didn't hit the driver, one round shot out the vehicles windshield as Ed was able to steady his gun and aim. As the Entity saw his chance of escape, he made a hard right turn at the intersection as he avoided the hit of two police cruisers coming fast at his vehicle. Ed afraid he was going to get hit by the impact, let go of his tight grasp of the windowpane as he was thrown by the car's tremendous speed from the turn as he flew through the air and he started to spin like a top as his body hit a parked car, left shoulder and backside as Ed came to a stop and hit the pavement. The Entity drove down Grand Avenue, as he saw the roadblock of police vehicles ahead of him, as squad cars began to chase him from behind. He knew he was about to be stopped, as he countered their offensive as he made a hard left turn and drove directly through the guard rail of the overpass, as the car sailed into the air as he leaped from the vehicle, as it was about to it the water below. He braced himself as he hit the water, and dove deep beneath the surface to avoid being seen.

Ed semiconsciously opened his eyes, as squad cars came to a stop at his location around him. As policeman rushed over to him and were asking him if he was all right, Ed who was in a tremendous amount of pain just closed his eyes as he heard the loud voices saying they needed an ambulance here right away, as Ed heard nothing after that but silence.

When Ed opened his eyes, he felt someone holding his hand as he was able to glimpse Stephanie sitting beside him as she held his hand. As Ed turned to his right and saw Rick along with Rob and a few other cops standing around his bed. As he knew he was in the hospital, as he saw a doctor in scrubs along with a nurse monitoring his vital signs through the heart monitor and blood pressure machines. As the doctor was looking into Ed's eyes with his small penlight, explaining to Ed he received a concussion from the hard impact, and heavy bruising to his left shoulder and ribs. But he will be fine in a few days, as he didn't break any bones or deep lacerations. As Ed thanked the doctor, as he told Rick to make sure Ed stays in bed the rest of the day, as it was now 4:30 AM. As Ed couldn't believe he was unconscious this whole time, as the doctor and the nurse left, as they informed Ed they will return with some pain medication for him.

Stephanie smiled at him and said besides being in pain how did he feel, as Ed remarked he felt like he got hit by an eighteen wheel truck, as Stephanie thanked God he was alive as she sat next to him on the bed and kissed his cheek. As Ed gently placed his arm around her, and said he tried to save them all tonight, as he looked at Rick and wanted to know the outcome from what transpired last night.

"After you were knocked off the car, and our cruisers pursued him until the vehicle roadblock set up at Grand Avenue, the suspect flipped his car into the stream bed below. As our divers and search boats scoured the stream and the banks for our man, but we didn't find any signs of him or his body. We did find a black nylon bag that belonged to him, still inside the black Monte Carlo as we raised it from the stream. The bag contained a few sharp knives and a short sword, along with a powerful night-vision scope and a hearing surveillance dish and microphone. He no doubt was watching you both and our own squads protecting your place, as he killed two more cops on the apartment's rooftop where he positioned himself to spy on you two." Rick informs Ed, as Ed just sighs in disbelief that he was unable to get a clear shot off and shoot the son of a bitch in the head. As he asked Rick, if they were able to trace the car back to any suspect. Rick told him the Monte Carlo was an old eighties model, as it was an abandoned vehicle at a local impound that was stolen. So they are still checking for forensic evidence, but they know their man is to good and cautious to be caught with his DNA left behind.

"Ed just relax now and get some rest, we have this hospital monitored by over fifty cops as well as the whole security force of the hospital. We will be back by noon time to see if you will be released by then, as Stephanie will be staying in the same safehouse as Rob and his family." Rick explains to him, as Ed thanks them for coming to see him, as they all leave the room so Stephanie can say goodbye to Ed before she leaves.

"You know that was the most stupid and crazy stunt I have ever heard of a cop trying to do, to stop a crazed killer. But I know it was a very brave thing you did in order to protect all of your friends and mostly me. I'm so happy you weren't seriously hurt tonight, just next time stay with me and hide indoors." Stephanie tells him, as she kisses Ed on the lips gently as he brushes her tears away with his hand. She tells him she loves him very much, as she rests her head on his chest. As Rob opens the door to the room, and tells her they are ready to move them out now. Ed tells her not to worry about him that he will be all right, as they kiss again as Stephanie tells him to rest that she will be back with his friends at noon. As Ed watches her leave the room with Rob, as the door closes as Ed then turns on the LCD television, hanging high up on the wall.

Ed listens as the newscast talks about the serial killer known as the Entity, had struck again tonight. Killing two more police officers and injuring others in the high speed chase, as he was again able to slip by the grasp of the police. As Ed became mad and shut off the television, he closed his eyes and then reopened them; "your chances are getting very slim with me, because the next time we meet. I will kill you this time, and then we will finally know who you really are." Ed says to himself, as he closes his eyes and gets some sleep.

He was able to get home in the cover of darkness, he was soaking and wet from the dark dirty water of the stream, that concealed him well. Until he swam downstream a few hundred feet, till he reached a clearing and broke the surface he rose from the water and found refuge in his second vehicle and made it home. He took off his black fatigues and burned them all as he did his others, in his old fashioned stove. As he placed the fatigues into the iron kettle stove, and pushed them far down with the iron poker. He placed the lid back on the stove, as the very hot flames incinerated his uniform of choice. As he was now standing naked in his home, as the lights were all off, he made his way to the bathroom to shower and relax himself. As the warm water of the shower, cleaned him from the dirt and foul odor of the stream, he thought back to the night Ed and Stephanie made love. He can't get her out of his mind, he know he has to stop killing now for a few days, for the police to become relaxed and set their focus away from him. But he knows he needs to plan this perfectly, he knows Stephanie will almost always be with Ed, or guarded by many policemen. As he cleansed his body with the liquid soap, and scrubbed his skin very hard as the warm water washed away the dirt from his strong physique. He smiled to himself as he thought of a plan, he shut the water off and pushed the shower curtain open as he exited the shower, and cleaned himself with a towel.

He stepped into his shower shoes and then walked into his bedroom, as he turned on the light to his mirrored hutch. He had many pictures of Stephanie taped to his mirror, as he took them from his old 35mm camera. He even had a few pictures of his nemesis Ed Brooks, as he took the pictures as he followed them all over the city. He stared at the one he took of Stephanie in her white dress, her first night here in San Diego as she looked so beautiful that evening. He thought at first she would be a prized kill for himself, but not anymore. Now he wants her for his own, as he picked up the picture of Ed Brooks and stared at it. "You think you're going to stop me, you think you can save her from me. I will kill you in due time, as I now know how to defeat you and get Stephanie for myself." He whispers out loud, as he crumbles Ed's picture in his left hand, as he stares deeply at Stephanie's picture in his right hand.

# Chapter 10

Just before 1:00 PM, Ed was changed into fresh clothes that Stephanie had brought for him from home. As the team with extra cops for their protection was now ready to move Ed and Stephanie, out of the hospital to Central division and then onto the new safehouse, as Ed walked with a slight limp from a pain that was felt from his left hip down to his foot. As he took Advil for the pain, he knew this little bruising hurt his ego more than himself. Because nothing was going to keep him from taking down the Entity as he was so deeply involved in the case, and very personally as well. As Ed and Stephanie walked outside to the parking lot, there were three large SUV's and over twelve police cruisers and unmarked cars. Ready to escort them to Central Division, as the couple got into the middle SUV with Rick and Rob, Ken and Jack got into the lead SUV. As Rick told them that his wife; Dr. Adams along with Dr. Diana Farrell, were in the last SUV along with FBI agents now assigned to the case. Ed was about to protest to Rick, if the FBI was going to oust him from the case, as Rick told him to calm down, that they will all be having a big briefing with the FBI, the forensic findings and most of all. Stephanie's profile of the killer, as Rick only admits to them, something is in the works for a counter option.

Rick let the two female Doctors begin to elaborate their findings of all the physical and DNA evidence in the case, as they read Stephanie's detailed profile of the killer, Dr. Diana Farrell with her expertise as a forensic criminologist gave her opinion on who the killer might be. As the team listened to her speak, there was also three FBI agents seated in the conference room, one of which was another top profiler to assist them.

"From studying how he conceals himself and the way he murders and his knowledge of not to leave any of his DNA evidence behind. I have no doubt that this suspect is an experienced medical Doctor, or from what we found with the carpeting fiber left in the victim's fingernail. He may even be a mortician, with skills to cut open a human corpse and remove organs and know exactly where the major arteries and veins are located on the body. As will he have a commercial van for use to transport the remains of body." Dr. Farrell tells them, as Rick and Ed drop their mouths open and Rob looks at Ken and Jack, as Stephanie tells her she is absolutely right.

Rick orders his men to hurry up and check for all local funeral homes and mortician's names, as the FBI agents, say they can get more done with the help of the Washington D.C. office, as the team runs out of the conference room to their office, to begin the search online. Ed asks Rob to stay in the room along with Rick and the women, as he wanted to talk to them alone about something.

"Look guys, we know this killer has an inside person leaking himself information about us. As he gained knowledge of where I live, along with Rob's residence and the first safehouse, so how about we beat him at his own game if we can't capture him in the act." Ed suggests to them, as Rick feels he may have a good plan brewing for them to capitalize on.

"You mean devise a plan to leave the door open for him to walk through, and we slam it shut fast once he's inside and take him down." Rick responds, as Ed smiles and tells him exactly. Rob and Stephanie tell them they agree as Cate and Diana, who are not law enforcement officials just agree with their plan, but ask how they are going to pull this off, as Diana reminds them that they are dealing with a person who is very smart and dangerous. Ed thinks to himself for a few seconds as he looks at his watch.

"First Rob is going to drive me back to my place and leave his car there for safe keeping for a few hours, then we follow up on all the mortician leads we have here in the city. Then if nothing breaks by at least 10:00 PM tonight, we just head home and call it a day." Ed tells them, as they all look at one another puzzled but Rick smiles, back at Ed and tells him let's get the wheels turning on this then.

Ed drove back to his home as Rob parked his car in Ed's garage, but not before Ed drove his Envoy and Fat boy Harley-Davidson motorcycle. As Rob pulled into the garage and parked his vehicle, Ed secured the garage door and put on his black biker helmet and thick padded leather jacket and gloves. As he handed Rob the keys to his Envoy, he told him they can return to Central Division now, as Rob was still confused as to what they were doing, Ed said he and Rick will explain when it got later in the day.

Doctor Diana Farrell returned to her office, as Stephanie went with Dr. Cate Adams back to the county examiners facility, to look at photographs and wounds to the first victim of Ashley Cook and compare them to the fatal wounds of the victims of Nathan Malcolm, as if Stephanie's theory is correct, that the killer is a close friend of Malcolm's. This new killer had to leave some kind of a new calling card to the police investigators to mock them, as Malcolm did when he placed the victim's organs in a symbolic mocking way to taunt the police. Cate stated to Stephanie and the others that she found no patterns of that, but Stephanie just wanted to check for herself being she is a profiler.

Ed and Rob returned to Division Command by 3:00 PM, as they entered Rick's office. Rick told him were everyone else was and the leads they were following up on, as Rob now asked them what this open door plan was all about; as Ed made sure the door was locked so they can't be heard talking by the others outside the office.

"Look, we have been beaten all the time by this guy with whatever we have done to catch him or hide ourselves from him. So I know his leak has to be someone within this Division of not our own team." Ed tells them, as Rob and Rick agree but they aren't so sure the leak is a trusted member of their team.

"So unless we can catch him on the phone telling the Entity where our safehouse if, or what leads and suspects we are looking at. How can we catch him, we are going to have to wire-tap the whole phone system in the building and then call every cellphone service carrier to do the same for all our team members to spy on them, that will take at least two or three days to cover. We don't have that time on our hands, as we are about to lose this whole thing to the FBI by tomorrow by what Chief Chase told Rick last night." Rob tells Ed, saying his plans of spying on his team members is very shaky at best, as Ed tells him that's not what he has in mind at all.

"Rick, where is the new safehouse we have Rob's family at, heavily protected by our people?" Ed asks him, as Rick turns in his chair and points to a location on his map of the city.

"The safehouse is here in North Park, a good sized home with three other homes we have our team members and surveillance set up all over the safe-house and the perimeters of University Ave. The major street to leads to that location," Rick tells him. As Ed's eyes light up as he stares at the location and the main road. He thinks to himself as Rick doesn't know yet what he has in mind.

"Good, we move Stephanie and me there around 10:00 PM tonight, as we don't mind spending the night with Rob and Antonella with Megan running all over the house." As Rick and Rob still don't know what Ed's plan is, Ed then goes over to the map with several colored thumb tacks and sticks them in the location of the safe-house and University Ave. As he turns back to his partners to tell them his full plan for the evening, as he asks Rick if they have a female officer, matching Stephanie's height and long black hair.

Stephanie and Cate had been going over the crime scene photographs for some time now, as Stephanie even brought with her, photographs of the Nathan Malcolm's victims and the five known photographs of, Jack the Ripper's victims. As Cate was very upset as she looked at the very upsetting picture, of Mary Kelly's crime scene photograph. As Stephanie told her this photographs belonged to Ed, as he has convinced her and Rob the murders of Malcolm and this new killer are related to the Ripper suspect, Francis Tumblety. As

Stephanie explained the whole connections to Cate, they looked again closely at the photographs of the victims as Cate asked Stephanie, did the Ripper victims have any wound patterns that stood out, or personal belongings missing.

"Victim Annie Chapman had two brass rings taken from her, as the only articles of clothing or jewelry that the investigators were aware of to be missing from any victim. As victim number four, Catherine Eddowes had deep v-shaped cuts into her cheeks. But Nathan Malcolm made no similar markings or had taken any jewelry from his victims, as our killer now." Stephanie explained to Cate, as Stephanie stopped and thought to herself for a minute, as she was thinking about the two brass rings as Cate asked her what she was thinking of.

"Oh it's nothing, I was just thinking of those two brass rings. I wish Malcolm had taken jewelry or something of significance from his victims, as he only taunted us with the placement of the organs like Francis Tumblety did with Mary Kelly, his last victim." Stephanie explains as Ed and his team members walk into Cate's office, the women are surprised to see all the men walk into the room as Stephanie knows they have some new plan in store to catch the killer.

"How are you two making out? Any new evidence or leads we are able to follow up on?" rick asks them.

"So far nothing really useful from the photographs of all the victims, past and present to also match them to the original ripper victim's, but sometimes the clue you don't expect will come to you when you keep looking for it." Cate tells them, as Stephanie asks Ed what they are planning to do next.

"We are going to set one more sting operation into plan to try and lure him out, since we know he has been following us and he has to have some inside source to learn all about our private lives and our supposed secret safehouses . Chief John Chase is giving us only till tomorrow to catch him, or try this one last plan to learn his identity." Ed tells her as Stephanie pulls him to the side to talk alone.

"Ed please don't tell me you're going to be in the heat of things again, he wants you vulnerable for him to kill us. Please we are close to ending this and then we can be together always, a life I never had to share with someone, but now I have you." She tells him with tears in her eyes, as Ed assures her he will not be in the way this time.

"I promise I am not going to be on the front line this time, Rick and I planned this one perfect a great diversion to lead him into a trap that we will spring with many cops and our top SWAT teams. We will have him I promise you, and we will get married soon enough." He tells her as Stephanie tells Ed she can't wait to start making wedding plans and looking at different wedding gowns and elegant halls to have the wedding reception at. As Ed was smiling and trying to act like he was happy, but he knew how expensive weddings are, as the thought of a lot of money leaving his bank account crossed his mind.

As Rick tells everyone is was getting late into the evening, that he wanted Cate and Stephanie taken back to Central Division for their safety till the mission was completed. As Cate just remembered she left her DNA report one the victims with Dr. Farrell at her office, she told Rick if she could pass by her office and get it first. As Rick made a sigh of breath as he looked at his wrist watch, the time was 5:30 PM. He wanted to get his team and all the vehicles into position within two hours tops, as Ken Rogers made a suggestion to Rick.

"Rick it's all right, I will take Stephanie and Dr. Adams to Central Command as soon as we get stop by Dr. Farrell's office and get the DNA report first. Jack can go with you guys to the safehouse and I will meet up with you guys there soon enough." Ken Rogers suggests to Rick, as his partner Jack Kerns just rolls his eyes at Ken, but Rick tells him all right, but to get back to the safehouse in North park by 7:00 PM. Ken tells him he will be there by then to get ready, as he leaves with the two women. Rick and Ed head down with Jack to get into his Envoy, as Rob drove his motorcycle to the safehouse and was waiting for them to arrive.

Just at 6:15 PM, Ken pulled into the parking lot of the medical facility where Diana worked. While they were driving on the freeway,

Ken noted that he felt as if they were being followed by another sedan behind them, but the vehicle stayed with the traffic on the freeway, as Ken to the exit ramp to get here. Cate was about to open her door and exit the vehicle, when Ken told her he will go get the report from Dr. Farrell, as he told the women to stay in the vehicle and lock the door that he will be right back. Cate and Stephanie followed his instructions, as Ken walked through the back door and was let in by a security guard.

Dr. Farrell was just putting away some of her files in her office and she was shutting off the lights in her lab, as she was getting ready to head home for the night. There was a knock on the door as she went over and looked through the glass window and smiled at Ken, as she waved to him to come inside as the door was open. As Ken walked up to her he asked if she was alone. As Diana told him her staff team had left for the evening and asked what was he doing here at this hour of the night?

"I was about to take Stephanie and Dr. Adams back to Central headquarters but Cate forgot her DNA findings of the victim's, do you have it?" Ken asks her, as Diana told him she did as she went to her desk to get it; she asked what was the task force's next plan to catch the killer? As Diana handed Ken the folder, Ken smiled and they embraced one another and kissed each other deeply. As Diana broke off the kiss and smiled at him, and shook her head no.

"Ken we have to be careful about this, you're still a married man and my colleague who I have worked with for a long time is here in your car. Please not now, but tell me what's going on?" She tells Ken they need to keep their sexual relationship very quiet from their friends and coworkers, as Ken reveals to her the teams plan to catch the Entity.

"Ed and Rick came up with the idea, if the killer is always following our team members around. The why not use decoys of Ed and Stephanie to lure him out, and get him out in the open. They are planning this tonight at the sight of the new safehouse in North Park." Ken reveals to him, as Diana is surprised to learn this now.

"Well you better get going Ken, you got to get Stephanie and Cate safe first." She tells him, as Diana curses to herself, as she just remembered she found matching evidence to one of the victims now, to Nathan Malcolm's victim's. A matching strand of female hair, as Ken tells her that's great. As she tells him she needs Cate to come up and look at this in the lab's microscope right away. As Ken calls Cate on his cell phone, to tell her to come up to the lab, Diana puts the labs lights back on as she also put on her lab coat.

Stephanie and Cate are seated in the backset of Ken's car patiently waiting for him, as Stephanie looks up and notices the lights come back on in the lab on the top floor of the building. As Cate asks what is taking Ken so long, as he cell phone rings as she answers it. Diana had called her to tell her about to new find of matching hair color and DNA characteristics of the victims. As Cate became astatic to the news, she told Diana she would be right up. As she got of her cell phone, Stephanie asked her what is going on.

"Diana just called; she found a matching hair link between victim Ashley Cook, and the first victim of Nathan Malcolm. I want to go up to her lab and look at it real fast as Ken is coming back down to stay with you." As Cate was exiting the car, Stephanie told her not to be too long that they needed to hurry. As she watched Cate enter the back door as the guard opened it for her.

Stephanie just looked around the deserted parking lot as the daylight was now gone, as the darkness of night fell over the city of San Diego, as a full moon cast it's rays down onto a reflecting mirror of a parked vehicle. As the light's reflection hit Stephanie in her face she looked in the direction of the light, and she saw two white vans parked side by side in the rear parking spaces. Stephanie knew they belonged to the facility for their medical use, as she remembered one of the witnesses describing a white cargo van. Stephanie unlocked her side door, and walked over to the vans still wondering what was taking Cate and Ken so long to come back down. As Stephanie approached the vans, she looked at the one on the left as it had black large painted lettering identifying it as, County Examiner. As she turned her attention to the vehicle on the right, she noticed there the lettering was covered by a magnetic sign on both sides. The sign read, fresh flowers as Stephanie removed one of the false signs knowing someone deliberately is trying to hide the van as a flower delivery vehicle. Stephanie quickly tried the side cargo door as it was locked, as she hurried to the back double doors. She tried the door handle as it was open; she opened both doors and looked to the right side of the upper right. She found what she was searching for, a torn piece of interior lining carpeting. Matching the same kind of material and color found in the victim's fingernail. As Stephanie thought to herself quickly; "I saw the ring on a chain around her neck?" She quickly took out her cell phone as she was going to call Ed right away.

Cate walked very slowly on the floor, as all the light that were turned on had been turned off again. As she made her way to Diana's lab, the door was still open as she called out for both Diana and Ken as she got no reply from them. As she found the light switch on the wall, and turned the lights on. She again called out for Diana, as she walked around the large center table she looked down and screamed in horror. On the floor was Ken Rogers, as he lay in a pool of his own red blood. As Cate screamed again, the security guard heard her screams and left his desk, and ran to see what was wrong.

Stephanie got Ed's voicemail as she heard Cate's screams she looked up as she then looked inside the van at the damaged material. As Stephanie, was leaving Ed a message; "Ed please listen to this and hurry, I found the cargo van used in the abduction of that young girl! It's one of the medical vans from Diana's office;" But before Stephanie could finish her sentence a gloved hand clamped over her mouth fast and tight. As she felt a tremendous shock to her right side, stunning her, the attacker shocked her with a stun gun. The low current power charge immobilized her muscles, as she dropped her cell phone to the ground. As the attacker forced Stephanie into the van and closed the doors behind them. Stephanie was still conscious but had no muscle functions from the shock, as her eyes fixed on her attacker; Dr. Farrell.

"My dear Stephanie, you're a very smart clever girl. You figured it out all by yourself along with your dear Ed. I wish I could kill you like the others, but someone very special wants you alive." Diana tells her is a soft voice, as Stephanie lay on the floor bed of the van, as she watched Diana reach into a plastic bag and take out a black dark cloth as she covered Stephanie's nose and mouth with it.

"Just breath in the sweet chloroform Stephanie, we are going home now and you're going to a have a new life for yourself." As the sweet potent fumes of the chloroform took effect on her, Stephanie slowly closed her eyes as she fell unconscious from the drug. Diana held the cloth in place a few seconds longer to be certain Stephanie was out, as she quickly placed the cloth back in the clear plastic bag and then into her jacket pocket. As she hurried into the driver's seat, and started the van and took off to her secret destination.

As the security guard discovered the body of Ken Rogers, he quickly used the phone in the lab to call the police as Cate called Rick on his cell phone to inform him what happened, Cate was screaming at Rick as he answered her. Ed and Rob, who were in one of the communication rooms together with other policemen, heard Cate yelling at Rick as they knew something bad has happened as Rick got off the phone.

"Ed and Rob, come on we have to go to Dr. Farrell's medical office. Ken Rogers is dead!" Rick screams to him, As Rick and Rob run to get into Jack's car. Ed runs to his motorcycle, knowing he can maneuver through traffic faster and the speed of his motorcycle will get him there faster than the car.

As Diana was driving on the Mission Valley Freeway, she kept a steady speed not to alert the attention of any police cruisers she would pass along the way. She looked at Stephanie in the rear view mirror and saw she was still unconscious. As she placed a call on her cell phone, as a man's voice answered her.

"I have her; she is safe I will be at the house in a few minutes. We have to move fast, because Ed and the rest of the police will be looking for her now. I had to kill my boyfriend, as he was about to find out it was me all along." Diana tells her friend, as he asks her is she harmed Stephanie in any way?

"No I only chloroformed her; she is safe I promise you. But we have to move her out now as soon as I get there!" Diana orders him.

"Don't worry about that; just get here as fast as you can unseen. I still have plans to make for my dear opponent." He tells Diana, as he hangs up the phone. As the Entity feels compelled that the first part of his plans are complete, he has Stephanie all to himself as he can now kill Ed Brooks and get out of San Diego with her.

Ed arrived at the facility before Rick and the others, as he ran up to the lab on the third floor he was met by Cate and a whole slew of uniformed policemen as they, were looking through Dr. Farrell's lab and office very methodically. As Cate was explaining to Ed what happened, he asked her where Stephanie was. She explained to him, she left her in Ken's car to come up and view the new evidence Dr. Farrell had found but she found only the body of Ken Roger's on the floor of the lab, and both Stephanie and Dr. Farrell are both missing now. Ed starts to look around the lab for clues, as he then takes out his cell phone and calls Stephanie on her cell phone as there was no answer. Ed knew right away she was abducted by the Entity as he was very enraged, but also knew he was helpless to help her, for not knowing where she was taken to, as Rick and the others entered the lab. Cate ran to Rick as they embraced each other, Rob went over to Ed and told him he found this cell phone on the ground of the parking lot ringing.

"This is Stephanie's cell phone, she's missing now." Ed tells them, as he listens to the new voicemail in his phone, it was Stephanie alerting him of the white cargo van she found at the facility, and the panel liner was damaged inside, as her voice then stopped and there was static before the call ended.

"She found the van that was used by the killer it was one of this medical forensic teams vans!' Ed tells Rob, as one of the policeman called to Rick to tell him he found something in the lab. He handed Rick a small bottle he found on the countertop, as Rick smelled it and made a face as he let Cate inhale its contents to see if she could identify what it was.

"Chloroform, it's used as an anesthetic to render someone unconscious," Cate tells him, as Jack Kerns made a face; he knew now all the pieces were coming together. As another policeman called to Rick and his team, as they ran into Diana's office, as they found interesting items in her locker.

Ed made his way over to the locker first, as he saw two black sets of scrubs, stitched together to form a black hood and sleeves, the Entity's style outfit. Ed said to himself, as he looked on the floor of the locker. There was a nylon black bag as Ed pulled it out and opened it, as he found black latex gloves and a picklock gun, along with a plastic case that held many steel sharp, post mortem knives. He and Rick looked at one another, and knew now that Diana Farrell was the Entity and she has abducted Stephanie.

"Right under all of us, no wonder there was any DNA evidence; she knew everything about us, where we lived the safehouses. She had deep insight to everything we were doing, and now she has Stephanie. Call dispatch and get them to tell us her address!" Ed yells to Rob as he takes out his cell phone, and calls dispatch. Rick see's the sad look on Jack's face and asks him what's wrong?

"Dr. Farrell knew everything about us and the investigation from Ken, he told me she had come onto him and they started having an affair. So I'm certain Ken told her everything we were doing on the case, and where the locations of the safehouses where. I told him he was going to get into trouble and end this relationship, but he kept telling me he could trust her and no harm was going to come out of it." Jack admits to them, as Rick curses and calls Ken a stupid idiot. As Rob quickly writes down the addresses he got from dispatch, as he then tells Ed and the others.

"Dr. Farrell has two homes, one all the way west of here in Village Center. The other home is 8542 Hill Street. The house right next to Nathan Malcolm's in Sunset Cliff Estates!" Rob tells them, as Ed shakes his head in disbelief.

"She's his daughter, it all makes sense now. She got him out of the house that night of the fire; he's still alive he has to be!" Ed screams as he runs to the parking lot, as Rick yells for him to wait.

"Jack call, Central Command and the FBI's office, tell them to get units to both locations and seal off every freeway and the airports and have check points set up at the marinas. Get an APP but out on all the vehicles of Diana Farrell along with the make and model of the cargo van!" Rick orders Jack, as he tells Rob to come on. As they race behind Ed to get to their car, as Ed didn't even put on his helmet. He started up his bike, and roared out of the parking lot towards Cliff Side Estates.

Ed peels through the intersection, as the light was red. He didn't care as the force of the heavy wind and air hit his face, as he sped up to 60 MPH on Van Horn Road, he didn't care as he made his way onto the freeway. He cursed at Nathan Malcolm and his daughter, for if they were going to harm Stephanie.

"You sick bastards, I'm going to kill you both!" Ed curses as he took the turn to the on ramp to the San Diego Freeway very fast. Ed excelled to 100 MPH, as he gunned his motorcycle as fast is it could go, as he was racing to save Stephanie's life.

# Chapter 11

Diana drove backwards up the long driveway of her home; as the double sided garage door was already opened for her arrival. She parked the van right next to her other vehicle, a dark metallic gray Ford Expedition. As the garage door closed once she was inside, as she met her ally who was waiting for them to come. He was all dressed in black; a he wore a black hidden face mask, as if it was a Halloween costume. He opened the double back doors to the van, as his eyes peered inside as he saw his prize still unconscious. He was caught with exhilaration of emotion, as he had only viewed Stephanie from a distance, as now she was here for him to have. He studied her as she was motionless, except her chest rising and falling from her breathing. He bit and grinded his teeth as with his gloved hand he gently touched her legs, and buttocks. As through her tight blue jeans, he knew her skin and figure was smooth and firm to his touch. He reached inside with both hands and gently pulled her writs towards him, as he then picked up her limp body in his arms. As Diana came around to meet him, she looked at Stephanie's face and then felt her wrist for a pulse, as she was satisfied Diana knew she would be awakening soon.

"We better get her inside the other truck, she will be waking up soon and we don't have much time. I will sedate her by injection to keep her out for as long as it takes us to transport her to our new home." Diana instructed the man in black, as he became enraged he had other plans first, as he answered Diana with his deep raspy voice, which echoed with anger.

"I told you, I want to confront Ed Brooks first, and then after I kill him we move her out. I know he is coming now, so help me prepare for him." He instructed Diana, as he carried Stephanie into the house and up the first flight of stairs, as they entered the large living room with that had an open kitchen. He placed Stephanie in a wooden chair, as Diana quickly tied her hands behind her with thick rope, as she also bound her feet together, as she fastened the rope to the bottom wood support of the chair. To make certain Stephanie will be unable to kick her legs free.

As Diana worked very fast to secure Stephanie, the Entity took off his glove as he was able to feel the very soft skin of Stephanie's face. He bent down and pressed his hooded mask against her soft hair, as he smelled her sweet perfume, he couldn't wait to have her alone all to himself. As Diana saw him getting allured to Stephanie, she became very mad now.

"You better contain your pleasure for Stephanie, as we are not safe yet. As most men fall to the weakness of a woman, you're about to jeopardize all we have planned and prepared for, just for this woman." As Diana finished binding her feet, she rose up to face him. As he stared at Diana through his mask, she couldn't see the anger she has just caused him to feel, as he made his right hand stiff and slapped her hard across the face, as he cut her lower lip.

"I started this whole ordeal in preparation for revenge, as I needed your help to regain my strength and plan the deaths of my enemies. I made you what you are, and I know you wanted me to kill her from the start, along with him. But my feelings for her changed, as she is very different from all those others I have killed. She is a pure soft soul, something that has been missing from you females for length of time. Now you can either help me, or I will slay you like the others here and now." He told Diana, as she licked away the blood with her tongue. As she then smiled at him, she then told him she is still loyal and willing to help him.

"Good, now hurry and start the Bunsen burner and heat up my blades. For he is coming now," As Diana turned to the kitchen counter top, and turned on the gas and used a match to ignite the very deep blue flame of the burner. The blue colored flame is the hottest point of the fire. As Diana held the handle of the very sharp steel dagger, as she passed the blade into the fire to make it very hot to burn human skin. As he watched Diana prepare his weapons for him, he heard Stephanie moan softly as he gently touched her face. As she was starting to awaken, her head tilted to the right as she tried to clear her thoughts and focus to where she was.

"That's it, awaken Stephanie, the end is almost here for my enemy. As a new beginning awaits us both far away from this place," the Entity spoke to her, as Stephanie squinted her eyes a few times, she finally opened her eyelids as her surrounding was very blurred to her. But she knew she had been drugged with chloroform. She shook her head hard to clear her vision, as she now saw the very large figure in black in front of her, as she turned around behind her, to see Dr. Farrell heating up daggers and two large swords with and open flame. As Stephanie tried to move, the Entity told her to be calm and no harm will come to her, as she tried to free her hands but couldn't.

"What the hell do you want? Where am I, who are you?" Stephanie yells at the Entity as she looks back at Diana who just smiles at her, she will let her counterpart explain everything to her now. As he started to speak through his dark face mask, he cleared his throat as much as he could for her to understand his deep raspy voice.

"Congratulations Stephanie, you and Ed did fit all the pieces of the puzzle into place and conclude who was; Jack the Ripper. But you didn't know who I was and my relationship to Francis Tumblety was, and why is my dear Diana involved." He tells her, but Stephanie is about to surprise him as she already knows all the answers to his questions and riddles.

"You're wrong! I know everything now, along with Ed. You are related to that sick son of bitch, Francis Tumblety, along with this crazy bitch who helped you all along. So who the hell are you now, show me your face!" Stephanie screams at the Entity, as he slowly

195

removes his hooded face mask, as his face was revealed to her. He was burned badly, all over his face as his hair and eyebrows had been singed away from the inferno that engulfed him, as Stephanie knew who he was but she was indeed surprised he was alive, Dr. Nathan Malcolm. She could still make out some of his facial features, as his eyes were still intact, as Stephanie whispered to him, he couldn't be alive. As he smiled at her, it was time he told her what happened that night four years ago.

"Yes I am still alive; I wouldn't be here now if it wasn't for the love and great support I received from my daughter Diana. She not only saved my life that night, we had planned our route of evasion for a year before then. I discovered through my father's personal items, who my great uncle was, and the greatness he achieved in life. As I showed Diana, the journal of our great uncle, Francis Tumblety, he wrote in detail of the whores he killed in England. In that foul dump known as Whitechaple, he was a true man who destroyed those whores who deserved to die. As I met them here in my own present life, starting with my own wife Jane, who abandoned me and left me all alone, but in time she got her retribution as she died a slow agenizing death. Diana grew older and stronger, as I let her read the journal, she knew what our family blood line detailed, and we were to cleanse the new world again in the present."

"So Diana is your daughter, she changed her last name from Malcolm to Farrell upon the death of your ex-wife. But how did you survive the fire at your house, and who was the person's body that even Dr. Cate Adams confirmed it was your badly burned corpse after the autopsy." Stephanie wanted to know the answers to these questions, as Nathan was about to tell her.

"I indeed fought with your daring Ed Brooks in the house, I was about to set the fire to a dead man's corpse when I was taken by surprise by him. Diana found a poor dear lost soul one dark night, who matched my height and weight. As we knew his face and fingerprints would be destroyed in the intense fire I was going to set, so Diana knew the only way to confirm the dead man's remains as my own, was through dental records. Diana took a mold of my teeth, with plaster and made a composite mold with the clear plastic invisalign braces, and fitted them into his mouth perfectly. So any autopsy expert would find my dental remains and confirm the corpse as my own. But I almost did die, at the hands of your dear fiancée. As I was burned beyond hell itself, as the fire raged in the house. Diana was waiting behind the stairwell door, as she covered me with a large fire blanket. As she guided me down stairs and out the back doors and into this home, that she had just purchased months before, a plan well formatted to work. But I was unable to kill Ed Brooks that night, as with Diana's help again and treating my wounds. I grew stronger, as I taught her how to use knives and kill our enemies. Together we were ready to extract revenge on everyone."

Stephanie now knew the whole ordeal that started and climaxed to this point, as she knew Diana was dressed as the Entity that night she killed so many of their friends at the safehouse. It was her driving the sports motorcycle through the mall, and able to quickly avoid being captured by her shear strength and quickness. The attack by the Entity at the lab, when Diana was injured that night while Rick and Cate were there, was all a set up to get guilt away from Diana. As Stephanie remembered seeing Diana wearing and old ring on a chain, around her neck one day, she knew it was one of the rings Francis Tumblety had taken from his fourth victim, and placed them along with his journal in the old wooden box. As Nathan took out the other ring, suspended on a gold chain around his neck, he smiled and told her, it was a true family treasure handed down by their uncle. To mark their victory in their will to rid the world of whores, and their enemies, as Diana told Stephanie, she felt very sorry for what her father went through from the pain her mother caused him. She knew her place was to help him, with all his needs and his revenge.

"So what do you want with me? Why not just kill me at the lab earlier?" Stephanie asks Diana, as she will let her father answer her question.

"Because Stephanie I had a change of mind and heart about you, I did order Diana to take your life when she had the chance, but I saw you making love to Ed one clear night in his bedroom. I studied you so deeply, you're a very beautiful woman that I want for myself, as we are going to take you with us to a far off place, where no one will be able to find you. As we will leave once Ed gets here and I kill him. You will be my future bride Stephanie," Nathan tells her, as he glides his fingers over her face and lips, as he reached down with his face. He wanted to kiss Stephanie on her lips, but she broke free of his quip and turned her head away from him.

"I'm sorry to tell you this, but I have a thing about marrying a serial killer, who is a crazed sick fuck! I am going to marry the man who is going to save me, and kick your ass!" Stephanie yells at Nathan, as he and Diana stare at one another and then start to laugh as she thinks Ed will be able to save her in time. As just then, there was the sound of a loud moving engine getting louder and closer. Stephanie knew it was the sounds of Ed's motorcycle. She screamed his name out, as Nathan yelled for Diana to pass him the flaming swords. Ed didn't stop as he jumped the curb to the house, as he drove straight through the large double windows and he leaped off the bike just in time, as Diana and her father jumped out of the way as the motorcycle crashed into the living room and stopped itself as it hit the large stove in the kitchen. As the tremendous impact, caused Stephanie to rock to her right side in the chair, and fall to the floor.

Ed dove to the front lawn just before impact, as he looked up he found his handgun as he jumped to his feet he leaped into the massive opening he created. As he saw Diana he didn't hesitate he took aim and started to fire at her, Diana leaped behind countertop just avoiding the bullets. As the Bunsen burner, fell to the floor as Diana accidently kicked it. Stephanie saw it on the floor right in front of her, as the flame was still lit. She fought hard with all her might to try and out stretch her tied hands to reach the hot flame, and burn away the rope. As Ed quickly dropped the empty magazine, he was about to insert the full clip into the gun. When Nathan hit him hard from behind with a hard shoulder tackle, from the floor Ed looked up at him. As Nathan was standing over him with both swords flaming hot in his hands, he screamed as he swung hard to strike Ed. As Ed quickly rolled to his right to avoid being hit, as he swept Nathan's feet out from under him, as he fell to the floor. Ed kicked him hard on the ground, as the two swords flew out of his hands, and ignited the carpeting in the living room and started a fire.

Stephanie leaned up and then crashed the chair back first to the hard marble floor, as she was able to break the back wooden frame in two. She was able to reach her hands up to the flame, as it started to burn away the rope, but Stephanie screamed in pain as it was burning her hands. Diana saw she was trying to free herself, as she picked up one of the daggers he charged at Stephanie to strike her. Ed caught her arm as he spun her around and hit her square in the face hard, as she flew backward to the floor. Nathan made it to his feet as he tackled Ed from behind; the two men hit the floor hard, as they exchanged furious blows to one another.

Stephanie pulled her hands free from the singed rope, as she reached for one of the daggers; she then cut the rope to her feet free. As Diana again charged at her, she kicked the dagger out of her hand as Stephanie kicked her in her thigh hard, stopping her in place. As Stephanie leaped to her feet as she grabbed Diana's long hair from behind with one hand, and punched her in the face with her right hand repeatedly, cursing at the her the whole time. As Diana bent her head down and then drove Stephanie into the wall hard, as both women fell to the floor. As the fire from the carpeting, now engulfed the large curtains and enflamed the walls of the home, as Ed knew this was a remake of his first encounter with Malcolm.

Ed pulled him up from the floor and with a thunderous blow, he smashed him in the face and then in his chest. As Nathan, reached behind his back where he had a sharp dagger strapped into its sheath. He quickly grabbed it, as he bend down to avoid Ed's in coming punch, as he stabbed Ed in his right thigh deep with the dagger. As he left it there imbedded into his muscle, as Ed fell to the floor screaming in pain. Nathan screamed as he kicked Ed in the face, and then bent down he pushed on the handle of the dagger, driving it deeper into Ed's thigh. As Ed screamed in desperation, he tried to get away from Nathan who reached out and picked up a flaming sword. Stephanie knew he was about to kill Ed with it.

She looked around for his gun but didn't find it, as Diana leaped to tackle her; Stephanie ducked down as Diana missed her and hit the refrigerator hard. As Stephanie kicked her hard on the floor, Stephanie found a can of aerosol oven cleaner. Stephanie picked up the burner with her left hand and sprayed the highly flammable liquid into the path of the flame, shooting a stream of fire directly into Nathan's face and eyes, as he screamed in pain. As the fire blinded him, he swung the sword furiously at her, as Stephanie dropped both the can and burner. Ed reached down and pulled the dagger out of his thigh, as he was about to get up. Diana kicked him in the gut hard, as Ed dropped the dagger. Diana grasped it with her right hand, as she swung it hard over her head to strike Ed. He caught her hand, and very tightly, fended off her thrust. As he tried desperately to free it from her tight grasp.

Ed then remembered the karate move Stephanie used on him, Ed bent her hand low and then back up, he held the dagger against her own chest as he threw Diana in the direction of her father who was still swinging the sword violently, as the flaming blade cut her neck like hot butter, decapitating his own daughter. As her head fell to the right side, and her body fell to the left side. Nathan was able to get a glimpse out from his right eye, as he screamed in agony that he killed his own daughter. He turned and saw Ed and Stephanie holding each other on the floor.

"You!" Nathan screamed as he was about to swing the sword at them, Rick and Rob together opened fire round after round from their guns, striking him in the chest and neck. As Nathan flew off his feet backward dead, as the flaming sword fell onto the fallen motorcycle, as it was leaking gas from its tank. Rick quickly helped Stephanie to her feet, as Rob with all his strength picked Ed up. As the four of them ran fast and then leaped out of the shattered windows, as a tremendous explosion ripped behind them, as they flew off their feet into the air, as the flames shot high over them. As they came crashing down to the grass face first. They kept their heads down low, as the flash fire ceased, as Rick looked up and then behind him, he yelled clear to the other. As Stephanie got up and ran over to Ed as she hugged him on the ground, she started to cry from both in pain, and very thankful Ed saved her life. As Rob and Rick got to their feet, they both stared at them. As Jack rushed over to Ed and Stephanie with a first aid kit from his vehicle, as many patrol vehicles with their sirens and flashers blinding deep into the late night. Came to a screeching halt, as the policemen exited with their guns drawn, as Rick and Rob showed them their badges as Rick ordered the head sergeant, to get and ambulances and the fire department to the location right away.

Jack started the clean Ed's deep knife wound, as Stephanie just held him in her arms as they kissed one another deeply, as Ed himself had tears of joy in his eyes, to know it was all over now.

"It's over Stephanie, he's gone, and Diana. I told you I wasn't going to let nothing happen to you".

"I know Ed, now just shut-up and let Jack heal you up, because you need to walk straight when we walk down the aisle as husband and wife," Stephanie tells him, as they just kiss deeply as Rob and Rick shake hands, knowing this how thing is finally over with. As Chief John Chase, just arrived with his staff and escorts, as Cate got out of one of the squad cars along with Rob's wife, as they ran to their husbands and embraced them, Chief Chase puzzled as to what was going on, as he watched the three happy couples together. He was then filled in by the head lieutenant on the scene, which Detective Ed Brooks was able to save the life of Stephanie Morgan, resulting in the deaths of serial suspects, Nathan Malcolm and his daughter, Diana Farrell.

Chase screamed to the arriving forensic teams, that he wanted immediate confirmation of the deaths of Malcolm and Farrell, and he wanted their remains secured right away, so no arriving media would be able to get photo graphs of the bodies. As the forensic team, moved in behind the firefighters who were containing the fire of the home, as the Chief walked over the ambulance, where Ed and Stephanie were being treated. He shook Rick's hand and then Rob's hand and congratulated them and Rick's whole task force, as he turned to Ed and Stephanie and told them he was very happy they made it, and they will receive high commendations from the city, for their excellent work on this case. As Chief Chase, then asked Rick to brief him and his staff of everything that happened, and who was involved. As Rick walked with the Chief, to get ready to brief the media, as the ambulance crew were finishing bandaging Stephanie's hand burns, and Ed's deep knife wound. As he was told he needed to receive staples at the hospital to close the wound. As Ed, smiled and told Stephanie; "at least this time, my wounds are not life threatening."

Two hours had passed since the deaths of Nathan Malcolm and his daughter, Ed and Stephanie watched together as their remains were placed into two black body bags, and loaded into a large sized coroner van. As it was escorted to the medical facility by four patrol vehicles; as the escort broke free of the media and gathering crowds of the neighborhood, that were getting ready to listen to the late media briefing by Chief of Police John Chase, and other high ranking staff members to announce the death of the Entity serial killer, along with his daughter and they will answer the rumors that he was related to; Dr. Francis Tumblety, who we all know now is indeed; Jack the Ripper. As Ed and Stephanie watch the brightness of the lights and the flashes of the cameras go off, around the podium that was set up right in front of the charred house. The ambulance doors closed behind Ed and Stephanie, as they were now enroot to the hospital to receive further treatment.

As Stephanie turned to Ed who was sitting next to her on the soft bench, she saw he was very upset; "Ed what's wrong, you look very mad now," she asked him as she held his hands.

"I lost my beloved fat boy Harley Davidson bike; I'm getting myself another one as soon as we get back from the honeymoon." He told her, as Stephanie just looked at him with tears in her eyes as Ed held her in his arms.

# Chapter 12

## One year later

Ed had married Stephanie; only two months after the most brutal serial slayings in the world came to an end. But what the couple didn't prepare for and expect was the rush of the media, in a strong surge to get them in from of every news correspondent and major news station. For repeated interviews, of how this team of a hardnosed detective and a vibrant and very intelligent FBI profiler, worked hard together to solve the most infamous serial cases ever known, Ed told every reporter and news host, in all the interviews that the couple had done, that he just followed up on the work of investigators and authors; who named Dr. Francis Tumblety as the lead suspect, as Jack the Ripper. With Stephanie's help, they were able to prove his distant nephew; Dr. Nathan Malcolm and his daughter, Dr. Diana Farrell. Carried on his tradition of multiple serial slayings, as Ed and Stephanie Brooks, told the whole world, they do not intend to write any books or make any deals for movie negotiations. As the couple has no plans to financially profit from their whole experience from this case, as they just repeated over and over, finding their love together was their true riches and rewards from this case. As they now were able to go on their long overdue happy honeymoon, as they agreed to take a long tour of the many beautiful countries and famous cities in Europe.

They visited Paris and Rome, along the way with stops in Zurich and Madrid. As they were now visiting England, as Ed wanted to visit one place in England, where this nightmare all started for everyone, and way back in 1888, they come upon the city of Leytonstone. As they were visiting St Patrick's Roman Catholic Cemetery on Langthorne Road, Ed wanted to have some self-closure from this whole ordeal. As Stephanie didn't argue with him, as she also felt a need to pay their respects to the resting place, of Mary Kelly. The last known victim of Jack the Ripper, as Stephanie laid a nice arrangement of fresh flowers by her tomb marker. Ed and his wife felt a deep sadness for her, because even though Mary Kelly lived a short life, many years before Ed and Stephanie were even born. Ed felt a touch in his heart for her, as he would look at her known photographs before her death. He and Stephanie knew, she was a young woman beautiful and full of life, that didn't deserve to have her short life end, at only 25 years of age. Ed found some recognition for Mary Kelly, as he was able to prove to the world who was her killer, and bring peace and closure to this beautiful young woman. That touched him in a way, many years and miles apart. As Stephanie reached over and held Ed's hand, as she rested her head on his right shoulder.

"You set out on what you wanted to do, I remember when we first met, you told me you wanted to prove to the world who committed these unspeakable acts, and to keep all the innocent and good people safe from harm. You are more than a hero Ed; you're a brave man who fights for just and good in the world. One of the qualities I fell in love with about you, and I know you retired from the force just a few months ago. But you are about to get a new job very soon, tough guy." Stephanie tells him, as Ed looks into her eyes as asks his wife, what she means.

"You're going to become a father, because I'm three weeks pregnant." Stephanie tells him with joyful tears in her eyes, as Ed picks her up off her feet and kisses Stephanie over this happy news. As they start to walk down the path and exit the cemetery on this clear autumn day. As they are holding hands, Stephanie starts telling him all the plans they need to make for the baby.

"Now Ed, I know we are still living in the condo, but we have to buy a three bedroom home in a good part of San Diego, as we have to search for a very good school system for all our kids to come. My parents and I talked about having them move to the city, so they can help babysit when we are busy with work and other things." As Stephanie begins to tell him about painting the nursery once they know the sex of the baby, Ed just smiles back at Stephanie and knows he is very happy for them, but his retirement was short lived.

# About The Author

Mark Barresi, spent four years in the Army in the infantry, where he trained at Fort Benning and then onto Fort Campbell. Where he combined both his military knowledge and skills, while going to college and taking creative writing courses, as he has followed the paths of his favorite established authors, James Byron Huggins and Clive Cussler. He has now authored four books and established himself as one of the new great talents of the Action and Horror genre. In his spare time apart from writing, he has been a strong supporter of conservative issues affecting our country's policies and directions. He follows the same paths and beliefs of iconic actors; John Wayne and Charlton Heston. He is a lifelong member and outspoken supporter of the NRA, for gun rights for private citizens. He enjoys traveling and collecting antiques and being involved as an animal rights activist, dealing with abused and neglected animals. He has plans to write two more novels in the near future, DAUGHTER OF AFFLICTION, and FOREBIDDEN PASSAGEWAYS. He currently lives in New York City.